Testing Midnight

by

Jane Drager

Midnight Sky, Book One

Testing Midnight

Cover Art by *The Wild Rose Press, Inc.*

The Wild Rose Press, Inc.
PO Box 708
Adams Basin, NY 14410-0708
Visit us at www.thewildrosepress.com

Publishing History
First Edition, 2024
Trade Paperback ISBN 978-1-5092-5563-4
Digital ISBN 978-1-5092-5564-1

Midnight Sky, Book One
Published in the United States of America

Dedication

To my Aunt Bub, an avid reader and my biggest fan.
I'll miss you.

Chapter One

Slowing to a stop, Skylar Dawson edged her motorcycle to the curb and used a booted foot to avoid scraping her precious baby against the concrete. After a grueling two-day drive, she finally arrived at her New Jersey destination, and her butt said thank you. She looked around and frowned.

She must have the wrong address. The house before her—more like a mini-mansion—stood like a grand lady in the bright afternoon sun. The structure sat in the middle of a manicured lawn with a curvy, interlocking, gray-brick walkway stretching at least five hundred feet to the front porch. Obviously, her GPS made a serious miscalculation.

Pulling a piece of paper from her jacket pocket, she double-checked the house number attached to a chest-high hedgerow, then the instructions on her bike's navigational display. *Oh, my.* Right street and right house. She choked on a cry, for the property was hers now, inherited from a great-aunt she never knew.

Ever since the news of this inheritance arrived in the mail, she walked around in a daze, and in Chicago, no one wandered without a mind on full alert. Nathan Kirby, the lawyer involved, did little to alleviate the shock. Surely, someone made a horrible mistake. How could a complete stranger leave her a house so picture perfect?

Killing the engine, Skylar released the kickstand, swung a leg over the cycle, and removed her helmet. While stretching her back and fluffing her short, cropped hair, she forced her racing heart to decelerate by taking several slow, deep breaths.

She fought tooth and nail not to come. Nothing irritated her more than to have her well-ordered lifestyle interrupted, which, by anyone's standards, bordered on mundane. Because of some weird stipulation in the will, her physical presence was required to finalize the estate. Who demanded such an archaic rule with the wonders of the Internet at one's fingertips? With little choice except to flat-out refuse the inheritance, she grumbled and complained to no one in particular, took a leave of absence from her bartender job, secured her house, and arranged for her neighbor to handle mail and whatnot. With the cycle's saddlebags packed and a duffel bag securely strapped in place, Skylar drove from Chicago to Woodstown, New Jersey, to face what might very well be a new future.

A boardinghouse. Her aunt was out of her ever-loving mind. But people lived here. Mr. Kirby talked about eviction notices and a whole bunch of other lawyer stuff, but she refused to kick the tenants onto the street without first getting a good look at the place. Now that she stood on the sidewalk practically gawking, she felt stunned. Why couldn't the place be something old and decrepit? Then, she'd do the tenants a favor by forcing them to find better living quarters, and she could sell and get back to Chicago where she belonged.

A rustling near the hedgerow drew her attention. Senses alert, she stiffened. With her luck, she'd be attacked by a guard dog and mauled to pieces before she had a chance to see the inside of the house.

From behind the shrubbery, a hunk of a man popped up. Leaves and dirt covered every inch of his six-foot-two frame, and an odoriferous stench filled the air. Sweat matted his brown hair, and his drenched blue shirt was completely unbuttoned to reveal a set of laddered abs.

Despite broad shoulders to go with that impressive chest, he reeked like he hadn't showered in ages. Ordinarily, she'd forgive any working man for doing his job, especially with June temperatures hot enough to make anyone sweat. They often stopped into the bar for a cold beer smelling like rotted garbage, but hey, as long as they paid. Some men even flirted, as if she considered a sweat-covered man sexy. She sneezed.

Mr. Garden Guy shot her a laser look that would cut through steel. Well, geez, could she help it if something tickled her nose?

"You must be Skylar Dawson."

Whoa. His deep, sexy voice sent a shudder straight to her steel-toed boots. If he didn't look and smell like a man allergic to soap, she'd hold out her hand. She'd be the first to admit dirt and her didn't get along. As a born and bred city slicker, she hadn't an iota of gardening skills. Every flower or plant she touched withered and died. She learned early in life to use plastic flowers for decoration. They lasted forever.

He reached behind the hedge. Metal clinked, and he approached with a forearm crutch on his left arm.

So, the garden guy was disabled. Still, she'd make a bet he'd satisfy a woman's lady parts—as long as he showered first. "Yes, I'm Skylar. I guess this is the right place."

Nathan Kirby never sent a photo with his registered letter. Then again, she'd miss this mind-boggling sight—the house, not the man. Scanning the huge front yard, she still couldn't believe this property was hers. And the building—*wow*. Without removing her gaze from the structure, she swallowed hard. "I had no idea what to expect. I pictured a dilapidated type of motel with rooms for the residents." A frog stuck in her throat. She coughed. "This place is magnificent!"

"It's one of the largest houses in the area. Your aunt's done a nice job with upkeep."

Nice was too mild a word. From where she stood, she couldn't see anything wrong.

My aunt. Despite living in North Philadelphia for the first three years of her young life, Skylar had no clue who Ginger Dawson was and, with both parents dead, had no one to ask. Her father's transfer to Chicago had cut them completely off from his side of the family which, according to Skylar's mother, was because he married a non-Catholic and not because they moved. Skylar never questioned the family dynamics. She had no idea how many aunts, uncles, or cousins might come sniffing around, but Mr. Kirby assured her of the legality of the will.

"You won't need to worry about anyone contesting, Miss Dawson. Your aunt left very explicit instructions. Being a shrewd businesswoman, she knew exactly what to say to ward off any problems. You alone inherited her entire estate."

And there it sat right in front of her—not like she had any idea how to run a boardinghouse.

Hobbling toward the sidewalk, Garden Guy threw

a thumb over his shoulder. "We have a parking lot along the side street. Probably safer for your bike."

She looked toward the area indicated. *Well, hallelujah.* An honest-to-God parking lot. "Okay, sounds good." Better than keeping her baby exposed to some idiot driver who failed to steer a car in a straight line.

Since the weather was warm enough, she removed her windbreaker and secured it and her helmet to the duffel bag. Then, hopping on, she hit the ignition, steered her bike toward the lot, and parked. From this position, she had a direct view to a wide patio built onto the rear of the mansion. Behind a row of tall evergreens, a rancher sat in full sun, and, to her left, a huge lawnmower blocked the entrance to an open garage.

Garden Guy hobbled over. "You might want to enter the house from the front. You know, like a first impression sort of thing."

"Good idea."

She followed Garden Guy along another brick walkway running parallel to the house. With his stench so strong, she'd rather be upwind—or was the direction downwind? Either way, she stayed several steps behind him, but her nose itched like crazy. "Do you live here?"

"Yes. Logan Greene." He adjusted his crutch. "Third floor, Room Number Ten."

A forearm crutch usually meant a long-term disability, but nothing obvious showed, and she had a fantastic view of his tight tush and thick thighs.

"*You have eleven residents who will need new leases, Miss Dawson, even if you sell. When you're ready, I'll handle all the details.*"

Funny how Kirby's words kept swirling around in her brain. The thought of owning a business frightened her. She had no background for such an endeavor, and at thirty, she wasn't willing to learn.

"I hear you're a bartender." Logan glanced over his shoulder. "We have another resident who's a bartender. You should have a lot in common."

Startled from her reverie, she snapped her gaze to his face. Dear Lord. She might have been thinking about Mr. Kirby, but her gaze remained glued to his butt. She rubbed her nose. "Oh, sure, we can talk about new beers on tap." She stifled another sneeze.

Garden Guy scowled.

As if *she* was the one who stunk to high heaven. *Geez*. She again rubbed her nose. No use. Two sneezes hit at once.

"I never met your aunt, but I heard she once ran a tavern." He continued on the brick path. "Have you tended bar long?"

"A couple of years."

Now, she was a landlord. The news had no appeal whatsoever. Bad enough she had to handle a virtual stranger's estate, but the possibility of tossing eleven people out on the street sat like lead in her belly. Yet, she couldn't stay. Her life was in Chicago. Although, truth be told, nothing forced her to hurry back. She'd be the first to admit she hadn't an iota of ambition. For as long as she could remember, she had no goals in life. She never dreamed of being someone famous or doing something heroic. All through high school, counselors encouraged her to accept the many offered college scholarships, but she hated school. It was too rigid and boring.

A car horn honked.

She and Logan turned to see a faded yellow clunker sputter along the side street with its engine out of timing.

The woman driver waved a hand through an open window.

As acknowledgment, Logan raised his crutch in the air. "That's Doreen Hashoff. She's another tenant and usually leaves for work around this time."

Skylar checked her watch. One in the afternoon, Chicago time. "I think New Jersey is an hour ahead of Illinois. So, it's two o'clock?"

"Sounds about right. Doreen leaves at two, unless she has errands to run." He gestured at her wrist. "That watch doesn't fit with the rest of your biker outfit. How come?"

She held out her wrist to show the only diamond-studded piece of jewelry in her possession. Considering how everything on her body was black, the watch stood out like a neon sign. "This watch was a gift from my father before he passed. I'll probably wear it forever, even when it breaks."

"Oh—well." He cleared his throat. "Sorry for your loss." Stopping where the side walkway joined with the front, he used his crutch to point toward the house. "What do you think of the place?"

Scanning the huge expanse of grass that extended from the sidewalk and down both sides of the house, she sighed. "I'm overwhelmed."

More like in awe. The three-story, graystone Colonial had corner cinder blocks painted white to distinguish the center structure from the two side wings, also gray but with vinyl siding. A front porch stretched from one side of the house to the other, creating visions of outdoor parties on cool, spring nights. White pillars and railings matched the white trim and shutters and gave the exterior an elegant appearance.

"Ms. Dawson?"

Logan waited midway on the four concrete steps.

The man must be in a hurry to return to work—or take a shower. She shook herself and followed.

On the wide, cement porch, two elderly gentlemen—one white and the other black—rocked on one of many available wicker rockers. Their gazes scrutinized her, as if she was a bad-ass biker ready to stick a knife in their gut. She never pretended to be the girly type who wore makeup and lace. She didn't even carry a purse. Because of the invention of cargo pants, she stuffed her wallet and keys in pockets. When she wore shorts, she buckled a small fanny pack around her waist. And, oh, yes, her entire wardrobe was black. Period.

"Oomph!"

Logan had stopped before the double-screened doors, and she collided with his broad back. At five foot eight and wearing boots, she was no lightweight, but he hadn't budged an inch. Cheeks flaming, she retreated a step and promptly sneezed. "Sorry. I wasn't watching where I was going." She rubbed her nose. "Is this a rest home?"

A dark cloud passed over his chiseled face, as if she just kicked his dog.

He twitched his jaw. "No, this is not a rest home. Can't a disabled person live in a boardinghouse?"

Whoa, defensive. Not good. "I don't have much information, Mr. Greene. I don't mean to offend." Well, hey, a boardinghouse could be a rest home, right?

Mumbling something inaudible, he yanked open the door and held it for her to proceed him.

A wide hall stretched before her with a long, narrow table against one wall and a carpeted staircase on the other. The stairs had tiny lights tacked along the edge of each step. Whether for safety or ambiance depended on one's point of view. Both ways worked. Near the main entrance, on the right and left, were two doorways into what appeared to be sitting rooms. From where she stood, every visible window was open to allow a gentle breeze through.

"This way, ma'am. You'll get the grand tour later."

Ma'am? How old did she look? She frowned at his back.

After the lengthy hall, she entered an enormous kitchen with two rectangular tables and—she counted—sixteen chairs, a double-wide refrigerator, and a six-burner stove where a woman in a flowery apron, over a white blouse and black slacks, stirred the contents in a huge pot. The aromas of onions, tomatoes, and basil floated in the air, and Skylar salivated. She hadn't eaten much since yesterday afternoon. Nerves, mainly. Or maybe the greasy burger at a fast-food stop got to her.

The woman at the stove glanced over her shoulder, started, then quickly turned with a smile. "Well, you're here at last." She rested the spoon on a ceramic holder before wiping her hands on the apron. "Let me have a good look at you."

She was an older woman, perhaps in her late fifties, with salt-and-pepper hair cut short to the neck. Behind a pair of speckle-framed glasses, her brown gaze scanned Skylar, giving no indication if she approved or disapproved of all the black. Not like Skylar cared, but the woman's smile was bright and gaze friendly.

Approaching, she stood directly in front of Skylar and extended her right hand. "I'm Fay Bartleson, the housekeeper."

Sky took the outstretched hand. "Nice to meet you." She released her hold. "I never knew my aunt, Ms. Bartleson, so I was shocked to hear from Mr. Kirby."

Slipping his arm from the crutch sleeve, Logan leaned against the counter near the open door leading to the patio. A screen door allowed a breeze through. Unfortunately, the air blew his stench into the kitchen instead of out.

His steady gaze scrutinized her, and his poker face told her nothing. Well, golly gee. She wasn't here for a popularity contest. Shifting her gaze to the housekeeper, she stuffed her hands into her cargo pants. "I thought my father's family lived in Philadelphia."

"They do, dear, or what's left of them, and call me Fay. Your aunt moved to Jersey—oh, gosh—a little over twenty-five years ago, not long after your family left for Illinois. She bought this place as a bed and breakfast but found more need for permanent residents. Ginger's Manor has been a landmark in Woodstown ever since."

One brow arched, Skylar turned to Logan. "Did I miss the manor sign?"

He shook his head. "It's on the mailbox, and it's positioned on the side street toward Ginger's house."

She gaped. "That rancher belongs to me?"

Chuckling, Fay removed her eyeglasses and cleaned the lenses with her apron. "I can see you have little knowledge about the estate, but we'll get into it soon." Angling her glasses toward the window light, she checked the lenses, then replaced the glasses to her nose. "For starters, I'm glad you met our resident gardener."

Skylar glanced at Logan and met a pair of guarded eyes the color of fine ale. In her book, fine ale had the rich hue of copper. Even sweaty with his hair matted and body odor strong enough to cause sinus congestion, the man oozed sex appeal. Thankfully, he buttoned his shirt to cover those gorgeous abs, but in the confines of the kitchen, his body odor nearly overpowered the soup.

****

Now that Fay stood between him and their new owner, Logan finally sucked in a long breath. The woman honest-to-God wore black—black T-shirt, cargo pants, and work boots. Even her big-ass cycle was black. What the hell happened to a woman's love of color? In every picture posted on the Internet, she never smiled, and along with her choice of clothing, the tough bitch image shined. Despite no smile, she was a damn beautiful woman. If he had any idea of her arrival time, he wouldn't be standing in a warm kitchen smelling like a week-old fish.

"He's one of the best gardeners in a long time."

Huh? Oh, hell, Fay had been talking about him, and he missed every word. With a nod, he acknowledged whatever she said only to prompt a smile from Skylar that nearly blew him away. Her smile shot straight into a pair of crystal-blue eyes. Damn, they were so bright and clear, like watching a starburst. She wore a no-muss-no-fuss haircut with spiked strands on top with a gradual tapering close to her neck. Jet-black hair along with killer-black lashes accented those gorgeous eyes and made them pop. To boot, he couldn't detect a drop of makeup.

Diverting his gaze to the stove, he grunted. "Something smells good, Fay."

With a snort, she turned to check the gas burner under the pot. "It's Mrs. Santini's soup recipe. I hope I got the proportions right, or she'll have my head."

No big deal there. At least once a week, Maria Santini chopped off someone's head with her verbal barbs. The tenants called her the wicked witch of Woodstown. She always demanded, instead of asked, and stuck her nose in the air, as if the manor was her castle. He expected Skylar to be the same, what with her unexpected inheritance. But no woman with such a beautiful smile should be placed in the same category as Mrs. Santini. Prim and proper Maria was no match for the laid-back attitude of Skylar Dawson.

"Well, come on, dear. Let me show you around." Reaching behind her waist, Fay untied the apron and tossed it over a chair.

Too haphazardly placed to stay, the apron slipped.

Catching the movement, Skylar snatched the garment before it hit the floor.

Logan inwardly smiled. The woman had excellent reflexes. That skill might come in handy, considering what she inherited.

"Help! Somebody come quick!"

He tensed. *Aw, hell. Now, what?*

Chapter Two

Skylar stiffened. The unknown voice shouted with pure panic, and Skylar shot her gaze at Fay. The housekeeper merely sighed, like such a cry was a common occurrence. Maybe it was. Curious, she followed the housekeeper through the hall with Logan, crutch clicking, not far behind.

Pausing at the bottom of the staircase, Fay gripped the banister and stared upward. "What's the matter?"

The white elderly man from the front porch stood on the second-floor landing and beckoned for her to ascend. "It's Margaret. She ain't moving."

With a brow cocked, Fay glanced at Skylar.

Oh, Lordy. Did Fay expect Sky to take charge five minutes after stepping through the front door? *I don't think so.* She held up her hands, palms outward. "Don't look at me. You're the boss here." What a way to start an orientation to her new inheritance. She hurried after Fay.

Stopping on the landing, Skylar glanced right and left. The second floor consisted of one large hall with doors to the rooms, some open and others closed. The carpet from the staircase extended across the hall floor and, from a few opened doors, into each of the rooms.

Fay had disappeared through one of the open doors on the left where the elderly gentleman stood peering around the doorframe. The eighty-plus-year-old hardly gave her a glance as she slipped by him to join Fay.

Positioned alongside the bed, Fay shook the woman's shoulders. "Margaret, wake up!"

Margaret was definitely *not* waking. Her complexion matched the white bedsheet, but as far as breathing? Skylar couldn't tell with Fay shaking the daylights out of the poor woman. Stepping to the bed's opposite side, Skylar lifted the woman's cold wrist and palpated for a pulse. Nothing. A carotid check on her neck confirmed the same. Sighing, she met Fay's gaze. "We're too late."

Fay slapped a hand over her mouth.

Logan hobbled alongside. "Are you sure? You're not exactly a doctor."

"No, but I know how to feel for a pulse. You'll be surprised how many people pass out in a bar." She also learned CPR, but no way would she give mouth-to-mouth to a bar patron. She wasn't paid enough for that hazard.

Frowning, Logan leaned over the bed. "Maybe we should start chest compressions."

While staring at the poor woman, Sky shook her head. "She's already like ice. She's been dead a while." Angling over the lifeless body, Skylar pointed to an abrasion on the right side of the woman's forehead. "Did she fall recently? This abrasion looks fresh." She glanced at the housekeeper.

Fay bit her lower lip. "Not that I know."

Lips pursed, Sky shifted her gaze from Logan to Fay. "What's the procedure in this state? In Chicago, we call 9-1-1."

"Same here. I'm on it." From his rear pocket, Logan whipped out his cell phone and limped toward the window to place his call.

"Is she dead?"

The question came from the elderly man by the doorway. Several others were gathered around him, all over the age of sixty.

Skylar stepped away from the bed. "Yes, she's gone." Thankfully, no one passed out from the news, but they whispered among themselves, as if talking too loud would wake the dead. With nothing more to do except wait for the authorities, she took a moment to look around.

The room appeared comfortable enough. It was a combination bedroom and sitting area, kitchenette with microwave, small refrigerator, and private bath. Cotton balls overflowed from the dead woman's trouser pockets and onto the bed. The little white pieces of fluff littered the floor, and an open cotton ball bag sat on the dresser. The woman was fully dressed and centered in the middle of the mattress, as if she settled in for a nap. She wore one shoe, and her hair resembled a cyclone hit. The woman's other shoe was by the bathroom door. Skylar leaned over the dead body. The woman had a small, split lip on the inside corner. Nothing about this scene looked normal, but hey, what did she know?

A light touch on her elbow shot a spark straight to her shoulder. Startled, she turned and locked into Logan's gaze, half-expecting to see him hooked to an electrical wire. Judging from his wide-eyed stare, he felt the same sudden jolt and retreated a few steps to put some distance between them. Since the humidity hung in the air like a blanket, the static definitely didn't come from the rug. Dropping her gaze, she cleared her throat and, like Logan, took a few steps to the side. His close proximity scrambled her brain. For Heaven's sake, why? The man was a prime candidate for a deodorant commercial. She fought the urge to grab one of the dead woman's perfume bottles to give him a good squirt.

To be truthful, she'd be better off if the guy stunk all the time. She hadn't traveled across the country to complicate her life by getting involved with a man, and body odor was a definite turnoff in her book. Besides, her aunt's estate created enough of a headache. Then, of course, she faced the decision of what to do with the place. She was a bartender, not a landlord—two entirely different careers. She kicked a few cotton balls to the side.

A commotion in the hall drew her gaze to the apartment door.

Acting like a bull in a china shop, a police officer broke through the small crowd.

With one brow arched, Skylar glanced at Logan. "Someone called the cops?"

Logan shook his head. "In this town, police respond on all fire and ambulance calls. They tend to arrive first."

After stifling a yawn, she studied the anxious faces peering into the room. Mr. Kirby hadn't mentioned anything about profitability. From what she observed so far, the kitchen, hall, and this room looked well maintained. Nothing appeared as if it was ready to fall apart or needed painting. She inwardly sighed. She had so much to uncover, and having a tenant die on her first day didn't help.

Five minutes passed before heavy footsteps thumped on the staircase. Emergency Medical Services personnel hurried through the door, followed by more uniformed cops. A woman in a black uniform carried a huge shoulder bag with the *New Jersey Paramedic* symbol emblazoned in white. She introduced herself as Tahira, lowered her case onto the floor, and started her preliminary assessment. With nothing to do but confirm death, the medic placed sticky pads on the dead body and then connected the leads to a monitor that printed out a flat-line strip. Finished, she repacked her case and left.

The police officer standing by the door held out a hand in a Stop position. "Everyone is instructed not to touch or move the body until Lieutenant Robert Monroe arrives."

Gaze narrowed, Fay jammed her hands onto her hips. "Why?"

He held up his hands. "I'm just the messenger, ma'am."

A bad feeling swept through Skylar. Why would a police lieutenant bother to leave his office for a dead woman when so many other cases crossed his desk? Really, though, one way or the other, she was too tired to care. If she didn't get some shuteye soon, she might fall asleep on her feet.

Five minutes later, a man wearing a dark suit and tie entered and overwhelmed the small room with his sheer presence. At six-foot-four and not an inch shorter, he had no neck, gray hair cut in crew style, and sharp, gray eyes. With one sweep of his gaze, he surveyed the area along with the woman on the bed until settling an intense gaze on Skylar.

Her palms itched. Why would the big man focus on her? Why not Fay or Logan? Just because she wore all black didn't mean she was an ax murderer.

Walking over, he extended a hand. "Lieutenant Robert Monroe, New Jersey State Police. You're the new owner?"

What an odd question! Did he know her aunt and that she died and left everything to her niece? If so, then he should know Fay. He didn't acknowledge her, though. In fact, he acknowledged no one except a woman who, for the first time, stepped foot in New Jersey. Stunned, she took his hand and nodded. "Skylar Dawson." Dear Lord, the man's fingers wrapped hers like a tortilla. For the first time in a long while, Skylar craned her neck to meet a man's gaze, and oh, my, his cologne smelled wonderful. He should stand next to Logan to mask his odoriferous stench.

Monroe turned to the two officers waiting by the door. "Garfield, I want pictures before we move the body. Your cell phone will do." He took Fay's arm. "You better go downstairs, little lady. You're looking a mite pale. Are you the housekeeper?"

Ah, so he didn't know Fay. Talk about confusion. Skylar reached for Fay. "I'll help her."

"No, Ms. Dawson. You stay." He waved toward the second officer standing by the door. "Escort her, will you? Then, make a list of everyone's names and have them gather in the sitting room. I'll talk to them shortly." After Fay and the others left, Monroe faced Logan. "Are you the one who called?"

"Yes, sir."

"All right, you stay. Let's move to the side so my man can take some photos." He ushered Skylar and Logan toward the window, but his cell phone rang. "Excuse me a moment." Turning away, he lifted the phone to his ear.

Skylar frowned at the lieutenant's back. "That's odd."

Removing his arm from the crutch holder, Logan stepped alongside. "What's odd?"

Facing Logan, she jerked her head in the lieutenant's direction. "If it's information he seeks, Fay is the logical choice. What makes him think I know anything?"

"He must have his reasons." He rubbed his left forearm. "For one, you don't seem ready to faint. Have you come across dead bodies before?"

"Only once." She shivered. "I found her in the ladies' room at the bar. We were closing for the night, and yeah, she felt like ice. She'd been dead a while." Luckily, she didn't know the woman. If she hadn't the urge to empty her bladder, she could have gone home without the memory embedded into her brain.

While she waited for Monroe to finish his call, Skylar stared out the opened window. Margaret's room faced the front of the property, and from this height, the view of the expansive lawn took away her breath. Keeping her voice low, Skylar leaned toward Logan. "Is this normal procedure to have state police on an EMS call?"

Snorting, he kept his gaze on the lieutenant. "Hardly. Maybe our local cops are busy, and they requested their help. The state police barracks isn't far from here."

After slipping his phone into his suit pocket, Monroe returned.

Logan cleared his throat. "Lieutenant, neither of us found the body. That was Anthony Powers."

Monroe acknowledged with a nod and turned to the officer with the camera. "That should be enough pictures. Thanks. Send the copies to my email."

"Yes, sir." The officer left, closing the door behind him.

Yawning, Skylar strolled over to a lounge chair and sat.

Logan hobbled behind her. "You okay?"

Glancing up, she forced a smile. "Tired, that's all. I left Pittsburgh at seven this morning. Traffic was horrible."

"At least, you didn't drive straight through from Chicago."

She shot him a wan smile. "I wasn't *that* anxious to get here, Mr. Greene."

He leaned over. "Call me Logan."

Oh, crap. His stench triggered her nose. She sneezed…twice. Shooting him a sideways glance, she shrugged. "I think I'm allergic to whatever is covering your clothes." She rubbed her nose. "My friends call me Sky."

Monroe slipped a notebook and pen from his shirt pocket. "I'd like to hear your honest assessment about this death, Ms. Dawson."

Brows high, she straightened in the chair. "Me? Why?"

"Let's say new eyes at the manor."

What in the world did *that* mean? She shifted her gaze toward Margaret. The poor woman was left on the bed like a slab of meat. Geez, not even a bedsheet. She met Monroe's steady gaze. "With all the pictures and statements, you're acting like this is a homicide."

"Standard procedure on unwitnessed deaths."

Yeah, well, whatever. Granted, the scene looked suspicious, but anyone could fall and hobble over to the bed on one shoe. Why would her opinion matter? She scratched her nose. The thing still itched. "What do you want to know?"

He poised his pen over the notebook. "Just a generalized impression."

She opened her mouth, then slapped her lips shut. Generalized, huh? Why did this feel like some sort of test? She didn't even know these people. "You're asking the wrong person, Lieutenant. I've only arrived. My bike engine is still warm."

After tilting his head, he met her gaze. "Let's say I want to see how observant you are."

Oh, brother. What was this, tenth grade? She glanced at Logan, who merely shrugged. The damn man was no help.

Pursing her lips, she nodded toward the bed. "I have questions more than impressions. I don't understand the abrasion on her forehead nor the fact her one shoe is by the bathroom door and the other is on her foot. She also has a cut lip, which might indicate she tripped and fell, then staggered to the bed." She wagged a finger. "What I find puzzling is why she centered herself on the mattress."

Narrowing his gaze, Monroe stared at the woman on the bed. "I see your point. Go on."

Skylar stifled a yawn. "She wears eyeglasses. She has indentations on her nose that tell of long-term use, but people who fall wearing glasses usually receive a cut from a broken frame. I've seen enough cut noses from drunks taking a fall."

One brow cocked, Monroe searched the floor.

"Over there." Logan pointed. "By the bureau, and yes, Margaret never went without glasses."

Monroe snapped a picture with his cell phone before bending with a handkerchief to retrieve a pair of red-framed spectacles. He placed them onto the bed. "No damage. She was probably holding them in her hand when she walked out of the bathroom." He wrote notations in his little book. "You have a sharp eye, Ms. Dawson. Nice work."

She rubbed her forehead, then peered up at him. "Did I pass?"

A smile tugged on the corner of his lips, but he said nothing.

Anyone who worked nights in Chicago better have their wits about them. Since she ended her shift after the witching hour and drove alone on a motorcycle, she always kept a careful ear and eye on her surroundings. Even then, her martial arts skill saved her on more than one occasion.

He tapped the pen on the notebook. "What else, Ms. Dawson?"

"What is this, twenty questions? If answered correctly, do I win a prize?" Fighting to control the onslaught of irritation, she met his gaze. "How do you know there's more?"

After shifting his gaze from her to Logan and back, he smiled. "Because I see the debate all over your face."

No one ever mentioned reading her so well. Maybe that was why she never won at poker. She smirked. "All right, yes. I'm curious about two more details." She waggled a finger in the direction of the bed. "Her hair is reminiscent of a struggle, rather than a poor night's rest.

And since she's already dressed for the day, then I assume she also fixed her hair."

Monroe shifted his gaze to the bed. "Or she fainted, fell, then hit her head and cut her lip."

Logan tapped his crutch on the floor. "It doesn't explain her shoes nor her position on the bed."

The lieutenant turned toward Logan. "And you are?"

"Logan Greene, sir."

"You're a resident?"

"Yes, room ten."

The man scribbled in his notebook. "Do you have anything to add?"

"Just that Mrs. Caine always had her hair perfectly combed. Also, she didn't join us for lunch." He leaned on his crutch. "Since Anthony found her, I assume her bedroom door was ajar."

"I'll be sure to ask him." Turning toward Skylar, he smiled. "Thank you. That will be all."

"Except I have a question for you." Standing, she lifted her chin and locked onto his gaze. "Who told you I'm the new owner? I haven't been here more than two hours."

Monroe's gaze twinkled.

If this man so much as said a condescending word, she'd flatten him—figuratively speaking, of course. No way would she attack a police officer.

Logan cleared his throat. "I told dispatch when I called, Sky."

Well, that didn't feel right, either. *I'm probably tired*. Nothing made sense. While pointing toward the floor, she faced Logan. "What's with the cotton balls?"

With a huff, Logan knocked a few with the tip of

his crutch. "Margaret liked to clean things with an alcohol-soaked cotton ball. Unfortunately, she always dropped them and couldn't bend because of a bad back." He nodded at Monroe. "If you check her trouser pockets, you'll find her small bottle of alcohol."

Approaching the bed, Monroe patted the woman's hips, then reached in to extract the bottle. Little cotton balls fell out, as well. Frowning, he shook his head.

People and their strange habits. Years ago, she met an old guy who collected rusty screws and kept them in his pocket. When he bent over, he showed everyone his butt crack.

Logan released a loud cough and lost the grip on his crutch.

Automatically reacting, she caught the crutch before it hit the floor. When she handed it over, she startled at the gaze exchanged between Logan and Monroe. *Uh-oh.* She probably insulted Logan's manly pride. Avoiding a glance at either man, Skylar left the room, and within seconds, she relaxed her shoulders and took a deep breath. She hadn't realized she was so tense. Then again, she rarely spent time in a dead woman's room. Moments later, she entered the kitchen.

At the table with a bottle of water in hand, Fay sat, staring at the floor, her face pale.

No one else was in the kitchen.

Lifting her gaze, the housekeeper forced a smile. "The police are questioning the others in the sitting room."

Skylar pulled out a chair and dropped to the seat. "Death is never easy."

Grunting, Fay rubbed her forehead. "I don't know why they're making a fuss over Margaret's death." She met Skylar's gaze. "Do they suspect foul play?"

The thought crossed Skylar's mind, especially after Monroe's interrogation. The big question was, why? She shrugged. "I'm too new here to answer you."

Fay sniffed. "Margaret was a nice lady, peculiar with her cotton balls, but funny to be around. I'll miss her."

Leaning back, Sky rested her arm on the table. "Have you known her long?"

"Six years." She took a swig of water. After plunking the bottle onto the table, she shook her head. "I've been with your aunt fifteen years and still can't get used to people dying." Reaching across the table, she patted Skylar's arm. "This isn't a rest home, dear. Ginger ran a home for all ages, but it's the elderly who stay the longest."

At the mention of rest home, Logan's response to the two words flashed through her mind. She mentioned his reaction to Fay.

"Oh, gosh, yes. He's defensive and has been since his arrival two months ago." She tapped her fingernails on the water bottle. "No man likes to be crippled, and I suspect that's why he's not overly friendly with anyone."

Sky cocked her head. "Has he said how his injury occurred?"

"Not a word. He's very private." She finished the last of her water and crushed the plastic bottle. "He's on welfare, you know. The state pays his rent."

At least, the man wasn't lazy. Tending to the property grounds couldn't be an easy job. She stifled another yawn. "Logan also mentioned Margaret missed lunch. Was she down for breakfast?"

"Yes, she ate her usual bowl of cereal. She seemed perfectly normal." Shaking herself, she slapped the table and stood. "Where are my manners? You must be exhausted after your drive. I'll show you to your living quarters." Tossing the crushed bottle into a marked *Recycle* bin, she stepped to the stove and turned off the burner under the big pot. With a wave to follow, she headed for the backdoor. "Come on, dear. Let's get you settled so you can see this marvelous estate your great-aunt left."

With a glance toward the archway to the kitchen, Skylar couldn't help wondering about Monroe's odd behavior. Why test her observation skills? She wasn't a doctor. Her training developed over years of being a good bartender and anticipating her customer's wants before they asked. Still, a nagging feeling lay in her gut like a rock.

Chapter Three

Hurrying after Fay, Skylar took one step out the backdoor and stopped. The concrete patio stretched across the entire length of the house and looked more like an outdoor dance floor. Chairs and tables stood on one side with grill and serving table on the other. Flowerpots full of orange marigolds decorated the perimeter, and in opposite corners, Irish gnomes with corncob pipes faced a set of concrete steps. The house had no awning overhead, but at this time of day with the rear of the house facing east, the patio sat in comfortable afternoon shade. "Wow!"

Already down the steps, Fay turned and grinned. "Nice, eh? Your aunt had this patio, the front porch, and the rancher's done at the same time. This way, dear."

Sky followed Fay along another interlocking brick path and past a row of tall, privacy evergreens to the rancher sitting in full sun. The structure was also gray-sided to match the manor's wings, but the design had more of a mini-me look without the elegance. An *Office* sign hung over a six-paned window door to what once looked to be an enclosed front porch with its array of windows around three sides. On the left, another brick path led to the side of the rancher, and a third path on the right disappeared around the side of the main house. A large mailbox on a wooden post stood outside the office door. As Logan said, *Ginger's Manor* was prominently displayed on the side. "Do all the tenants receive their mail in this one box?"

"Most of them, yes. I usually collect and distribute whatever comes."

A yapping dog forced Skylar to turn. Closing in on her heels was a small terrier-poodle mix with a mop of white hair.

A little boy with fair skin and light-brown hair ran full tilt after the mutt while yelling commands the dog ignored. The animal circled Skylar, yapping all the way.

Not in the least afraid, she stared at the bouncing fur ball to make sure the creature didn't pee on her boots.

Bending and with stern expression, Fay wagged a finger at the dog. "Mind your manners."

The animal immediately sat on its rump and whimpered.

Straightening, Fay frowned. "This is your aunt's pet, Yapper."

Skylar laughed. "Appropriately named, I see."

"This young man is Tommy Hashoff." She adjusted her eyeglasses. "He and his mom are residents. Tommy, meet our new owner, Ms. Dawson."

Backing away one step, Tommy squinted from the sunlight. "Are you gonna sell the place?"

The very question she asked herself about a half-dozen times. "I have no idea what I'm doing, Tommy." She might as well be honest with the kid.

"I'd rather own a baseball stadium."

Yeah, wouldn't we all.

Judging from his height, Tommy couldn't be more

than ten years old. His hair stood on end, as if he stuck his finger into an electrical socket like a Saturday morning cartoon character. Dirt covered the knees on his blue jeans, and his sneakers looked one wash away from falling apart. His wrist and elbow bones protruded from his short-sleeved shirt and gave him the appearance of being a trifle malnourished. But what did she know? Her parents didn't follow in true Irish tradition with lots of children. Having a brother or sister would have been nice.

"I've been taking care of Yapper for ya, but he's real excited with all the cop cars around." Tommy puffed out his small chest. "We're great pals."

As much as she loved animals, she didn't need the burden of caring for one while she sorted through her inheritance. She smiled. "Then, would you mind continuing with his care until I figure out what I'm doing?"

"Sure. No problem." With a broad grin, he turned on his heel. "Come on, Yapper. Let's go talk to more cops."

Tommy and the dog raced across the yard and around the corner of the house.

Fay stared after Tommy. "Your aunt had a strict rule about no pets, but one day, Yapper appeared on her patio, all mangy and starving. She couldn't turn him away." She clucked her tongue. "He's become a mascot of sorts. You know, the Ginger's Manor cheerleader. Everybody fell in love with the little mutt." She shot Skylar a glance. "Almost everybody." She inserted a key into the office door. "I keep the dog food in the main house. I wasn't about to let Yapper have the run of the rancher." She smiled over her shoulder. "Since

Tommy's caring for the dog, the boy is much happier. His appetite's improved, too. I think the little guy is much too skinny." She opened the door.

Following, Skylar entered a sauna without the steam. Dear Lord, the heat was stifling. Not a breath of air stirred. She almost turned on her heel to stick her head out the door to fill her lungs with fresh air.

Fay waved a hand. "As you can see, this is the office."

More like a torture chamber, but no sense being rude. While the heat opened every pore on her body, she scanned the interior.

Typical office furniture filled the space. A worn, wooden desk with a cushy chair and a contoured pillow faced an array of front windows, which were half shaded by partially closed blinds. Two metal filing cabinets rested against the wall to the left. On top of the desk, a combination fax machine and printer along with a computer, portable telephone, and rotary card index told her Aunt Ginger joined the twenty-first century. Everything about the room was neat and orderly, but more than blinds were needed to keep out the hot, afternoon sun.

Fay pointed toward a large white unit on the right wall. "Since this was once the rancher's front porch, heating and air conditioning had to be added. The unit works both ways. The remote is in the top desk drawer."

With fresh batteries, hopefully. Whew. Too hot. The sweat dripped between her breasts, and she pulled her top away from her chest.

"Your aunt only turned on the AC when she sat at the desk. Even then, she kept it on low." Removing a key ring hanging on a hook by the door, Fay jangled them. "These keys are for the main house and all the residents' rooms. I have a similar set in my bedroom. All are labeled. The garage key—two keys, actually—are included." She returned them to the hook and removed a smaller set from her trouser pocket. "Ginger never used the garage for her car. She preferred to park under the carport alongside. Consequently, the garage became a catch-all place for junk, including all the lawn equipment. These keys I'm using—which are yours, by the way." She spread the keys onto her palm and pointed to each. "Office door, rancher's front and rear door, manor's front and backdoor, and the car's fob."

Fay approached a side door, heavier and more ornate than the office door. "This is the main entrance to your living quarters." She inserted the key. "Since I knew you were coming, I gave the place a good cleaning with the help of Rita, another of our tenants. The air conditioner has been serviced, and I turned it on this morning. So, the house should feel a lot better than the office."

Thank God for that. After one step over the threshold, Skylar sighed as cool air hit her skin.

"This is your home away from home, honey."

The saying hit like a brick. Yes, this was her house, her property, and maybe her new life. She had so much thinking to do. Yawning, she scanned the interior.

A welcoming brightness greeted her. The combination living-dining room had opened drapes on two sets of double-hung windows surrounding a rear door. Daylight flooded the room and allowed her a nice view of a wide backyard. Closed curtains covered the front windows, probably for privacy from office visitors. A large sofa sat in the middle of the floor with its back cushions covered with colorful afghans of yellow and orange. White doilies protected the furniture from lamps and knickknacks, and a bookcase along the wall held no books, only a collection of beer steins, large and small. Overall, a comfortable home for an elderly woman.

Fay glanced over her shoulder. "I wasn't sure if you wanted to sleep in your aunt's bed or the guest room. I prepared both."

At this point, any bed would do. She was about to collapse on her feet. "Thank you, Fay. The guest room is fine."

"This way."

Turning left toward a hall, Fay pointed at the thermostat on the wall. "Heat and air conditioner. Digital settings." She continued down the hall.

Skylar passed a folding-door closet, a full bath, and a laundry room before reaching the two bedrooms. Dark carpeting covered the entire floor of the house, with the exception of the laundry room and bath.

Fay stopped and waved toward the left bedroom. "Ginger's room has the master bath." She turned into the right bedroom.

The room was nice and bright, thanks to two windows with opened drapes. A white chenille spread covered a queen-size bed with nightstands on both sides. On one wall, a white dresser with a mirror sat between the two windows. A matching white chest of drawers and a small vanity completed the furnishings. Everything looked clean and cheery.

Sighing, Fay faced her. "Because of Margaret, your introduction to your inheritance was a bit skewed.

When you're ready, return to the manor, and I'll give you a proper tour."

By then, this strange numbness might dissipate from her brain. She still couldn't believe all this property was hers. Stifling another yawn, Skylar followed Fay to the living room. "I have one question before you go. Why did my aunt leave everything to me?"

Gaze steady, Fay chewed on her lower lip. "Your father's dead, right? If he was alive, he'd explain. Come over here." She led the way across the living room to a dining table loaded with framed photographs. "Most of these faces are tenants who lived at the manor. A few are relatives. However—" She lifted one framed photo and handed it to Skylar. "This is why."

Skylar stared at the picture of a woman who resembled Skylar in every way, except for a head of tight curls. She had the same small nose and prominent cheekbones. But the woman was older than Skylar's thirty years, perhaps in her late fifties. With both brows high, she turned to Fay. "Aunt Ginger?"

"Yes, the family resemblance is strong." Fay smiled. "She was so proud of you." She took the photo and replaced it onto the table.

Sky gaped, then slapped her mouth shut. "Proud of what? I'm a bartender."

"But that's how she started, dear. After graduating from high school, she waited tables, elevated to bartender, and then to owner of the bar. You're unknowingly following in her footsteps." She retrieved another photo. "Recognize this one?"

A little dark-haired girl leaned against a seated Ginger in what appeared to be someone's living room.

Both faces smiled brightly for the camera. Skylar stroked the photo. "It's me."

"I don't think you were more than three years old. She told me she fell in love with you and hadn't stopped. You two actually look like mother and daughter." While pointing to the photo, she smiled. "Your father snapped the picture on one of his visits."

Tears clouded Skylar's vision. "I have no memory of her." Replacing the photo to the table, she looked at Fay. "Why the secrecy?"

Fay chewed her lower lip, then sighed. "I don't know. Ginger always claimed not to be much of a family person. Yet, she treated her tenants like family—me, especially. I started as the housekeeper, and we became good friends. I thought for sure she..." She stared at the table. Then, she shook herself and smirked. "Well, never mind. You have a few relatives still living in Philadelphia, but Ginger said they aren't worth a plugged nickel. If I were you, I'd be careful if they come sniffing around. They never bothered while she was alive, and you know how relatives crawl out of the woodwork when money is involved." With a curt nod, she tapped the table.

"So, now you know. Get yourself settled. Here are your keys." She dropped the ring into Skylar's open palm and turned toward the front door. "I'm afraid your refrigerator is empty. I figured you'd do your own shopping. You should dine with us tonight. That way, you'll meet most of the tenants." With her hand on the knob, she glanced over her shoulder and paused. "Dinner's at six. Now"—she squared her shoulders— "let me see what this Lieutenant Monroe is up to. Margaret's family needs to be notified."

Alone at last, Skylar stood in the middle of the living room and stared at the keys in her hand. She owned a boardinghouse and rancher and, according to Mr. Kirby, whatever else came with the estate. Some people would call her blessed to have such a generous aunt, but she felt numb. The property might be worth a ton of money, but what about outstanding debts or a mortgage? What if the manor operated in the red? She wasn't a woman with money growing on trees.

Too many questions for her tired brain, and standing in the middle of her aunt's fully furnished house only created a lost feeling. Not like the rancher was huge. The kitchen sat at one end, the two bedrooms at the other, with the main living space between.

Skylar rubbed her eyes. The stress of travel and seeing this beautiful estate was taking its toll. A quick nap might be nice. She checked her watch. She had time, so she headed for the bedroom and flopped onto the bed.

"Sky."

Her shortened name sounded intimate coming from the deep, male voice.

"Come on, Sky. Wake up."

Leave me alone. No, on second thought, talk to me. I love your voice.

A hand touched her shoulder.

Reacting on instinct, she grabbed onto a thick wrist and yanked, sending whoever he was flying across the room.

The ensuing crash and shocked cry knocked some sense into her foggy brain. She bolted upright in bed and scanned the bedroom. Dear Lord! She threw Logan clear across the room.

He lay in a heap under a window. "Skylar, what the hell?"

Jumping from the bed, she hovered over him. "You shouldn't sneak up on me." She wasn't sure whether to feel sorry for him or mad. The poor guy looked more stunned than anything. Straightening, she jammed her hands onto her hips. "How'd you get in here?"

"Ouch." Wincing, Logan eased to a sitting position. "I knocked, but when you didn't answer, I walked inside. You left the front door unlocked." Scowling, he met her gaze. "I don't know how you do things in Chicago, but we lock doors around here. Help me up." He extended his hand.

"Wait. Before you stand, are you hurt?"

"Only my pride." He shifted his hips. "I outweigh you by at least eighty pounds, and yet, you threw me like a five-pound sack of potatoes. How'd you do that?"

"Practice." Skylar clamped onto his wrist and silently questioned how to help a two hundred pound disabled hunk of muscle to his feet. As it happened, she provided some leverage as his fingers circled her wrist in the universal soldiers' grip until he righted himself. She handed him his crutch.

Well, she hadn't expected a thank you, but she did get a quick once-over, which she reciprocated and did the same to him. She almost didn't recognize him. He had showered and changed into a white shirt and black jeans, with both garments hugging the muscles on his body. His light-brown hair was clean and finger-combed, and something woodsy filled the air. For some reason, she was mesmerized. The man was an extraordinary example of manhood with biceps straining his short-sleeved shirt. If the muscles grew any larger, the sleeves would cut off circulation to his hands. Breaking her ogling, she tugged on her shirt's hem. "Why are you here?"

"Dinnertime. Fay sent me."

"Oh." She should have set an alarm. "Okay, let me splash some water on my face, and I'll be right over."

Gaze twinkling, he leaned close. "You love my voice, eh?"

Oh, rats. She said the words out loud? Heat flushed her face, but the embarrassment took a backseat as she locked onto his copper-colored eyes. They were gorgeous. Since he stood so close, she watched tiny flecks sparkle, like pieces of fudge floating. She cleared her throat. "Sorry, Logan. I guess I talk in my sleep, but you do have a nice voice." Might as well be honest. She had yet to see a smile. Maybe his teeth were rotted and ready to fall from their sockets. And one other thing…she gasped. "I don't feel like sneezing."

Narrowing his gaze, he huffed. "I trimmed the forsythia bushes today. You're probably allergic to the pollen." He pointed to her face. "You have chenille indentations on your cheek."

Smirking, she shook her head. "I'll be fine." And thank God, she hadn't undressed for her little nap. Shaking the sleep from her eyes, she glanced at the tall figure rubbing his right hip. "Are you okay?"

He grunted in answer and hobbled toward the door. "I put your duffel bag and helmet on the sofa. Wouldn't want anyone to drive by and steal them." He stopped in the doorway.

"Thank you. I appreciate your trouble, but next time, announce yourself before touching me." His aftershave swirled around the room, and she resisted the urge to suck in a deep breath. She cleared her throat. "Wait for me at the house, Logan. I'll be along in a minute."

"Right. Remember to lock your doors." He hobbled from the room.

Was she in some high crime area? In Chicago, sure, she double-bolted doors and checked all locks on windows. Her cycle she kept in a garage. Sighing, she hurried into the bathroom to splash cold water on her face. Like Logan said, chenille indentations marked her cheek. She pinched and rubbed until her skin responded. Satisfied, she headed for the living room when her cell phone mooed. *Aw, crap.* Her boss. She assigned him a special ringtone because he was built like a cow. She aimed for the sofa where Logan said he dumped her stuff and fished through her windbreaker. Grabbing the phone before it switched to voicemail, she swiped the Accept button. "Hi, Kevin."

"How're things going?"

"I arrived a few hours ago and am just settling in."

"What do you mean? Your last shift was Friday night. The house should be halfway empty by now."

Oh, good heavens. The man should learn to listen. She flopped onto the sofa's armrest. "I told you. I needed Saturday to pack, gas up, and give my neighbor the key to the house. I left Sunday morning and stayed overnight in Pittsburgh."

"How come you didn't drive straight through?"

She'd like to see his fat ass on a slim motorcycle seat for a cross-country trek. The man couldn't get into his sedan without a grunt and a groan. "I don't drive my cycle in the dark, Kevin, especially on the turnpike."

He snorted. "You should have worked the

weekend, Midnight. You missed some good tips."

Since the staff pooled their money, *he* missed the good tips. The man took a cut for just sitting on his rump.

"So, when are you coming back?"

Was he for real? She stared at her phone, as if her glare shot through the lines and directly to his face. Taking a deep breath, she replaced the phone to her ear. "I've scheduled a month off. Remember?"

He humphed. "Well, everyone misses you."

"Thanks for the compliment, but I've an estate to settle. I'll keep you posted. Okay?"

"Yeah, yeah. Call me tomorrow."

He disconnected.

Again, she stared at her phone. When she asked for the month off, she watched his face change from pale to red in five seconds flat. She swore up and down he'd have a stroke right in front of her. Sighing, she pinched the bridge of her nose. She needed to find a bar in a more upscale neighborhood, one with a better boss who wasn't such a tightwad. Did her aunt experience the same frustration? Was she tired of working the bar so, instead, bought one?

After tossing her phone onto her jacket, she headed for the main house. With a knot growing in the pit of her stomach, she stopped midway along the brick path and stared at the manor's screen door. Her emotions were all over the place today. Logan and Kevin aside, her stepping into her aunt's shoes might be the ultimate topping on the cake. She was the new landlord and about to meet the tenants. *What the hell were you thinking, Aunt Ginger?*

Chapter Four

All right, I can do this. Dinner with a bunch of strangers wasn't at the top of her to-do list, but after years behind a bar, she talked to all sorts of people. Interacting with the tenants should be no different. Besides, they were probably as nervous. Technically, their fate was in her hands. She'd simply show them Skylar Dawson had backbone and wasn't a woman to be pushed around or intimidated…much. Sucking in a calming breath, she hopped onto the porch and opened the manor's screen door. She stopped dead.

A woman blocked the path. She stood by the door with her hands on her hips and looked about as imposing as a Chihuahua confronting a Bull Mastiff. Thin, frail, and barely reaching Skylar's shoulders, she had to be in her seventies with brown-dyed hair cropped short and permed. Her wide, brown eyes surveyed Skylar and then twinkled as a smile stretched across her wrinkled face. Grabbing Skylar's hand, she shook like a pumping machine.

"PPE, PPE."

Dumbstruck at the woman's odd greeting and strong grip, Skylar managed to move her tongue. "Nice to meet you, too."

"Ya-ya."

The woman nodded like a bobblehead.

What the hell?

Fay strolled into the kitchen, chuckling. "I see you met Gilda." Approaching, she wrapped one arm around the woman's small shoulders and squeezed. "She's our only tenant who developed a medical condition and is still able to function on her own. Right, Gilda?"

"Ya-ya."

Grinning, Fay dropped her arm. "Gilda is a retired high school physics teacher and, believe it or not, helped Tommy win first prize in a science contest this spring."

"Ya-ya. PPE." Gilda hurried to the stove.

Skylar stared at the woman's back. "What kind of medical condition?"

While watching Gilda, Fay released a heavy sigh. "A few years ago, she suffered a stroke. It robbed her of everything pertaining to language. In other words, she can't form coherent words nor can she read. But, she understands us perfectly." She touched Skylar's arm. "When you talk to her, ask *yes* or *no* questions. Sometimes, she gets frustrated with her limitations— like the time she discovered one of the tenants dead in the bathtub. She tried to tell me, but getting nowhere, she grabbed onto my arm and dragged me upstairs. Gilda, honey, don't let that pot boil over."

"Ya-ya." She adjusted the burner.

Gaze following Gilda, Fay stuffed her hands into her trouser pockets. "Her stroke happened during that horrible COVID pandemic. Personal Protection Equipment—or PPE—was the one phrase she heard over and over. So, naturally, she latched onto it. She won't say anything else." Pausing, she faced Skylar. "As a rule, tenants who develop a medical condition that involves nursing care are asked to leave. This facility is a licensed boardinghouse and not a nursing home. Excuse me." Turning toward the stove, she clicked all the burners to the Off position. "Okay, honey, drain these two pots, and we're ready." She removed another pot's lid and placed it to the side before returning her attention to Skylar.

"Tenants must be independent, take their own medication, and not require wheelchair assistance. We do not have an elevator, but every bathroom has handlebars. Gilda is very much independent. She just can't talk." She waved toward the archway to the hall. "You won't meet everyone tonight. Some of the tenants still work—like Tommy's mom. She handles the dinner shift at a diner in Woodbury and comes home around nine. Mr. Chang sometimes gets stuck in traffic, but for the most part, he joins us. Joe Ryan leaves for work at five every night." She waved toward Gilda. "Okay, honey, ring the bell."

Gilda rushed out the rear door.

Seconds later, a bell clanged.

A real dinner bell! Steeling herself for the tenants' arrivals, Skylar stood off to the side.

An African-American woman rushed through the archway, grabbed the dishtowel, and wiped dinner plates already clean and set. She moved like a whirlwind, and the breeze lifted the edges of the paper napkins.

Smirking, Fay nodded in the woman's direction. "She's Rita Garrett. She has OCD. Rita, meet Skylar Dawson."

Rita waved the towel in the air but continued around the tables.

Skylar realized a little too late that she resembled a

guppy gasping for air. She slapped her mouth shut. First, the woman with a cotton ball obsession, then a woman with a speech impediment, and to add to the list, a woman with Obsessive Compulsive Disorder. What kind of boardinghouse did she inherit?

The two elderly gentlemen from the front porch entered. One, an African-American, extended his hand. "Tyrone Houser. Nice to meet you."

Skylar shook a strong grip. "Likewise."

He jerked a thumb over his shoulder. "Behind me is Anthony Powers. He's the one who found Margaret."

"Yeah, lucky me." Anthony offered his hand. "I'm sorry I went upstairs to take a pee. I shoulda used the bathroom under the stairwell." After shaking Skylar's hand, he yanked a chair from the table. "What's for dinner, Fay?"

Fay turned from the stove with two large platters in hand. "You'll find out in a minute. Just sit." She placed a platter on each table.

As an only child in a quiet house, Skylar had no experience with a large crowd at the dinner table. Being here with all these people was like standing in the middle of a carnival. Everyone talked at once and behaved like one big, happy family.

Another older woman entered, followed by an Asian man.

The woman shot a quick glance at Skylar and, without a word, took a seat at the table, being careful to fold her dress skirt before she lowered onto the seat.

While rolling his white shirt sleeves to the elbow, the man walked over.

He was perhaps in his forties with necktie loosened and top button unfastened. He wasn't a tall man by any means. In fact, if age wasn't a factor, he and Gilda matched in height and would make a cute couple.

Extending his hand, he smiled. "Michael Chang. I liked your aunt a lot."

"Yeah, yeah, we all did." Anthony tucked his napkin into his shirt collar. "Sit down before we starve to death."

Fay placed identical plates of food onto each table and then clapped her hands. "All right, everyone. Eat. Skylar, sit next to me." She patted the empty chair between Gilda and her own.

Whether by design or chance, the men gathered at one table and the women at the other.

Tommy ran in and hopped onto a seat next to Michael Chang, who served the boy as the platters passed.

The unfamiliar woman sat one chair away from Fay and was the lone tenant somewhat dressed for dinner with pearl necklace and matching earrings. She glared at Skylar through veiled lids.

Fay positioned her chair closer to the table. "You haven't met Maria Santini. Maria, this is Skylar Dawson."

"I know who she is."

Whoa. Sky liked to reserve her judgment of people, but she recognized a bitch when she saw one. "Nice to meet you, Mrs. Santini." All right, so she lied. Her parents raised her to be polite, and since she was new here, she'd keep her snarky comments on a back burner.

The clink of Logan's metal crutch echoed in the hall. Seconds later, he hobbled in and took a seat with the men. "Sorry I'm late."

Since his position was directly opposite, he locked onto her gaze and frowned.

Sky inwardly sighed. The man should give her some semblance of a smile, right? You know, politeness and all. If he kept with the frown, he'd develop a permanent crease between his eyes. Lowering her gaze, she slipped her napkin onto her lap.

Fay tapped a spoon against her glass. "We're eating Mrs. Santini's soup tonight." She leaned toward the woman. "I hope I prepared it right. I had to triple the recipe."

Sipping a spoonful, Mrs. Santini grimaced. "A little too much salt."

Skylar tasted the soup full of little pasta noodles, chunks of vegetables, and diced tomatoes. "It's good."

At which, Mrs. Santini shot her a glare.

Oh, brother.

Fay passed Skylar the salad bowl. "I don't know how you eat in Chicago, but here, we eat everything at once. Nothing fancy."

Taking the bowl, she placed a heaping portion onto her plate and passed the salad to Gilda before taking the next plate coming her way. Since the death of her mom, Skylar rarely had a home-cooked meal. Fast food and frozen dinners became her normal diet. When the cooking urge hit—which was once in a blue moon—she cooked enough to freeze.

Rita sprang to her feet, grabbed the iced tea pitcher, and poured into everyone's already full glass.

The woman had ants in her pants. She hadn't stayed in her seat for longer than three minutes.

"Rita, will you sit and eat!" Tyrone pointed toward her chair.

"I've too much to do."

"Everyone is fine, honey." Fay grabbed the pitcher and set it on the table. "Now, sit."

Maria cleared her throat. "My son's a lawyer."

Groans echoed around the table.

Skylar almost laughed. She assumed the comment was for her benefit.

"He's a damn public defender." With a knife, Anthony jabbed his beef. "Fay, this meat is a little tough."

Fay grunted. "You've needed new dentures for months. Break into your bank account and buy some."

Skylar half listened to the chatter. She did her best to keep her gaze away from Logan, but the man sat with a small twist to his lips while he watched her, like he wanted to smile but forced himself to hold it in. Even that tiny gesture was cute. If she wasn't careful, she could swim into the depths of his beautiful eyes and never bother to come up for air.

****

Good food combined with an extraordinary woman in full view, what more could Logan ask? Well, privacy would be a start, along with a nice bottle of wine, and maybe Skylar sitting next to him, instead of clear across the room. This separation of men at one table and women at the other was so high school. But as the newcomer, he followed their strange protocol. Ten to one, no man wanted to sit near Mrs. Santini.

At least, the constant debate was over. For the past two months, the topic at the dinner table centered on their new owner and the questions surrounding their fate. The predominant fear among the tenants was the soon-to-be homeless question, and justifiably so. Skylar lived a lifetime in Chicago. Why would she hold onto the manor when the incentive to sell would amass a small fortune? So, until her intentions were clear, he and the rest of the tenants had their lives on hold.

One way or the other wasn't his concern. A loner by choice, he traveled from place to place and worked the odd jobs necessary to earn his keep. Whenever he arrived at a new location, he interacted with people primarily for information. Nothing and no one affected him, but holy hell, he wasn't prepared for Skylar Dawson. Even though he studied her photos on the Internet, when she stepped off that motorcycle, he truly had no idea what hit him. She had the most expressive pair of blue eyes. Given the opportunity, he'd swim in their depths and drown a happy man.

In his short time at the manor, he'd gotten acquainted with these quirky characters. Tyrone Houser, for example, secretly drooled over Rita, but the woman wouldn't stop cleaning long enough to look into his doe eyes. To spend alone time with her, the poor guy allowed her to clean his room. Talk about desperate.

Grumpy Anthony felt abandoned by his children and complained about everything. The other tenants labeled him the resident grouch, but underneath, the guy was sharp as a tack. Tyrone and Anthony were like two peas in a pod. If one wandered into the room, the other followed.

For a man who developed computer programs all day, Michael Chang was a puzzle. He worked in Delaware at a tech firm and commuted every day. On an IT salary, he made enough money to afford an apartment in Delaware and save himself travel time, especially during the summer when out-of-state cars clogged the roads heading to the Jersey shore.

Doreen Hashoff and Tommy needed Ginger's Manor to survive. After her husband deserted, Doreen lost everything. Faced with no family support, she wound up in one of Ginger's furnished rooms with a suitcase full of clothes. The manor turned into the godsend she needed. Logan reached for a roll to sop up the soup that wasn't half bad.

Joe Ryan was another oddball. He socialized very little and always preferred to lay on the sofa with the TV playing and a Wild West paperback in his hands. He quoted the Bible like he was a former preacher, but all records list him as a thirty-year Navy veteran. Like Doreen, he ate dinner with the group on a night off.

Then, there was Gilda, a woman with a masters in physics. Despite her stroke, she still surprised him with her remarkable brain. Like the day the vacuum died. She took the machine apart, replaced a broken wire, and put everything together in record time and all without instructions she couldn't possibly read. Sometimes, he wondered whether she faked her language disability.

He cut into his meat and chewed. Yeah, Anthony needed new teeth. The beef was perfect.

Fay, of course, worked at the manor for fifteen years and knew every aspect. She'd kept the tenants informed of Ginger's great-niece and ran the manor without a hitch. All in all, a decent bunch of people— on the surface. Logan knew better than anyone how looks deceived.

After an apple pie dessert, Skylar stood with her empty plate in hand only to have Rita whip it from her faster than a card dealer at a casino. Sky glanced his way with those gorgeous blue eyes wide, and he suppressed a chuckle. She looked so darn cute.

Skylar touched Fay's arm. "Thank you for dinner, and good night to everyone. I'm hitting the sack early." She headed out the rear door.

Grabbing his crutch, he followed. "I'll walk you."

Stifling a yawn, she met his gaze. "Why?"

She had a nice mouth with plump lips. Kissable was a good word. He'd bet they were soft and pliable. Realizing he was staring like a fool, he cleared his throat. "I need to put away the mower." As good an excuse as any.

Halfway along the brick path, he glanced over his shoulder at the house. No curious faces peered through the screen door, which surprised him. He lived among a bunch of Nosy Nellies. Gossip was their biggest entertainment. Stopping, he nudged Skylar's elbow. "What do you think happened to Mrs. Caine?"

Halting her steps, she turned to face him. "What do you mean?"

"I didn't say anything with the lieutenant standing nearby, but questions flashed across your face. You're suspicious of something."

She shrugged. "More curious than anything. The abrasion on her head is too high for a fall. She'd have to hit the floor with her chin tucked to her chest."

Yup. This woman was sharp. Another good trait. He adjusted his crutch. "So, what are you saying, someone hit her?"

"I don't know what I'm saying. I'm not a cop."

"But bartenders have an innate ability to read people."

Snorting, she slipped her hands into her front

49

pockets. "Being able to tell when someone has had too much to drink isn't much of a skill." Chewing on her lower lip, she stared at a car driving along the side street. After a moment, she shook her head and started toward the rancher. "I'm sure her death was by natural causes. My suspicions will hardly raise a concern."

He was right. Skylar Dawson had a keen eye for observation, and what she saw was murder. What possible motive would anyone have to kill the little cotton ball lady?

****

Skylar needed her head examined. How could she have this unfathomable attraction to a man she hardly knew? She only met Logan earlier in the day, but every time those copper eyes locked onto her, she struggled not to jump into his arms—those gorgeous, muscular arms attached to his mouth-watering chest. So ridiculous. She never experienced such a feeling with any man, so why him? *Fatigue? Definitely fatigue.*

Letting herself in through the office door, she entered and bolted the lock. Despite the setting sun, the stifling heat settled within the enclosed porch like an oven. Hurrying through, she opened the house door, stepped into the living room, and again bolted the lock.

The house needed light. After switching on one lamp after the other, she walked to the backdoor and tugged on the knob. Locked. Since Logan had her slightly paranoid, she checked the locks on the windows, then closed the drapes. Alone at last and feeling like she should do something but hadn't a clue what, she wandered toward the photos on the dining table. Scanning the array of faces, she recognized no one except…

The framed picture of a man and woman with a little dark-haired girl caught her attention. Picking it up, she smiled. Her mom and dad, both squatting to Skylar's height, smiled brightly for the camera. Dressed in a frilly pink dress, Sky looked to be around two years old, and even at that age, her notoriously straight hair hung like wet strands. To this day, she hadn't a hint of a curl and finally admitted defeat. She kept her hair cropped short and close to the neck. No muss, no fuss.

Her chest squeezed as she slowly traced a finger along the image of her father and then her mother. She missed them so much. Her dad had been dead ten years from a heart attack that took everyone by surprise. He just dropped at work. Her mom fought breast cancer for seven years until the disease finally won. That was two years ago. Why hadn't Aunt Ginger made her existence known? They could have become acquainted, and Skylar wouldn't have felt so alone in the world.

Setting the photo to the front of the group, she lifted the one of her great-aunt. The resemblance was remarkable—except for the curly, dark hair. "I'm not sure whether to thank you or cuss you, Aunt Ginger. For some reason, I think you disrupted my well-ordered routine on purpose." Yeah, some routine. She ate, slept, and worked. She had some friends, but no one close. Most of the time, she kept to herself. Being here with all these people was definitely new. So often, she imagined life in a big family, and tonight was a taste of something she never had. The whole scenario felt weird but nice. Sighing, she replaced the photo onto the table and meandered toward the kitchen.

New cream appliances and sparkling linoleum floor gave the kitchen a showroom appearance. A round table for four sat near two double-hung windows that faced a gazebo—a peaceful view, no matter what time of day. She opened the refrigerator, then freezer. Everything was empty except for an ice cube tray with hardly any water left. She placed the tray into the sink.

The cabinets were next. She found plenty of dishes and glassware, including a collection of shot glasses and one opened bottle of a top-label brand of Irish whiskey, some cans of chicken noodle soup, tea bags, but not much else—and worse, no coffee! She scanned the counter. No coffeemaker, either. *Oh, Lordy.* Bending toward the lower cabinets, she flung open one door after another. Nothing but pots and pans. *Aggh*! Skylar Dawson wasn't a morning person and required several doses of stimulant to wake her brain. First chance tomorrow, she'd ask Fay if Ginger had a machine packed away somewhere. Otherwise, her to-do list included a trip for food and the purchase of one very urgent appliance. She strolled toward her aunt's bedroom and hit the wall switch.

Another afghan covered the foot of the bed—a pretty blend of purple, pink, and yellow. A hairbrush with matching hand mirror was on the dresser along with a glass tray full of bottles of nail polish and makeup. A half-empty aspirin bottle sat under a small lamp on the nightstand, and a dark-blue housecoat hung on a hook on the outside of the closet door.

A wave of melancholy swept over her, and she wrapped her arms tight around her torso. She stood in the middle of her late aunt's bedroom, looking at her life. What was she like? Was she happy? "I don't even know how she died."

Suddenly, according to Mr. Kirby's letter—which

told her nothing.

Even before Kirby's letter arrived, Skylar had thought long and hard about what to do with her life. She liked her job, but she lived alone and rarely dated. Loneliness sometimes hit, and she couldn't do a damn thing about it. Now, here she was, standing in her aunt's bedroom, wondering if her great-aunt just threw down the gauntlet.

Chapter Five

After a relaxing shower and a decent night's rest, Skylar woke the next morning ready to conquer whatever anyone threw her way. Figuring the day would be as humid as yesterday, she ditched her boots for sneakers, cargo pants for cargo shorts, and T-shirt for tank top. Black, of course. As much as she enjoyed a quiet cup of coffee in the morning, she'd bite the bullet and grab a cup from the manor. With luck, the tenants weren't in a chatty mood. She stepped out the office door.

From the corner of her eye, she caught a glimpse of Yapper bolting around the evergreens that separated the rancher from the manor. With a whirl to avoid the dog, she collided with Tommy who was in hot pursuit. She remained on her feet.

Tommy went sprawling onto the grass. Propping onto his elbows, he grinned. "Hey, sorry, Ms. Dawson. I just took Yapper behind the garage to do his business." After jumping to his feet, he cupped his small hands near his mouth. "Yapper!"

The canine trotted over, tongue dangling. He immediately sniffed Skylar's sneakers.

What a duo! They were practically inseparable. She smiled at Tommy. "Where's your mom?"

He brushed dirt and grass clippings from his shirt. "She's putting clothes in the washing machine, but I don't need someone watching me. I'm almost nine and a half."

Oh, wow, old age.

Biting his lip, he glanced up. "Mom says I can keep Yapper if you don't want him."

How could she say *no* to this lovely, little boy? She waved her hand. "He's all yours."

Eyes wide, he gaped. "You mean it? Wow, thanks. I'll tell Mom. By the way, your motorcycle is so cool. Can I have a ride?"

Oh, dear. She'd never given anyone a ride, least of all a child. How in the world would she strap him down? She coughed. "We'll get permission from your mom first, okay?"

"Yay! Come on, Yapper." He and the dog hopped onto the manor's patio and hurried through the screen door.

Speaking of her cycle, she'd left her baby exposed to the elements. Fay said something about a garage so Skylar ambled along the secondary path leading to the bedroom side of the rancher. The bricks ended at a large concrete slab and, ultimately, the garage with its wide-open doors. Grass covered what was once a driveway, but judging from the lawn equipment cluttering the interior, a car hadn't been sheltered inside the building in years. To the left of the garage, a white car was parked under a metal carport. After unloading her saddlebags, she'd move her cycle under the vaulted roof to protect it from the weather.

She stifled a yawn. All right, time for coffee. Following Tommy, she entered a kitchen full of the wonderful aromas of coffee, bacon, and eggs. She sucked in a deep breath. "Smells wonderful in here.

Morning, everyone."

To her relief, only Logan, Tommy, and a woman sat at the men's table. The woman looked about as inviting as typhoid fever. She shot daggers from a pair of hazel eyes, and her lip curled into a sneer. *And a good morning to you, too.*

Fay turned from the sink, grabbed a dishtowel, and smiled. "Morning. I've scrambled eggs and bacon. Want some?"

"I'd love it." She sniffed. "Any coffee left?"

"On the counter." Fay gestured with her head. "Everyone drinks coffee around here. You'll always find a fresh pot. Help yourself."

Three coffee machines lined the counter—one carafe full, the next marked Decaf, and the third empty. Since Skylar required a kick-start every morning, she grabbed one of the stacked ceramic cups and poured from the full pot—hopefully, high-test. After savoring the first sip, she turned to the table.

For such an early hour, Logan looked a little worse for wear. Grass clippings stuck to his hair and shirt, and a smudge of dirt streaked across his forehead. She gave a careful sniff. No odoriferous stench…yet.

He slid his empty plate to the side and sipped his coffee. "Sleep well?"

She took a second to realize the question was meant for her. She smiled. "Like a rock." Which surprised her. She slept in a strange house and bed and not once had she stirred.

Locking onto his gaze, she struggled to force air into her lungs. Yesterday, whatever covered his clothing created the tightness in her chest. She had no excuse today. The man caused a funny feeling to swirl inside her, and for the life of her, she couldn't figure out why. Yes, all right, he was handsome, but so what? A lot of good-looking men frequented the bar. She never once felt the need to suck on an inhaler. She broke eye contact.

Leaning back in his chair, Logan nodded toward the woman on his right. "You haven't met Tommy's mom. This is Doreen Hashoff."

Doreen sported a beautiful head of long, blonde hair. Too bad she'd rather look like a sourpuss than offer a friendly smile. Skylar acknowledged the introduction with a polite nod. "Nice to meet you."

No "Hi" or "Go away," not even a grunt. Blondie merely stared through slits over the rim of her coffee cup. Didn't her aunt screen her potential tenants for manners? Skylar approached the table and lowered onto the chair next to Tommy. "Where's Yapper?"

While swinging his legs under the chair, Tommy glanced from his cereal bowl with a mouth dripping milk down his chin. "He's outside. I fed him earlier." With his hands, he lifted the bowl and slurped the remaining contents. Clanging the bowl onto the table, he wiped his milk mustache with a forearm. "I'm done, Mom. Can I go?"

She smirked. "Sure, but stay out of trouble."

Tommy bolted straight out the backdoor.

Fay slid a plate of scrambled eggs and bacon in front of Skylar. "Toast if you want some. White, rye, or wheat. Help yourself."

"Thank you, Fay. This will do." Comfort food. Just what she needed. She picked up her fork. "So, what are the rules of the kitchen?" She dug in.

Fay returned to the stove. "I prepare breakfast

between eight and nine. Early risers can make their own, as long as they clean any mess. Not all tenants eat breakfast, but nearly everyone drinks coffee. Lunch is between twelve and one, and of course, dinner at six. Anyone is welcome to a snack or drink anytime." She placed the frying pan in the sink.

"So, Doreen—" Skylar crunched on a strip of bacon. "I hear you work the dinner shift at a diner."

Mouth pinched, Doreen leaned a nudge toward Logan. "I do what I can to provide for Tommy."

Logan patted Doreen's hand. "You're doing a fine job."

Blondie responded with an adoring gaze.

Oh-kay. Obviously, these two were a couple. Skylar crunched on more bacon. The crispness was perfect.

Doreen stood and bumped Logan with her hip. "Are you taking a look at my car?"

Nearly spilling his coffee from the jolt, Logan stared. "Now?"

Hissing through tight teeth, she glared. "Yes, now."

After gulping what remained in his cup, Logan shot Skylar a raised brow, grabbed his crutch from the wall, and followed Doreen outside.

Fay clucked her tongue. "That woman has the hots for him."

Unfazed, Skylar finished the last of her buttery eggs. "They make a nice couple."

"Honey, you don't know what you're talking about." While wiping her hands on a towel, she approached the backdoor and peered left. "Logan's been here two months, and the girl hangs on him whenever she can." She turned toward the table and sat next to Skylar. "FYI, Doreen's husband deserted, leaving her and Tommy flat broke and without any viable means of support. Since our rooms have one bed, Ginger purchased a small cot for Tommy and took them in at a reduced rate. To return Ginger's generosity, Doreen works on the flower beds."

Another child's psyche destroyed by a worthless sperm donor. What was it with people who had children but never stuck around to enjoy them? Finished with her meal, Skylar wiped her mouth with a napkin. "My aunt did a noble thing."

"Oh, absolutely, and not the first time, either." Leaning close, Fay thrust her face at Skylar. "Are you listening?"

Skylar jumped. Mouth agape, she stared. "Yes, of course. I heard every word."

Leaning against the table, Fay slapped an open palm onto the surface. "Then, why do you look like you're stuck in la-la land?"

Was she? She thought she kept her expression neutral. So what if Blondie and Logan were a couple? They were no concern of hers. She frowned. "Travel fatigue, I guess."

"Uh-huh." Straightening, she snickered. "Come off it, honey. I saw the way Logan looks at you. You can't tell me you didn't notice."

Aw, phoo. Her cheeks grew hot. She sipped her coffee—which only increased the heat coming from her face.

Fay tapped a finger on the table. "Logan's handsome, for sure. It's a damn shame he hobbles around on a crutch."

Having no desire to continue this particular

conversation, Skylar rotated to face the housekeeper. "Does my aunt have a coffeemaker?"

Sighing, Fay nodded toward the counter. "The clean one was hers. She gave up coffee last year."

Oh, sacrilege. Her aunt couldn't possibly be related.

Fay glanced into Skylar's cup. "If you're finished, how about a tour?"

Should she forgo that second cup of coffee and opt for the tour? Her system should survive on minimum caffeine—at least, for today. Besides, she was anxious to see the place and could always grab a cup later. "That would be great." She stood.

Fay also stood and waved her arms in a wide circle. "As you can see, the kitchen is quite large. Ginger had the dining room wall demolished to accommodate all the tenants and family gatherings. Over here—" She opened a door to a descending staircase. "This leads to the basement, which is quite a size. Down there is the laundry area. Everyone is responsible for their own laundry, including bedsheets and cleaning their own rooms. The rancher, of course, has its own washer and dryer." She shut the door but lingered with her hand on the knob.

Skylar brushed her arm. "You okay?"

The woman shook herself. "Yes, I'm fine." She proceeded to the center of the kitchen. "Meals are included. Each room comes equipped with a small refrigerator and microwave, and anyone can volunteer to cook. Many of our tenants have favorite recipes to share—like last night's soup." She gestured with a thumb over her shoulder. "My bedroom is down this short hall off the kitchen. After my husband died, I spent most of my time here. Ginger was getting on in years, so she suggested I sell my house and move in permanently. She built my bedroom especially for me. It's twice the size as the others with a larger sitting area."

Fay made no move to show Skylar the room, which was fine. Even though she owned the estate, she still felt like an intruder. "My aunt never married?"

Stepping toward the main hall, Fay snorted. "Afraid not. She was a shrewd businesswoman, though. Ran a bar in North Philadelphia for years before selling to buy this place. Most of our tenants are seniors, and occasionally, we'll rent to the younger ones like Doreen and Tommy. Logan is another young one, along with Michael Chang. After a few years, they usually move on." She cocked her head. "Logan was the first tenant I took on after Ginger's death. I hope you don't mind."

How could she mind? She hadn't a clue what she was doing here. "To be honest, I'd like you to continue running the place until I get an idea of what to do." Gaze steady, she held up a finger. "But let's not take in any more boarders, okay?"

Brows furrowed, Fay peered. "You selling?"

"Truthfully, I don't know."

Fay studied her for a moment, then nodded. "Okay." She led the way toward the front door and entered the room on the right. "This is the main sitting area—or TV room."

Skylar stood at the threshold of an enormous room containing four sofas, several wing-back chairs, and a large screen TV with some kind of fishing program showing. *Ugh.* The guy was gutting a fish. Just what she wanted to see after eating. The single occupant was an older man stretched across one of the sofas, flat on his back, and gaze glued to the TV. He wore an old pair of gray work trousers with a faded-red T-shirt and socks that had seen better days. Normally, people glanced at whoever entered a room. Not this guy. His gaze never strayed from the TV. How interesting could a fishing program be? Big deal, put a worm on a hook, and throw the line in the water. Lower the ball cap over the eyes and sleep. That's how her father fished, anyway.

Fay strolled over. "This is Joe Ryan. Joe, meet our new owner, Skylar Dawson."

Never removing his gaze from the screen, Joe extended his hand. " 'Many that are first shall be last, and the last shall be first.' "

Huh? Dumbfounded, Skylar took the outstretched hand and shook, puzzled over his reluctance to glance her way.

Fay chuckled. "Joe likes to quote the Bible. Half the time, I can't make heads or tails of what he says."

She wasn't the only one confused. Another oddity to add to the tenant list?

"Joe tends bar at night—like you. Whenever he's off, he's stretched out here. He, like Doreen, is rarely around for dinner. Right, Joe?" She slapped the bottom of his foot.

"Yep."

Chuckling, Fay pulled on his sock. "Skylar is a bartender, too, Joe. The two of you have something in common."

"You don't say?" He shifted his gaze toward Skylar. "Do you like your job?"

Skylar smiled. "Yes, I do."

"No snobby college education?"

"Nope." She emphasized the *p.*

He nodded. "Then, you're all right. Just like your aunt. Welcome to Ginger's Manor."

Obviously, the man had something against college-educated people. Following Fay, she crossed the hall and stood in another room, also quite large, but this one contained two card tables, two more sofas, and a wall full of books. She felt a definite vibe in this room, like if she spoke too loud, she would be shushed.

"This is our card room and library. Folks who don't want to stay upstairs or join the others in the TV room come in here. You'll notice both rooms are great for family gatherings."

"You mentioned gatherings earlier. Do you have many?"

"We have the occasional birthday party. Some large, some small. A lot of our tenants have family living in another state. They'd rather stay here than move."

Behind them, Rita flew through the door with a dustrag in one hand and a spray can in the other. Without a word, she shot a pinched look at Skylar and set to work at the card table while spraying and wiping with rapid motions.

Dear Lord, if Rita rubbed the furniture any harder, she'd strip the finish.

Leaning close, Fay spoke near Skylar's ear. "Rita's main OCD is cleaning. Ginger reduced her rent because she keeps the downstairs immaculate." She straightened. "I did the same for Logan. He cares for the lawn and does minor repairs around the property. If you find anything needs fixing, let him know. He's handy."

Rita stopped mid-wipe. "You want me to clean the rancher again? I will, you know. Half the residents won't let me in their rooms, and some need a good cleaning."

Taken aback by the rapid-fire words, Skylar blinked. "Thank you, Rita, but no. The place is still spotless."

She jerked her head. "Good to know. Now, excuse me. I've work to do." She flew over to the bookcase.

With a crooked finger, Fay gestured for Skylar to follow into the hall. "Messy people aggravate Rita. We had a little guy who dropped candy wrappers all over the house. He nearly drove her batty."

Glancing back into the room, Sky watched Rita saturate a table with polish. "How about Margaret with her cotton balls?"

Fay grunted. "That, too." She lifted a foot onto the staircase step and glanced over her shoulder. "You've seen Margaret's room. Most are the same." Again, she leaned close. "I notified her family."

Skylar nodded and ascended behind Fay. The carpeted staircase rose to the second floor with a carved banister on one side and a straight wooden rail on the other. Along with the tiny lights to brighten the way, three small chandeliers hung from the ceiling.

Fay stopped in the middle of the second floor's wide hall. "We have twelve bedrooms total, which includes mine. The door behind us is a utility closet for cleaning supplies." She opened another door. "This is the tub room. Each apartment has a small bath with shower, but sometimes, the tenants want a long bath."

Seeing a clipboard hanging by the door, Skylar

leaned forward to read.

"You're looking at the sign-up sheet. This way, we won't have any arguments. No one's allowed more than an hour, and they must clean the tub afterward. Violators are banned for three months."

Skylar stepped into the room and marveled at a beautiful claw-footed tub, a wide vanity and mirror, and shelving full of towels and soaps. *Nice.*

In between two of the rooms was another flight of stairs. With an arched brow, Skylar pointed.

"Those steps lead to the attic. We have nine rooms on this floor and two rooms in the attic. Logan and Tyrone reside on the third floor. Those are the only rooms with balconies." Turning toward the descending staircase, Fay waved for Skylar to follow. "That completes our tour of the inside. You can mosey around outside whenever the mood hits you. Any questions?"

"Why doesn't Logan move to the second floor? We have the room, right?"

She shrugged. "I gave him a choice, and he insisted on the third floor." She gripped the banister. "Don't ask me to analyze male logic. Maybe you can mention it later, in case he changed his mind." Fay stopped on the last step. "You met Mrs. Santini last night. Her late husband was the mayor of some small town down by the shore. She acts like he was president of the United States." Moving to the table in the hall, she fussed with a colorful array of white daisies arranged in an ornate vase. "The woman is a bit antisocial and hates it here. Her son lives in Penns Grove, which isn't too far away. She'd rather live with him." Fay started for the kitchen. "He's still single and doesn't want his mother hanging over him. Knowing her as I do, I understand perfectly."

She entered her domain and gathered the remaining dishes from the table. "You taking the coffeemaker?"

"Absolutely." Skylar stopped to open a door under the stairwell. A small powder room with a sink and toilet looked fairly new. After closing the door, she approached Fay. "I also need groceries. Any stores nearby?"

Fay loaded the used dishes into the dishwasher. "There's a shopping center at the intersection of Routes 40 and 45. That's a good place to start." Straightening, she faced Skylar. "You're welcome to eat with us."

"Thank you, but I'll spend some quiet time going through my aunt's stuff and eat when I'm hungry." She picked up the third coffeemaker. "Did my aunt have a reason for eliminating coffee?"

Folding her arms over her chest, Fay released a heavy sigh. "Her heart, mainly. She stopped beer, too, and never drank any hard liquor with the exception of Irish whiskey—her favorite." Turning, she closed the dishwasher. "I disposed of all her prescription meds. I left the aspirin bottle on her nightstand, in case you needed one. For an old woman, your aunt didn't have a whole lot of pain." After adjusting her glasses, Fay hit the Start button and then nodded toward the backdoor. "Ginger's car is the white sedan parked alongside the garage. It's yours now."

A car at the ready, a house of her own, and a business taking in steady income…wow, how her life had changed—and all from an aunt she never knew. She clutched the coffeemaker to her chest and left the kitchen.

Halfway across the path to the rancher, she glanced in the direction of the parking lot to see a faded yellow car with Logan, Doreen, and Tommy bent over its engine. In the sunlight, a similar glow of gold rose from both Logan's and Tommy's hair. One would think they were father and son.

Blondie's close proximity to Logan, along with her bending over to show a little cleavage, confirmed Fay's got-the-hots statement. Unfortunately for Doreen, Logan had the intentness of a man concentrating on the task—namely, the engine.

Spotting Skylar's movement, Logan glanced up.

Doreen's gaze followed, and she shifted to block his view.

A blatant maneuver, for sure, and Skylar suppressed a smile. Shaking her head, she reached for the office doorknob.

"Stay away from him!"

Whoa! Nearly dropping her precious appliance, Skylar whirled to face a woman with fire shooting from her gaze. "Excuse me?"

Doreen shook a finger in Skylar's face. "I know you can throw me and Tommy on the street to have Logan all to yourself, but I'm telling you, he's Tommy's father. He's back in our lives and wants to make amends."

Logan is the absentee father? She shot her gaze toward the car. Logan and Tommy were nowhere in sight. "That's wonderful news, Doreen." What else could she say? She only met the man yesterday.

Blondie folded her arms over her impressive chest with a triumphant lift to her chin.

Bad enough the woman had beautiful waves through her long hair, but why be blessed with a nice set of boobs? With a peek down at her own small chest,

Sky cleared her throat. "Look, Ms. Hashoff, I'm here to settle this estate. Nothing more." She leaned close, gaze narrowed. "I will keep your secret. Just don't threaten me again, or I *will* throw you out." The last thing she wanted was to get involved in some family drama. She had enough problems of her own.

Chapter Six

Skylar slipped the coffeemaker onto the kitchen counter and stood, staring at the machine. What a way to begin a morning—as if she gave two cents whether Doreen and Logan reconciled into a happy, little family. Damn people should leave her alone. She had more important things to do, like food shopping.

After finding a memo pad and pen, she itemized a list of essentials with coffee and filters at the top— double starred. Her list complete and pockets stuffed with wallet, phone, and keys, she exited through the front door and headed for the garage. While studying the array of buttons on the car's key fob, she— "Oomph."

Strong hands caught her shoulders. "Well, well. Who have we here?"

Dazed, she stared at a tall male with hazel eyes and dark, curly hair. *Holy moly*. At the sound of his smooth voice, she fought to keep her tongue from slipping down her throat. He was breathtakingly handsome in that drool-worthy way. Casually dressed in summer shirt and trousers, he wore an unbuttoned collar to reveal a tanned neckline circled by a gold chain. To top this example of male perfection, his smile weakened her knees, and spicy aftershave enticed her nose. She almost leaned into him for a good sniff. Stepping back, she forced herself not to gape. "Depends on who's asking."

Gaze twinkling, he dropped his hands. "Philip Santini. My mother lives here."

Ah, yes, the lawyer. She returned the smile. "Skylar Dawson."

He rocked his eyebrows. "You're Ginger's niece?" He shook himself. "Mother said they were expecting a frumpy old maid."

Somehow, the comment didn't surprise her, especially coming from Mrs. Santini, but really...frumpy? "I suppose no one knew what to expect, Mr. Santini."

"Philip, please, and don't defend her. She lies all the time." Frowning, he scratched his ear. "I'm sorry about your aunt. She was a nice lady."

"Philip!"

At the shrill voice, Skylar jumped, as if caught in a passionate embrace. Whirling, she spotted Mrs. Santini leaning out her second-floor window. Her face held an expression bordering on murderous. *Wow, jealous much*?

Releasing a low growl, Philip waved but tilted close to Skylar. "She sits by the window and watches for my car. Too bad these evergreens aren't hiding the parking lot." He straightened. "Mother depends on me for her social entertainment when she's surrounded by a great group of people." Sighing heavily, he squared his shoulders. "I better go before her head explodes. I'll catch you later." He winked and hurried for the manor's backdoor.

Be still my heart. He could catch her anytime. With Logan's ruggedness and this man's good looks, were all Jersey men this mouth-watering? Not like she had time for dating, but holy cow, maybe she should give one of them a try. Smiling, she watched him disappear into the manor, only to feel Mrs. Santini's dagger glare. Waving to the old biddy, Skylar headed for the garage.

So, Philip was the son whose mother wanted to invade his space. Being handsome, he was, no doubt, popular with women. A mother in attendance would definitely crimp any man's style. Chuckling, she passed the opened garage.

With a deep scowl wrinkling his forehead, Logan emerged, carrying a wrench. "I see you met Mr. Casanova."

My, my, such a sourpuss.

But over at the faded yellow car, Doreen wore a similar expression.

This was so ridiculous. If Sky wasn't careful, she'd bust out laughing, but just to tempt fate, she smiled at Logan, knowing full well Blondie's blood might boil. "What's the matter? Don't you like him?"

Snarling, he shot her a glare. "I detest the very air he breathes."

Oh, good heavens. A little green-eyed envy? While both men had the potential to earn a chunk of change at a bachelor auction, Logan, with muscled arms and chest, caused a woman to pray he'd strip to his skivvies. His biggest flaws included a crutch and no viable means of monetary support. Doreen's statement also raised the question of his marital status.

Philip, the lawyer, wore expensive trousers over long legs and had a trim physique, but his mother would end any relationship before one began. Both men might know their way around a woman's body, but she wasn't anxious to discover which one had the better map. Suppressing her smile, Skylar met Logan's stormy gaze. "Philip seems rather nice."

The storm intensified.

What was wrong with this man? His ex was fuming by the car and ready to spit nails. If he came to Ginger's Manor to reconcile, he'd better hurry to her side before she used the wrench on his head.

Grunting, he gestured toward the white sedan. "Going out?"

"Yes, for food. When I return, I'll park my cycle under the carport, even if the car's tail end sticks out."

"It's your property. You can do whatever you want." He nodded toward the vehicle. "I filled the gas tank over the weekend. So, you're ready to go. Where're you heading?"

"The shopping center. Fay gave me directions."

He scowled in Doreen's direction. "If I wasn't busy, I'd drive you."

Since Skylar had enough daggers in her back for one day, she turned toward the car. "I'll see you later." *Let them figure out their own problems.*

The key fob opened the door to a newer model, four-door sedan. She still had her mother's sedan and only drove it whenever she needed a big trunk. Now, she had her aunt's. She was beginning to feel like some privileged princess. Sighing, she slipped her butt onto the cushy leather and started the engine. After adjusting the seat and then the mirrors, she lowered the windows and drove off.

Before Kirby's letter arrived, she had given some serious thought about what to do with her life. For some reason, she had gotten antsy and considered changing jobs. Money worries weren't a concern. Her bar job paid the bills, and she inherited her family home free and clear. But with her parents gone, she felt stuck in a rut. Maybe this trip to New Jersey would provide some answers or, at least, give her some clarity. She sucked in a large breath of humid air and sneezed. *I'm allergic to New Jersey. Case closed.* She rubbed her nose.

After following Fay's directions, she found the shopping center and maneuvered the car around a large parking lot with its array of stores and fast-food restaurants. Choosing an empty slot near the supermarket, she pulled in, closed the windows, and killed the engine.

A shadow in her rearview mirror stopped her from unlatching her seatbelt. A black sedan had stopped behind her vehicle and blocked any chance of her backing out. Two men, wearing sport coats but no ties, approached the driver's door. She tensed.

Gripping the steering wheel with one hand, she double-checked the door locks with the other. She knew nothing about crime in the area, with the exception of Logan's warning to lock the doors. Would she be beaten and robbed for the pittance of cash in her wallet and all in broad daylight?

One of the men used a knuckle to tap on her window.

Even though she expected it, she jumped anyway. She rotated her head to see both men lift part of their jackets to reveal gold badges clipped to their belts.

They were cops? Did she miss a stop sign or something? Eyebrows high, she activated the ignition to crack open the window. "Yes?"

The older one bent to her eye level and lifted his lips into a soft smile. "Are you Skylar Dawson?"

To be addressed by name from a complete stranger took her aback. She rotated in her seat and peered. "Yes."

"Lieutenant Monroe wants to see you at headquarters, ma'am."

Her mouth fell open, then snapped shut. "Why?"

"He'll explain. We'll go in our car."

No way in hell would she step into a car with two strange men. That was like asking for an automatic death sentence. Muscles tense, she tightened her grip on the steering wheel. "I need a better reason." She'd rather not die her first week away from home, thank you very much.

With a smile lifting one side of his mouth, he leaned closer to the window. "I'm sorry for the secrecy, and we're not forcing you, but the lieutenant wants to speak to you privately."

Why, to scare me to death? Geez, Monroe could have called or met her at the rancher. Why so mysterious? She scanned both men. "Can I see some official ID, please? Anybody can buy a badge." *My momma didn't raise no stupid child.*

Both men whipped out thin, black billfolds with IDs prominently displayed. The older man was Michael Burke, Detective, New Jersey State Police, and the other, Timothy Carlyle. The New Jersey state seal embedded their photos.

Detective Burke gave a curt nod. "Lieutenant Monroe said you were sharp."

Flattery wouldn't get him anywhere, not when suspicion rattled every nerve in her body. She cleared her throat. "Why don't I follow you?"

"No, ma'am. Someone might recognize your car."

That made not an iota of sense. Rather than have him elaborate, she unclipped her seatbelt and stepped outside. Using the fob, she locked the doors.

She wished Logan had come. At least, someone would know she was about to step into possible oblivion. She had neither Logan's nor Fay's phone numbers. Her aunt's lawyer, Nathan Kirby, was in her phone. His number was probably the better one to have, in case she found herself locked in a cell.

Detective Carlyle held open the sedan's rear door and waited.

Sucking in a calming breath, Sky slipped onto the seat while the men sat up front. "How far are we going?" She fastened her seatbelt. Damn, her hands shook.

Detective Burke, sitting on the front passenger side, gestured with a nod. "A little over a mile. The barrack is on the outskirts of Woodstown." He smiled over his shoulder. "We'll have you back to shop in no time."

Oh-kay. Not like she was worried about shopping. Living long enough to shop dominated her thoughts. To help calm her nerves, she released a slow breath.

Once clear from the busy commercial center, Carlyle drove by open farm fields until he slowed for traffic congestion.

Leaning against her seatbelt, Skylar craned her neck. The majority of cars were turning left where a big barn-like structure stood. At the curbside, a huge cowboy statue, complete with red shirt, blue jeans, white hat, and big smile, marked the entrance. "What's this place?"

Carlyle glanced into the rearview mirror and

smiled. "Cowtown Rodeo, ma'am. Popular place. The flea market draws the crowds every Tuesday and Saturday, year-round. The rodeo is every Saturday night in summer. Tuesday is the better day to visit. Less crowded."

Less crowded? But today was Tuesday, and the adjacent parking lot looked packed to capacity. She hated to see what Saturday was like.

"We're here, ma'am."

After clicking on his turn signal, Carlyle pulled into a parking lot with the New Jersey State Police sign out front, but instead of using a parking slot near the road, he drove to the rear of the building and parked among several patrol cars.

Burke unfastened his seatbelt. "We're using the side entrance for privacy reasons."

More secrecy. The statement did little to settle her nerves. What next? A shroud over her head?

Leading the way, Burke ushered her through the side door where she got her first glimpse of the state police uniforms. Up until this moment, she believed the uniformed cops at the manor were part of Monroe's department, but obviously, they were local police. No way could she mistake these gorgeous uniforms of light blue tops with yellow triangular insignia. The men were just as gorgeous. Quite a few who passed in the hall had their hair shaved close to the scalp and resembled walking bulldozers with muscular chests and arms. If she hadn't felt Burke's hand on the small of her back, she'd have stood by the wall and gawked.

The detective led her past a series of offices to the end of a long hall and knocked on a door with *Lt. Robert Monroe*'s gold placard prominently displayed.

"Come in."

"This is where I leave you, ma'am." Burke opened the door and stepped aside.

With the door closed behind her, Skylar stood in an office too small for the large man behind the desk. The room was ordinary, with desk and computer, two wooden chairs for guests, and a leather sofa against one wall.

Lieutenant Monroe lifted his gaze from his paperwork, then stood with a smile. "Ms. Dawson, thank you for coming. Please sit." He motioned toward the two chairs in front of his desk.

Feeling like a trapped animal, Skylar resisted the urge to ball her hands into fists. "What's this about, Lieutenant?"

He cocked his head. "Please, sit. I'll explain everything."

She wasn't sure why her skin itched. She had no criminal record and lived her life pretty much on the quiet side, but Monroe's serious expression put her on edge. With little choice, she slipped onto the chair and waited with spine stiff and gut in turmoil.

Before sitting, Monroe grabbed a pen and flung it at her head.

Reacting with a skill that took years to perfect, she intercepted the projectile and glared. "You threw that on purpose." She tossed the pen onto his desk.

Nodding, he smiled. "I wanted to double-check your reflexes, and I must say they are quick." He reclaimed his seat. "You caught Logan Greene's crutch with the speed of some super woman. I've never seen anyone move so fast." He wiped the smile from his face and furrowed his brows. "I'm sorry for the secrecy, but you'll understand soon enough."

Intertwining his fingers and placing his hands on the desk, he narrowed his gaze. "I know a lot about you, Ms. Dawson. I know you have black belts in Jujutsu, Aikido, and Tai Chi. Your IQ is noted to be around 140, which makes you quite intelligent. Yet, you never attended college, refused all offered scholarships, and basically, remain content to work in a small Chicago bar for the rest of your life. Why?"

She started. How could he possibly know so much? For crying out loud, they just met. She studied him. "Why, what?"

"You have the potential to make something of yourself. Why don't you?"

What was this, the Spanish Inquisition? First, he threw a pen at her head, and now, he spieled off her bio like her life was an open book. Her Irish temper flared, and she shot to her feet. "Who are you, my father? I happen to despise school on all levels." Forcing herself not to walk out the door, she paced.

"It's highly unusual for someone with your intelligence to go about living without purpose. According to your martial arts masters, you have the skills to be a world-class Mixed Martial Arts champion. What you need is a challenge."

Whirling to face him, she gripped the back of her chair. "You contacted my instructors? Why?"

"Because I'm about to offer you that challenge." He waved toward the chair. "Please, sit, and I'll explain."

She remained standing, arms crossed, and peered with as much suspicion as possible. If truth be told, she was curious as hell. "How did you find out about my black belts?"

He pointed to his computer. "Obviously, you haven't typed your name into a search engine to see what materialized. Otherwise, you'd see where your instructors posted an impressive list of videos. One, in particular, has over a million hits."

Eyes widening, she opened her mouth to speak, then slapped it shut. Why didn't she know this? She avoided social media because she had nothing to post, and here, her masters were making a big deal over her skills. They wanted her to compete and to teach. She wanted neither. After pinching the bridge of her nose, she sighed. "Why are you going to so much trouble, Lieutenant?"

"Because I'm always cautious whenever I'm about to ask someone to do something out of the ordinary, maybe even dangerous."

Dangerous? Monroe talked as if he had some secret agent stuff—of which she was woefully under-qualified. Forcing herself to take a deep breath to slow her heart rate, she dropped to the seat. "All right, I'm listening."

He leaned back and steepled his fingers. "Did you know that over the past year and a half, four accidental deaths occurred at the manor?"

Great. The manor's being sued. *And I'm getting a damn headache.* Although, why should he care? She rubbed her temples and then met his gaze. "Not unheard of if the accidents involved the elderly."

"As a matter of fact, all were over the age of sixty." Sitting forward, he opened a folder on his desk pad. "The first accident was an elderly man who fell down the stairs."

She rolled her eyes. "Falls are the leading cause of death for the elderly, Lieutenant." Where was he going with this? Anyone who turned on a television heard the statistics.

Without commenting, he closed the first folder and opened another. "The next death occurred seven months later. A woman who loved bubble baths drowned in the tub. Her death was ruled accidental."

Oh. Probably the woman Gilda found. She shrugged. "Okay. So what?" Did she somehow slip into another dimension, because this conversation was making no sense? She crossed her legs. "Why question the incident?"

He flashed a brief smile. "Your aunt expressed curiosity about the water on the bathroom floor."

Water on the what? She gaped and then, realizing she had that guppy look again, shook herself. "I'd question water on the wall but not the floor." When someone stepped from a tub, water dripped before…*oh*! The woman never got out of the tub. *Duh*. She cocked her head. "You obviously have more to tell me."

"I do indeed." He closed the folder and opened a third. "Our next victim died of a heart attack."

What was he trying to prove? She shifted on her butt. "A heart attack is not considered accidental. Death is the result of a medical condition."

Nodding, he quirked his lips to the side. "I agree, but the victim was deathly afraid of the dark, and the tenants found her in a locked basement at night with the lights out. Being eighty-six years old with a weak heart, the outcome was inevitable."

Brows high, she stared. "You mean someone locked the woman in the basement on purpose?"

"Yes. The lock only works on the kitchen side. Do you know how your aunt died, Ms. Dawson?"

From the sound of his tone, she wasn't sure she wanted to hear. Her gut already jumped all over the place, and damn, the man made her skin itch. Studying his face for any clue and finding none, she uncrossed her legs and gripped her thighs. "All I know is she died suddenly."

While watching her, he rocked his chair. "I understand she had a weak heart."

The realization of his words hit like a sledgehammer. Eyes wide, she gasped. "Are you telling me—"

"I am. Your aunt was victim number three."

"But a heart attack is definitive."

"Being locked in the basement tells another story." He rested his arms on the desk and again intertwined his fingers. "Several months ago, your aunt came to me with these wild accusations about tenants being murdered. She originally went to her local police, but they told her to go home and bake some cookies. I listened and let her talk. Then, I asked for proof. She said she'd get it and call me. A week later, she was dead." He tugged on his ear. "I don't put too much stock in coincidences."

Her eighty-six-year-old aunt was playing amateur detective? Was she nuts? Sky drifted her gaze to the diplomas and awards on the wall. Judging from the array, Monroe wasn't an idiot, but her aunt somehow convinced him. Frowning, she chewed on her lower lip. "I never knew my aunt, Lieutenant, but I know how stress can cause sudden death. My father died that way."

"Yes, and your mother died from breast cancer." With closed lips, he smiled. "I said I knew all about you. Let me continue." He switched folders. "Victim number four is the woman you found. Normally, a death like this would bypass the coroner's office and go straight to a funeral home, but I pushed for the autopsy. Here's the preliminary report." He drew a paper from the folder and slid the sheet across the desk.

Reaching, she took the report and read. She met Monroe's steady gaze. "Death is ruled as natural causes with time of death estimated between nine and eleven in the morning. It seems rather straightforward." She threw the paper across the desk. "Wait a minute." Sitting back, she eyed him with a steady gaze. "That's why I'm here. You don't believe the report."

He returned the paper to the folder. "No, I don't. I believe we have a clever killer on our hands. Each death appears like an accident or natural causes. At present, you are the lone resident free of suspicion."

Slumping in the chair, she groaned. "You want me to play cop. I can't do that. I'm not qualified."

He wagged a finger. "You're sharp, Ms. Dawson. I want you to go through your aunt's possessions and look for her proof. You might not find any, but suppose you do? Without this conversation, you might throw the evidence in the trash. Even worse, suppose you found something and mentioned it at the dinner table? You'd put a target on your back." Sighing, he drummed his fingers on the folders. "We have four different deaths and no clear motive for any of the victims—except for your aunt. I've a strong suspicion she confronted the killer and threatened him or her with exposure." Rising, he ambled around the desk.

"I have no probable cause to exhume the bodies for autopsy. I will if you find evidence to the contrary." Extending his hand, he helped her to her feet. "I can't force you to do this, but all I'm asking is to look for any proof your aunt found. Bring it to me right away and tell no one. And here." Reaching into his shirt pocket, he extracted a business card. "Office and cell. Call if you see or hear anything that arouses your suspicions."

This wasn't really happening, right? Maybe she was still in bed, dreaming. If what the lieutenant said was true, one of her tenants was a cold-blooded killer.

Chapter Seven

As Skylar slipped onto the backseat of the detectives' vehicle for her return trip to the shopping center, she rested her head against the headrest and closed her eyes. None of this could possibly be real. Monroe had to be out of his mind and playing some sort of practical joke. So what if he researched and found the three black belts attached to her name? Those skills didn't make her a detective, and throwing a pen at her head only proved her reaction speed. Even more important—and what got her into this mess in the first place—what made her aunt suspicious of a fall down the stairs or a drowning in the tub? In either case, how in the world could anyone prove murder?

The car hit a pothole and jerked her eyes open.

Really, though, from her first day, Skylar saw the possibility of foul play. Sure, Margaret Caine's official cause of death was natural causes, but what if someone bopped the woman on the head as she left the bathroom? That scenario would explain the location of the abrasion on her forehead and the eyeglasses clear across the floor. The one shoe on and one off probably meant she was dragged to the bed. The split lip was a puzzle, though.

Gad, what a dilemma, and she silently cursed her luck. She had neither the time nor desire to help Monroe, but she owed her aunt. If the woman died a calculated death, then Sky had to uncover the killer and help bring him or her to justice. And Monroe was right. She couldn't ask questions without putting a target on her back.

"Shall I drop you off in front of the supermarket, Ms. Dawson?"

Startled by Carlyle's voice, she glanced out the window. Gracious, they were already at the shopping center. "Yes, that's fine, Detective."

He maneuvered the car close to the curb.

Officer Burke jumped from the front seat to open her door and leaned close. "Remember, not a word about your meeting with Monroe."

"Right." All this covert stuff was for the birds. She was a bartender, not a cop. With a wave, she entered the market, grabbed a cart, and whipped out her list.

In no time, she had the car loaded with groceries. After a quick stop at a fast-food restaurant for a burger and fries, she headed toward the manor and guided the car to its spot alongside the garage. With all the ground surrounding the rancher, she wondered why her aunt hadn't erected a separate garage for her vehicle. Even if she hardly drove, parking in a garage was a lot better than leaving the car out in the weather. After pressing the button to release the trunk, she alighted.

A red sports coupe pulled into the parking lot, and a quick toot followed.

With a bright smile, Philip Santini jumped from the driver's seat and waved before rushing around to the passenger side.

With her nose in the air, Maria stepped out with her eyes covered by dark sunglasses.

Oh, joy. Mommy, dearest. Skylar almost laughed.

A sports coupe wasn't the best vehicle to cart around an elderly woman. So, kudos to the lawyer-son for keeping it.

Philip hooked his mother's arm through his but, instead of taking the walkway to the back patio, he tugged her toward Skylar's car.

Yes, tugged. Maria resisted, like a child protesting to be released. Philip deserved another set of kudos for keeping a firm grip on her arm.

"Want some help with your bags?"

Nice of him to offer, but his mother clearly frowned at his words. Obviously, her precious son didn't do menial labor. Shifting her gaze toward the trunk, Skylar stared at the bunch of canvas carryall bags. She'd love some help but not at the risk of Maria's ire. "Thanks, Philip. I can manage."

Maria pursed her lips. "She's not helpless, Philip. Come. We must continue our discussion."

"You're not moving in with me, Mother." He patted the hand on his arm.

"Well, you certainly need to reconsider because this woman will probably sell the manor."

A brow cocked, he glanced at Skylar. "Is this true?"

Skylar shrugged. "I don't know what I'm doing." She attempted a reassuring smile, but Maria's scowl wiped any nice gesture on Skylar's part. The old crow would scare away a nest of hornets.

Maria huffed. "You'd be a fool to stay when your life is out west somewhere."

"Chicago."

"Yes, gangster country. So uncivilized." She shuddered.

Philip rolled his eyes. "Forgive my mother. She believes the world turns primitive outside of New York, Philadelphia, and Washington DC."

Maria whipped off her sunglasses and glared at her son. Fire flew from the woman's gaze, and she jerked his arm. "Don't laugh at me, Philip Santini. You wouldn't be where you are today if your father and I hadn't sacrificed to put you through law school." Scowling, she replaced the sunglasses onto her nose. "Now, take me to my room. The sun is too hot." She yanked his arm.

Philip tightened his arm against his body and, again, patted his mother's hand. "I can still carry a few bags, Sky."

Oh, my. The woman's glare could peel paint off a wall. "Thank you, but take your mom inside." *Before she melts.* Then, Monroe's disturbing news came to mind. *Hmm.* Sky turned to watch them enter the manor. Maria had to be in her early seventies and appeared in reasonably good health with no hearing aids or obvious signs of dementia. So, why was she living in a boardinghouse when she'd do as well in a small apartment? Even more important, could Maria be the elusive killer?

****

From the open garage window, Logan watched and listened, but finally, the pain-in-the-ass and her precious son left. Even Mrs. Santini recognized Philip's attraction toward the beautiful new owner, and that fact alone complicated matters. Logan was half-tempted to charge through the doors and growl like some crazed animal, but he'd look ridiculous—and jealous. He was just…protective. Logan hobbled from the garage toward Skylar's car. "Let me help with those."

Skylar straightened from the trunk, one brow arched.

He sensed hesitation. Most women envisioned the crutch as a weakness. Men, too. But hell, he had one free arm. He peeked into the bags. "Which one has eggs?"

She pointed.

Avoiding the bag indicated, he grabbed four large ones by their handles. He liked how her pretty mouth dropped open. *So cute*. He'd happily carry all of them, but the crutch was a necessity. He nodded toward the open trunk. "I left you two."

With a smile curling one side of her mouth, she lifted the remaining bags, closed the trunk, and headed for the rear of the rancher. After placing her armload onto the patio table, she fumbled with the key ring and found the needed key. Successful, she swung the door wide and held it for him to hobble through. "Put the bags on the kitchen table, Logan."

Twice, he'd been in Ginger's rancher—once for a quick inspection and the second to wake Sky from her nap. The place was a little too cluttered. More than three dozen pictures covered a dining table, and the glow from all the glass was a trifle blinding. It had this strange mirror-like reflection made more so from Rita's excessive polishing. Two full-to-capacity magazine racks overflowed by the recliner, and cheap knickknacks rested on doilies. He hated doilies and considered them nothing more than dust collectors. He placed the bags on the kitchen table.

She followed and slipped her packages alongside, then turned with a smile. "Thank you, Logan. You saved me several trips."

Leaning over the table, he peeked into a few bags. Fruits and vegetables filled one, but the second stopped him cold. Pointing, he gaped. "Really, Sky, TV dinners? They're no good for you."

"They're fine when I don't have energy to cook." She lifted five boxes from the bag and tossed them into the freezer. "This brand is actually my favorite. They taste pretty good. Some of the others hit your tongue like cardboard." She emptied another bag.

Seeing what she placed on the table, he smirked. "Three packages of pretzel nuggets?"

"Hey, don't touch." Grinning, she gathered them in her arms. "I'm trying brands we don't have in Chicago. They're my biggest vice." She opened a bare cupboard to slip the packages onto a shelf. "Beer and pretzels, Logan. Can't beat the combination." She faced him. "Your supermarkets don't sell beer. I asked."

"No liquor stores in town, either. I buy my beer in Swedesboro. If you want, I'll grab you a six-pack on my next trip."

"Thanks. None of the lite stuff, okay?"

A woman after his own heart. He suppressed a grin. "Okay."

With a slight frown, she studied him. "You know, Logan, I have yet to see you smile."

He shrugged. "No reason to smile."

"Bad teeth?"

Grunting, he furrowed his brow. "My teeth are fine."

"Until I see them, I'll withhold my opinion." After an audible sigh, she opened the refrigerator and slipped in the perishables. "You're much too serious."

"I'm a serious kind of guy. Look, Sky." He cleared his throat. "I hadn't meant to eavesdrop on your conversation with Philip, but you stood right outside the open garage window. He eyed you like candy."

"Yeah, well, his mother doesn't want him to rot his teeth." She placed a bottle of dish soap near the sink and cleanser in the cabinet beneath.

"He's a good-looking guy."

She met his gaze. "So are you, Logan, and don't think for one second a crutch will scare women. Some, yes, but not all." She lifted two cans of coffee, one for each hand, and clapped them together. "I can't live without this stuff." She set them in the cabinet above the coffeemaker, along with filters and several boxes of cookies. "Will you tell Fay I'll eat in here tonight?"

"Sure, but what's this?" He pointed to her take-out bag. "You call this dinner?"

"It's my lunch, and no, I don't have enough to share." She folded the canvas bags and piled them on a chair. "Did you fix Doreen's car?"

The memory of Doreen hanging all over him gnawed at his gut. Whatever was on her mind, he wasn't interested. Frowning, he shifted on his crutch. "Timing is out of whack. She needs a real mechanic."

"At least, she snuck in a little alone time with you."

Yeah, alone time he didn't need. Thank God for Tommy being underfoot. Although, since Skylar's arrival, Doreen changed from flirtatious to clingy. All her excess attention annoyed the hell out of him. Glancing out the kitchen windows, he watched Tommy and Yapper race around the gazebo. "Tommy played the perfect chaperon. He can't stop asking questions, and he loves that dog."

"Well, the dog is his now." After double-checking for any forgotten perishables, she faced him. "Thanks for your help."

Sensing his dismissal, he gave a quick salute and headed for the door. With his hand on the knob, he turned to meet her guarded gaze, and his grip slipped. The look surprised him, but better for her to be on guard than to wind up like Margaret Caine.

****

From her position in the kitchen, Skylar had a clear view to the backdoor, and she swept her gaze along Logan's strong physique. Crutch aside, he drew a woman's attention with rippling muscles under form-fitted clothes. Back, tush, legs—*oh, my*. She couldn't keep her eyes still. His crutch was definitely *not* a deterrent. What puzzled her were his subtle flirtations. He didn't appear to be a man reconciling with his ex-wife.

Finished with her groceries, she re-heated her fast-food burger, poured a glass of lukewarm juice, and sat for her first meal in the rancher.

My rancher. Her chest filled with…something. Pride? Or how about anxiety? What in the world would she do with the place? Should she clear out Aunt Ginger's stuff to make the house her own or clear it to sell? Chicago had been her home for her whole life. Could she be happy relocating to New Jersey? What about her job at the bar? Well, all right, she had thoughts about doing something more meaningful, but never in her wildest dreams had the word *landlord* popped into her mind.

After swallowing the last of her meal, she tossed the wrappers in the trash and washed her glass. Before she started any other project, she had to protect her motorcycle from the sun.

Patting her pocket to feel for the cycle's fob, she hurried to the parking lot with a bath towel in hand and covered the hot seat. Then, she hopped on and pressed the ignition. Once under the carport, she emptied the saddlebags and then covered her precious vehicle with its canvas tarp. She had too much work to think this would be a short trip. Right now, she had two pressing problems—look for clues for a possible killer and, secondly, what to do with all her aunt's stuff. She had no idea where to start. So, she might as well be systematic. After her own possessions were unpacked and tucked into drawers, she headed for her aunt's bedroom.

Ginger Dawson hadn't many clothes in her closet—some slacks, blouses, and a few day dresses. Nothing fancy. Shoes were the sensible kind, mainly low-heeled pumps in black or brown and several pairs of slip-on sneakers. The top shelf held a heating pad and a variety of purses. Since she came into the bedroom without a thought about packing supplies, she left everything in its spot until she talked to Fay. For now, a quick inspection was best.

The bureau drawers were next, mostly underwear and a few sweatsuits. Junk filled the bottom drawer. A catch-all place filled with old eyeglasses, several wristwatches, loose keys, rubber bands, and stained doilies.

A large gold-quilted jewelry box sat on the dresser. She opened the lid and...*whoa*. Packed full. Box in hand, she propped herself onto the center of the bed, crossed her legs, and sorted through the stuff.

Her aunt had a lot of colorful costume jewelry. An oblong black box revealed two pearl necklaces—one long, the other short—but whether they were real or not, she couldn't tell. A collection of the little cards funeral directors printed for the deceased were wrapped with a blue ribbon. On another day, she'd read them to see if any were relatives.

A tiny drawer at the bottom of the box contained rings—a school ring for Saint Maria Goretti High School, a pink pearl surrounded by diamonds, and—Skylar gasped—a diamond engagement ring! Her aunt was engaged. But to whom? And what happened? "So much I don't know about you, Aunt Ginger."

Oh, good heavens. Talk about not knowing anything. She totally forgot about Mr. Kirby. She promised to call for an appointment. Taking a quick look at the bedside clock, she sighed. Four-thirty already. More likely, he was gone for the day. She made a mental note to call him in the morning.

A loud chime echoed through the house. Hurrying to the living room, she threw open the front door to see Fay standing in the office with flat cardboard boxes tucked under one arm and a box of trash bags under the other.

Fay motioned with her head at the office door. "I still have keys to all your doors. Do you want them?"

"Since I have no idea what I'm doing, keep them." Eyeing Fay's armload, Skylar waved her in. "You must be psychic."

"I figured you'd need them." She handed Skylar the box of trash bags. "Bags for clothes for donation and trash. The boxes are for everything else." She trudged toward the sofa and propped the folded cardboard against the armrest. "We have a donation truck that comes around for small appliances and clothes. You can let me know, and I'll schedule a pickup." She tugged on her disheveled top and faced Skylar. "We've had our fair share of tenants dying over the years. Ginger always kept supplies handy for packing."

"You're saving me a trip to the home store." Or the junkyard. When her mother died and left her the house, she removed enough clutter to make cleaning easier, but here, this house was another story.

Fay picked up a ceramic bunny rabbit. "I imagine a lot of these knickknacks will find a place on one of our yard sale tables."

"All of them probably, with the exception of the beer steins. They might be valuable." She sighed. "Aunt Ginger doesn't have many clothes."

Grunting, Fay returned the rabbit to the doily. "Not for lack of money, that's for sure. She hated to shop. Half the time, I bought her something she needed."

The woman was like a daughter to her late aunt. Fay should have inherited the house, not a niece who had no clue. She waved a hand about the room. "Is there anything you want, Fay, you know, like a memento?"

Puffing her cheeks, Fay scanned the living room. "I don't think so. I have enough photos of us together. I miss her, though. She had this cackle that drove Mrs. Santini crazy." Her eyes misted.

Skylar touched Fay's arm. "If you change your mind, let me know." Dropping her hand, she crossed her arms over her chest and leaned against the sofa. "I'll probably start in the office tomorrow. Anything I should know?"

Fay glanced toward the open door to the office. "You'll find the tenant folders in the desk drawer. Your aunt's computer looks impressive sitting on top of the desk, but she rarely used it. She was old school and wrote everything out by hand. Basically, she and I used the computer for ordering supplies." She faced Sky. "A few years ago, Ginny put me on her checking account. I keep the checkbook in my room to pay bills and deposit tenant checks. So, any time you're ready to switch the account to your name, just say the word."

"Keep it for now." She rubbed the back of her neck. "Tell me about the tenants. Who is long term?"

"Well, let me think." Frowning, Fay pursed her lips. "Gilda, Joe, and Tyrone are the longest. I'd say at least five years or more. The others…oh, probably a couple of years with Logan being the newest. People come and go. Or die. Why?"

"I'm getting a feel for things." Hell, everyone was suspect…with the exception of Logan. All she had to do was clear him of Margaret's death. Right or wrong, she had to start somewhere.

Fay turned toward the door. "Don't forget. You're welcome to eat with us any time." She paused with her hand on the knob. "If you want, I'll lock the office door on my way out. There's an outside bell should anyone need you."

"Thank you, Fay. I appreciate your help."

"Pleasant dreams, dear."

After Monroe's news? More like nightmares.

But dream she did, of two men, both handsome—one with abs to die for, wearing some kind of bearskin vest, and the other trim and tall in sparkling armor.

They were faceless, but she grasped who they were. They fought with swords while she stood to the side like Maid Skylar in a black medieval dress. Naturally, she woke before the duel concluded. *The story of my life.* By daybreak and fully awake, she stared at the ceiling.

This inheritance placed her in an uncomfortable category. She wouldn't know who to trust. The sparkle in a man's eye could be the glow of dollar signs.

Chapter Eight

The next morning, after a quick breakfast of coffee and buttered bagel, Skylar called Nathan Kirby's office only to be told by an answering service that he began his day at ten. Since she had time on her hands, she emptied the hall closet and placed the coats and hats on her aunt's bed. Then, she started the process of gathering clothes. As a precaution, she checked all pockets before folding and placing everything into neat piles. The garments were in decent shape with some hardly worn. And sweatsuits always came in handy. Before stuffing the array into donation bags, she'd offer the women tenants a chance for a free shopping spree.

Satisfied she had every piece of clothing for the ladies' perusal, she shot a glance at the bedside clock—nine thirty. Still too early for a call to Kirby, but the tenants should be done with their breakfast. Leaving the rancher, she hopped onto the manor's patio and entered the kitchen.

Five tenants surrounded the table—Logan, Anthony, Tyrone, Michael Chang, and Doreen, with Blondie once again sitting next to Logan. Coffee carafe in hand, Gilda refilled the cups on the table while Fay loaded used dishes into the dishwasher. From somewhere down the hall, the distinct whirl of a vacuum cleaner echoed. "Morning, everyone."

Fay glanced from the dishwasher and smiled.

"Morning. Did you eat?"

"Yep. Thank you."

Tyrone stretched his lips into a broad grin. "Well, morning, Missy. Nice to see your pretty face to start the day."

Anthony elbowed Tyrone. "Don't flirt with the new owner. You're too damn old."

While shaking his head, Tyrone waved aside the comment. "Don't listen to him. He hates being here, hates the food, and his neighbors."

Gaping, Anthony sat back. "I do not! I'm sittin' next to you, ain't I?"

Skylar suppressed a grin. "Good morning to you, too, Anthony."

Grabbing his napkin, Tyrone wiped his mouth. "Breakfast was a little late this morning. Fay had trouble with the stove until Anthony and I fixed it."

"What do you mean *you* fixed it?" Anthony grunted. "I'm the one who figured out what was wrong."

These two guys were a trip. They probably debated everything, no matter the subject. Chuckling at their banter, she slid her gaze around the table before skidding to a halt on Logan. The man shot her a look that bordered on anger. Ever so quickly, the expression disappeared, making her wonder if she imagined it. Not like she was an expert, but her years tending bar taught her a few things about reading faces.

Catching their locked gazes, Doreen grabbed onto Logan's arm.

The move was a possessive one, like a child who grabbed a toy from another child. Just in case, Sky took a quick inventory of the weapons on the table—butter knives and forks. Okay, nothing too dangerous.

An elderly man strolled in while carrying a coffee cup. He wore a white T-shirt with gray trousers and slippers on his feet, and wow, his head nearly brushed the top of the doorframe. She thought she met all the tenants, but how in the world could she miss this giant?

The man smiled, revealing tobacco-stained teeth. "Morning, Ms. Dawson."

He knew her? With a raised brow, she glanced at Fay.

Fay chuckled. "He's Joe Ryan, Sky. Nobody recognizes him the first time they see him standing."

The guy from the sofa? Skylar stared at Joe, who was, without doubt, six foot five or better. He probably doubled as the bar bouncer. "Hi, Joe."

" 'All flesh is grass, and all the goodliness thereof is as the flower of the field.' " He grinned. "I'm here for more coffee." He held out his cup for Gilda to refill and, with a nod, left the kitchen.

Skylar stared at his slim back, once again feeling at a loss to understand the meaning of his words. She glanced at the others to see them shaking their heads.

Still chuckling, Fay closed the dishwasher and pressed the Start button. "Joe lies on a seven-foot sofa, Sky. No one realizes how tall he is until he stands. Because of his size, Ginger bought him an extra long bed."

"Yeah, you should see the monstrosity." Anthony lowered his cup to the table. "Practically takes up the whole room."

Tyrone sighed. "You say that every time someone mentions his bed."

Anthony huffed. "Well, it's true. The rooms aren't

that big."

After downing the remainder of his coffee, Logan grabbed his crutch and mumbled something inaudible before hurrying out the door.

As if pulled by a string, all heads turned toward the open backdoor—except for Doreen. The damn woman had a victorious glint in her gaze as she tilted her head and smirked. *What is this girl's problem?*

Tyrone craned his neck. "Wonder what's eating him?"

Anthony grunted. "Maybe he's got jock itch. Makes all us men moody."

After pushing her chair back, Doreen stood. "I'll talk to him." She hurried out.

Be my guest. Skylar leaned against the kitchen counter and wondered why the hell she didn't wait another ten minutes to avoid all this drama.

While everyone's gaze returned to the table, Michael's lingered on the door.

Well, well, if the longing look was any indication, the guy was interested in Blondie and probably had no clue about the connection between Logan and Doreen. *And so the plot thickens.* Sky stuffed her hands into her front pockets. "Michael, I didn't expect to see you at the breakfast table. No work today?"

Tearing his gaze from the door, he lifted his cup to his lips and sipped. "Twice a week, I work eleven to seven. Beats a lot of traffic."

"He never has a set day." Fay grabbed a dish towel. "He keeps surprising us by showing up for breakfast." While wiping a glass with the towel, she frowned at the door. "Before Logan, Doreen hung all over Philip."

Wow. So, Michael never had a chance. Poor guy.

Anthony pushed his empty cup to the side. "Logan's a man on welfare. Philip or Michael is a better choice. Right, Mike?"

Michael snorted and sipped his coffee.

Cup in hand, Tyrone stood. "Philip's interested in our beautiful new owner." With a wink in Sky's direction, he handed his cup to Gilda.

"Well, so is Logan." Anthony tapped a crooked finger on the table. "Ya can't help notice how his eyes light up whenever she enters the room."

Really? A moment ago, she saw anger, not any bright lights. But if this conversation continued, her face would turn into a beet, and she'd be the next one to bolt out the door. She cleared her throat and faced Fay. "I came to see if anyone's interested in Ginger's clothes."

While staring at the floor, Fay pursed her lips. "Let me think."

"Don't burn a fuse," Anthony bellowed.

Fay shot him a pinched look, then turned to Skylar. "Ginger was a size twelve. That eliminates Doreen and Gilda. Mrs. Santini wouldn't be caught dead in secondhand clothes, so she's out. That leaves me and Rita."

Smiling, Sky nodded toward the backdoor. "Well, go over whenever you're ready. Everything is on her bed."

Anthony coughed. "I could use a bra."

Skylar laughed. She liked grumpy Anthony. He had a way of lightening the mood.

The screen door flew open with a bang. Without a glance at anyone, Doreen ran through the kitchen and down the hall.

Tyrone stared through the archway. "I'd say she's upset. Rita, will you shut off that damn vacuum for an hour and relax!"

The machine drowned his words.

"Ya-ya. PPE." Gilda pointed toward the door.

With a cluck of her tongue, Fay nodded. "Yes, obviously, Logan said something to upset Doreen. Men can be harsh sometimes." She nudged Skylar's arm. "You should talk to him."

"Me?" She held up her hands. "No way, Jose."

Rising, Michael handed his cup to Fay. "I'll talk to her." He hurried from the kitchen.

Anthony shook his head. "Logan's got a handicap. Makes him feel less of a man. That's why he works in the yard all day, to prove something to himself."

All day? Every day? This might be her chance to establish Logan's alibi for the time of Margaret's death. How to go about it without raising suspicion might be tricky. Approaching the table, Skylar gripped both hands onto the back of a chair. "The guy seems to like his job. On the day I arrived, he smelled like he'd been working for hours."

Snickering, Fay stood alongside. "He's usually not so bad. Most days, he starts early to beat the heat, but that morning, he drove to the home store for a new mower blade and some light bulbs. He left soon after breakfast."

Anthony humphed. "Yeah. Then, he returned and stayed out front as much as possible. Heard we were expecting a pretty owner and dollar signs flashed in his eyes." Squinting, he shook a finger. "You be careful with him."

Okay. She now had some semblance of an alibi for

Logan Greene. She wasn't an expert, but she'd accept the possibility he had nothing to do with the death of Margaret Caine. The news lightened the weight on her shoulders.

Fay nudged Skylar's arm. "Talk to Logan. He'll listen to you."

Oh, yeah, like being a bartender gave her a degree in psychology. Groaning, Skylar stared at the chair. "I don't know Doreen well enough to interfere. They might be having a lovers' spat."

Anthony snorted. "Just give Logan a pill. You can buy anything over the counter these days."

The front doorbell rang and echoed from a silver box above the hall archway—a true saved-by-the-bell moment.

Gilda hurried into the hall and, a minute later, returned with an armload of shipping boxes.

Tossing her apron onto the counter, Fay pointed. "Put them on the table, sweetie. I'll sort them."

Gilda obeyed and then jammed her fists on her hips and stared at the cartons.

Shifting one package after the other, Fay read the shipping labels. She handed one to Gilda. "This is for Rita. Shove it under her nose so she'll stop sweeping for fifteen minutes."

"Ya-ya." She left.

The vacuum stopped.

"Hallelujah!" Tyrone released an audible sigh.

Fay slid two boxes across the table to Anthony, then held two more, one in each hand. She lifted her left hand. "This one is for Mrs. Santini." She glanced at her right hand. "This one is for Logan." With a cocked brow, she looked at Skylar and held out the package in her right hand. "Here's a good excuse to approach Logan."

Skylar rolled her eyes. Was this part of the landlord's responsibility to mediate disputes? Maybe she should look for some sort of landlord training guide. Sighing, she extended both hands and waggled her fingers. "I might as well go all out. I'll take Mrs. Santini's, too." Shaking her head, she tucked the cartons under one arm. "I'm a glutton for punishment. What's Santini's room number?"

Stepping alongside, Tyrone patted her shoulder. "Number Two, the one with the *Do Not Disturb* sign tacked to the door. But if I were you, I'd be careful. Her package might be a bomb from one of her many admirers." He chuckled at his own joke.

Heaven forbid. Leaving the kitchen, Skylar entered the hall, scooted around an upright vacuum, and sprinted up the stairs. She stopped in the middle of the second-floor hall and scanned for Room Two. Walking to the left of the attic stairwell, she knocked above the *Do Not Disturb* sign.

"Yes?"

"A package for you, Mrs. Santini."

The door opened.

The woman stood in an elegant dressing gown looking like she belonged in a mansion. After glancing at the label, Skylar handed her a box.

Taking the parcel, Maria frowned. "Thank you, dear. At least, you're useful for something."

Jaw tight, Skylar lifted her chin. "You have a habit of insulting the owner, Mrs. Santini." Maybe the woman hoped to get thrown out. Then, Philip would have no choice but to take her in.

Maria waved a ring-covered hand. "A woman's place is in the home catering to her husband's needs, not going around catering to others. Your aunt was a prime example of a woman who took the wrong path." She scanned her from head to toe. "I'll admit owning this establishment is far better than working in a bar."

This time, Sky couldn't help it. She gaped at the comment. *How archaic*! No wonder Philip kept his mother here. If she lived with him, she'd wipe his ass every time he used the john.

Shifting the remaining box so her arm wouldn't crush the contents, Skylar stifled a growl. "If Your Highness will excuse me." She turned toward the stairs.

"One moment, dear. I see that package is for Mister Greene. Will you kindly tell him to stop thumping around? His room is above mine, and I find the noise positively irritating." She tilted her chin upward. "As the new owner of this establishment, you can have him evicted."

Skylar arched a brow. "Because he requires a crutch? Really, Mrs. Santini, you're out of line."

"Hardly, dear. I'm within my rights as a paying tenant." She peered down her nose. "I can tell my son to take legal action."

Yeah, good luck convincing a jury. But to keep the peace… "I'll talk to him. Do you know if he's in his room?"

"It's always quiet when he stays outside. So, no, I don't think he's upstairs."

She'd probably prefer Logan sleep in the garage. Gad, what a woman. Resisting the urge to curtsy, Skylar ran down the staircase and out the front door. Stopping by the porch rail, she drew in a large breath.

What an insufferable woman! If anyone should be thrown out the door, the committee would pick Mrs. Santini, no question. How had her aunt tolerated such tenants? This wasn't a hotel where one changed their room on a whim.

She stared at the package in her hand. Should she take the coward's way out and leave the box near Logan's room door? That would be the sensible course. *And when have I ever been sensible?* Sighing, she headed for the garage.

Stopping at the open double doors, she scanned the interior. The man barely had room to move. Garden tools, wood boards, and scrap from Lord knew when crowded every spare space. Some old windows were stacked overhead, supported by what looked like two-by-fours. Who in their right mind saved old windows?

Since he wasn't in the garage, she'd leave the box by his room door, but just her luck, she caught a glimpse of him through the window that overlooked the carport. With his broad back to the garage, he leaned against the white car's front fender while staring at the side street. From this angle, Sky couldn't see his face, but his usually squared shoulders had a slight slump.

She bit her lower lip. Maybe Doreen told him about Tommy. What possible words could she say to help the situation? He'd tell her to go pound sand, and she'd happily comply. *Yeah, I'm a glutton for punishment, all right.* Straightening her shoulders and, with parcel in hand, she exited the garage. Before rounding the car, she cleared her throat.

He rotated his head and scowled. "What do *you* want?"

What was it with people today? For crying out

loud, shouldn't they show a little respect to their new owner?

"I'm not in the mood, Sky. Go away." He, again, stared at the street.

Why was she here? Logan and Doreen were none of her business. She should just let him sulk alone. Praying for a little logic as to why she bothered, she lifted her chin. "Package delivery, courtesy of Ginger's Manor." She extended her arm, box in hand.

With a snort, he took the box and read the label. "My mother still sends cookies like I'm starving to death."

His mother should take a good look at her son's physique, for he definitely was *not* a starving man. She coughed. "Mrs. Santini is complaining about your thumping."

Cutting her a glare, he sneered. "So, what else is new? Why do you think I spend so much time on the balcony? If I belch too loud, she complains."

"I never asked Fay why only the rooms on the third floor have balconies. Do you know?"

"Fire escape reasons. Tyrone and I have rope ladders."

"If you—"

"Yes, dammit, I can use a rope ladder."

Touchy, touchy. She fought the urge to turn on her heel and ignore him. Instead, she folded her arms over her chest and smirked. "I was going to say if you want, you can move to the second floor. We have two rooms available."

He stiffened. "Why would I want to move?"

"One flight of stairs is easier on the hip, and your thumping won't bother Mrs. Santini."

"I happen to enjoy the freedom of the balcony." He shook the box in her face. "Thanks for the delivery." He turned his back.

She was summarily dismissed. Well, maybe she wasn't ready to go. She tapped a finger on his shoulder. *Wow*. Like tapping on a rock. "Anything you want to talk about? You know, like why Doreen ran through the kitchen practically crying her eyes out?"

Cussing softly, he shot a quick glance over his shoulder. "Yeah, so?"

For a brief moment, his face showed remorse, which made her think she needed glasses. The emotion was so fleeting it could be nothing more than a simple twitch. Slipping her fingers into the rear pockets on her shorts, she cocked a hip. "I know it's none of my business, but do you want to talk? I've a good ear."

Pushing away from the car, he turned with a sneer. "You must think you're some kind of psychiatrist." He bent to retrieve his crutch, slid his arm into the holder, then faced her with a growl. "She's after me—like you."

Mouth agape, she staggered and dropped her hands to her sides. "I hardly know you."

With fire in his eyes, he shook a finger in her face. "I told Doreen, and I'm telling you. I can't perform for a woman. Get it?" He hobbled toward the front of the garage.

Ordinarily, she wouldn't bother with a man and his hurt pride, but facts didn't jive. Had he suffered nerve damage in the pelvic region that led to the limp and erectile dysfunction? He bent without difficulty. That was a positive sign, right? "Why are you so angry when you're the one initiating reconciliation?"

Shoulders jerking, he whirled, eyes wide. "What?"

Uh-oh. She might have stepped into a rabbit hole. Frowning at his tone, she narrowed her gaze. "Doreen told me."

He peered. "Told you what?"

"You're the ex who deserted her."

Chapter Nine

Logan sucked in a breath so hard Skylar swore the pressure collapsed his trachea.

For indeed, his crutch dropped to the ground, his face paled, and then, he coughed and sputtered before falling against the garage wall with his chin hugging his chest.

Smart man that he was, he held onto the cookies from his mother. She extended a hand—in case he keeled over. "You okay?"

Lifting his chin skyward, he closed his eyes and thumped his head against the wall. "Did she say Tommy was my son?"

"Yes." Realizing a little too late her fingers stroked along the thick arm muscle, she dropped her hand.

Lowering his head, he met her gaze. "I am not her ex, Sky." He bent to retrieve his crutch.

Well, all right, someone was lying, but who? She frowned. "Why would Doreen tell me otherwise?"

He stared into the distance. "She's been after me. I have no idea why she'd want a cripple."

A nice-looking cripple, but hey. Whatever damage he sustained certainly ruined his confidence. But who should she believe? Not that it mattered. She had neither the time nor inclination to figure out these two. She passed her fingers through her hair. "You and Doreen are none of my business." She turned to leave.

"Sky, wait." He caught her wrist.

Lordy! As gentle as his touch was, sparks flew from his fingers, just like in Margaret's room. What was it with this man? No rug under his feet, no electrical wire attached to his leg. If this continued, her heart might flutter to death. Turning, she saw his package nearly crushed under his crutch arm. *So much for whole cookies.*

Clearing his throat, he dropped his hand. "Look, Sky. You're a threat to Doreen. You're beautiful and own a boardinghouse. She's a struggling food server with a son."

Beautiful, really? Men at the bar said the words every night, but she hardly ever experienced a reaction. She just figured they were stone drunk. With Logan, her whole body tingled. *Has to be his voice. No other explanation.* She jutted her chin. "Yeah, so? Despite your accusations, I'm not competing for your affections." *There. Swallow that statement, big guy.* His egotistical idea of her chasing him grated on her nerves. Skylar Dawson never chased men. Period.

Besides, even a cripple playing the sympathy card could be after her inheritance. She shot Logan her practiced bartender face—a combination of stern and firm. "You need to talk to a counselor about your anger issues. It's unhealthy to mope around feeling sorry for yourself. Have you discussed your erectile dysfunction with a doctor?"

Back going ramrod straight, he yanked his package from his armpit and adjusted his crutch. "No." He hobbled toward the front of the garage.

She followed. "Doctors can do a lot for the problem. You know, medication and such."

"This discussion is over."

"Doreen has no need to feel threatened, Logan. You should talk to her."

He glanced over his shoulder. "She should apologize for fabricating such a ludicrous story." He reached the front of the garage and stopped. Shoulders slumping, he stared at the ground. "I'll admit I have a problem, but I can't discuss it."

"Fair enough, but go easy with Doreen. A deserting husband can leave a woman vulnerable for a long time." Feeling like she'd done her good deeds to last an entire month, she turned on her heel and headed for the rancher. People created entirely too much drama. They should learn to just chill out and let things slide.

As Skylar slipped through the office and entered the main house, she heard giggling. Coming up the hall, Fay and Rita emerged from the bedroom with clothes draped over their arms and hats on their heads while chattering like two schoolgirls after a shopping spree.

Fay held out a flowery blouse. "I hadn't realized Ginny owned so many unused clothes. Look, this still has the price tag." She extended the sleeve to dangle the tag. "Rita snatched all the new bras."

"And most of the sweatshirts." Rita flashed a big grin. "We're both too tall for her slacks, but I always loved her overcoat." She patted the coat draped over her arm. "I'm taking two of the cardigans for Doreen. If she doesn't want them, I'll keep them for myself."

Skylar smiled. "I'll pack the rest of the stuff tonight."

Rita waved aside the comment. "Already done. I left the bags in the bedroom." She wagged a finger around the living room. "If you want help with all these knickknacks, let me know."

"Thank you, Rita. I will." The woman was a marvel. She'd have everything packed in no time.

Fay patted Skylar's arm. "Join us for dinner tonight. We're having pizza."

Oh, yum. But sharing the kitchen with Logan tightened her gut. If Doreen was off work, she'd be at the table tossing daggers. Between the two of them, she'd never enjoy her meal. *Talk about drama.* "Thanks, Fay, but I've work to do." As much as she loved pizza, she spent far too much time with the tenants and not enough settling the estate. If she didn't move her butt, she'd be here longer than her allotted month.

After the women left, Skylar stood by the front door and stared at the office desk. She hadn't taken a whole lot of time searching for her aunt's proof—if any existed. Logically, Aunt Ginger could hide her information anywhere. With the clothes packed and ready to be hauled away, she might as well start in the office.

Clicking the porch air conditioner on high, she adjusted the blinds and flopped onto a squeaking desk chair. Her butt easily slipped into the cushion's indentations, and a wave of melancholy swept through her at the vision of her aunt sitting in this very chair. Ginger left her so much, and Sky had no possible way to thank her.

Pushing aside the thought, she stared at the desk computer. If Fay was right and Aunt Ginger hardly used the computer, then a search for information about a supposed killer would be a waste of time. She hit the Power switch anyway. The computer took no time to load and wasn't password-protected. Double-clicking on one program after another, she found each and every one displaying a *Welcome and Let's Get Started* page. Several icons took her directly to social media and shopping sites.

With the computer eliminated, she hit the Shut Down command and opened the largest drawer on the right. File folders with neat handwritten labels hung on a metal rack with each listing the names of the tenants. *Hmm.* She might be sitting at this desk for a while. So, why not take everything into the kitchen and relax with a cup of coffee?

She clutched the chair's worn armrests to push onto her feet when a movement outside the front windows caught her eye. Logan. She half-expected Doreen to follow, but he limped alone. Curious, she reclaimed her seat and closed the desk drawer.

Knocking first, he stepped inside and stopped short, brows high. "I didn't expect to see you at the desk. Can I talk to you?"

"Sure."

After shutting the door, Logan faced her. "I want to officially decline your offer for a second-floor room."

"Duly noted. I'll make the same offer to Tyrone. He'll probably accept since he'll be closer to Rita."

He curled one side of his mouth. "I see you already picked up on his feelings. Is this bartender psyche?"

Chuckling, she leaned back and propped one foot onto the chair's cushion. "Anyone can see how his gaze follows Rita whenever she's in the room. I'm guessing she's too busy with her OCD to notice. And FYI, I suspect Michael has more than a casual interest in Doreen. He dotes on Tommy like he's a son. Have a seat." She waved toward the wooden chair alongside the desk.

After slipping his arm from the crutch sleeve, he settled onto the seat and lowered the metal staff to the floor. "I apologized to Doreen, but she needs to apologize to you." He shot Skylar a glance.

His voice caused pleasurable chills to travel the length of her spine. For a man with erectile dysfunction, he should, at least, talk with a gruff manner since a romp in bed was out of the question. In any case, she wasn't a woman who took sex lightly. Call her crazy, but the joining of two people had to mean something. Avoiding his gaze, she grabbed a pen and twirled it between her fingers.

"Are you going through your aunt's files?"

How in the world...*oh*. She'd left the drawer partially open. *Duh*. She stared at the green folders. "I just sat down, Logan—which reminds me." She threw the pen onto the desk. "Excuse me while I make a phone call."

"I can step out."

"No, this won't take long."

Too lazy to retrieve her cell phone, she dropped her foot to the floor and stretched across the desktop for the rotary card file. She found the lawyer's card easily enough and dialed from the desk phone. While it rang, she glanced at Logan. "I need to finalize the paperwork with my aunt's attorney."

"Nathan Kirby's office."

"This is Skylar Dawson. I'd like to—"

"Yes, Ms. Dawson, hold on. I'll transfer you to his assistant."

Well, that was unexpected. The woman acted like

her name was important.

Fifteen seconds later, the assistant answered. "Mister Kirby has been waiting for your call. Would you like to come in tomorrow, say around ten?"

"Perfect. See you then." She disconnected and stared at the phone.

Logan cleared his throat. "I understand Kirby pressured your aunt to sell. Is he doing the same to you?"

She returned the phone to its holder. "Not really." She frowned.

"Are you contemplating world peace?"

Jerking, she met his gaze. "What?"

"Your face, Sky. You look so serious."

"Oh." Smirking, she shook her head. "This inheritance makes me question everyone's motive. Thanks to my aunt, I'm more than a bartender." She wasn't sure she liked it, either.

"Take one day at a time, Sky."

She studied him. When he wasn't defensive, the man acted like a good friend. If only she could trust him. She so desperately wanted a confidant. But just because his demeanor relaxed her didn't mean she'd blurt Monroe's news without sounding like her brain had a loose screw.

"Okay, then." With the help of his crutch, he stood.

Their gazes met and held. Her breath hitched at the warmth probing her face. *Dear Lord Almighty*. His muscles tempted her eyes, his voice played with her libido, and his steady gaze robbed her of all sense of concentration. If he didn't leave, then she'd do something foolish, like invite him to dinner.

With a hand on the doorknob, he turned. "How

about I drive you tomorrow? I'm due for a haircut."

His hair looked perfect for a woman's fingers—not too long, not too short, and clean. She loved clean hair. But she wasn't about to tell him to let it be. She grinned. "All right. My appointment's at ten."

Smiling, he winked. "See you at nine forty-five."

He finally smiled, and the transformation nearly bowled her over. Bright, white teeth showed, and truth be told, the smile changed him into the sexiest man alive. Thank the Lord Logan left before she melted off the chair.

Shaking away his effect, she gathered the tenant folders into her arms and headed for the kitchen. While waiting for the coffee to brew, she skimmed through the file folders. Everyone had a signed lease agreement and emergency contact information, but her aunt also included a handwritten note with some personal observations. Since anyone could look into the folders, her aunt's information had to be vague enough not to raise suspicions. With coffee cup in hand, Skylar settled at the kitchen table and opened the first folder.

Room Number One: Rita Garrett. Widow.

Former occupation: housewife. Daughter in Arkansas, son in Maryland.

Her aunt's notes were handwritten with a beautiful script.

Rita can't sit still. The poor girl goes berserk when tenants are sloppy, and it takes me or Fay to calm her down. OCD used to good advantage to help Fay with housekeeping. I reduced Rita's monthly rent by forty percent.

Would an OCD kill in a fit of rage? A possibility to consider, but she was no expert. Sky opened the next folder.

Room Number Two: Maria Santini. Widow.

Former occupation: politician's wife. One son, Philip, resides in Penns Grove, NJ.

Keeps to herself. Spends most of her time by the window in her room. A very unhappy woman who resists all efforts to socialize.

Several of Maria's complaints were included and all handwritten on personalized stationery—one about Michael Chang closing his door too heavily, another about Tommy making too much noise on the stairs, and quite a few about Rita. Petty stuff. Petty enough to kill? Sky continued.

Room Number Three: Michael Chang. Single.

Works as an IT specialist in Delaware. Parents reside in New York.

Known asthmatic, controlled by inhalers. Complains about Rita's strong cleaners and Darla's bath salts. Taught me how to use a computer. Still hate the blasted things. Wonderful tenant, but don't know why he doesn't find a place closer to work.

Now, there was a clue. An IT specialist should make decent money, right? Why stay in Jersey and commute? And who was Darla? She opened the next folder.

Room Number Four: Anthony Powers. Widower.

Former occupation: engineer. Two sons—one in Philadelphia, the other in Pittsburgh.

Complains about everything. Never pays his rent on time. Claims his memory is failing. Big-time bullshitter. The man designed several patents for large engine projects, but the company kept the rights. He resents the fact he never received a dime.

Bitterness changed a lot of people, but was it enough to cause a man to go on a rampage? Definitely something to keep in mind.

Room Number Five: Gilda Mongrief. Widow.

Former occupation: high school physics teacher. No family.

Had her stroke while a resident. Robbed her of speech and reading skills. Memories intact. Has a severe allergy to cilantro and keeps epinephrine in her nightstand drawer.

Lots of personalities change after a stroke. Her neighbor across the street, for example. The old guy was a miserable bastard. After his stroke, he never stopped smiling. *Talk about a one-eighty turn.*

Skylar leaned back and sighed. Too bad her aunt hadn't written a note about a tenant having murderous tendencies. Suppose the deaths were true accidents? Aunt Ginger's heart attack in the basement could be nothing more than bad timing. Someone saw the light on, called down, and hearing no answer, turned off the light and locked the door. She swallowed the last of her coffee, then stood for a stretch.

Outside her window, Tommy and Yapper chased each other around the gazebo.

Alongside the two entry steps grew clusters of rose bushes with blooming red buds where Doreen worked with a garden spade.

About twenty feet away, picnic tables sat under large elm trees. The chest-high hedgerow from the front of the property continued along the side, separating the grounds from the gorgeous Victorian neighbor next door. After refilling her mug, she returned to her seat and continued with the folders.

Room Number Six: Joe Ryan. Widower.

Occupation: bartender. No family. Retired from the navy.

I ordered a longer bed for Too-Tall Joe. Fay's good at making sheets to fit. He doesn't socialize much and quotes the Bible like he was a former preacher. Works for my good friend, Babe, at her bar in Westville. Babe has an apartment above the bar should Joe want it, but he seems content to stay with us.

So, something is keeping Joe at the manor. Definitely another fact to consider.

The next folder, Room Number Seven, was empty.

Room Number Eight: Margaret Caine. Widow.

Former occupation: executive assistant. One daughter in Arizona.

Another OCD resident. Must own stock in a cotton ball factory. I've told her about the balls all over the house. She should buy a hand gripper thingy to use, but she's a stubborn old bird. The arguments between Margaret and Rita make for some uncomfortable dinner conversations.

Another clue? Clash of the OCDs?

Sky might drive herself crazy with questions.

Room Number Nine: Doreen Hashoff and son, Tommy.

Occupation: food server. Divorced. Husband deserted.

Our first time with a child at the manor. Tommy is well-behaved but lonely. Plays with Yapper. Doreen helpful around the garden. Unknown whereabouts of Tommy's father.

Maybe Sky should ask Monroe to find Tommy's father and determine once and for all whether the man actually exists. What if Doreen buried him in a field somewhere? Serial killers have been known to relocate to continue their killing spree. She could be one of them.

Room Number Ten folder was Logan's, empty except for the lease. According to the payment section, the State Welfare Board paid his rent. Everyone else paid with a personal check. In the occupation section—*unemployed. Well, no shit.* Fay probably felt sorry for him. Skylar sipped her coffee.

Room Number Eleven: Tyrone Houser. Divorced.

Former occupation: hospital maintenance man. Three daughters, all in California.

Can fix anything. Gets along well with grumpy Anthony, although the debates can be endless. Refuses to move to California to be with his daughters.

If the daughters want him in California, why stay here? Another clue?

Skylar drummed her fingers on the table. Three people had the option to move—Michael Chang to Delaware, Joe Ryan to above Babe's bar, and Tyrone Houser to the West Coast. Yet, here they stayed. Was this significant?

After placing her empty cup in the sink, she gathered the folders and carried them to the office. Before replacing her armload, she inspected the drawer for any loose papers, then dropped the folders onto the wire rack. The small drawer above was full of staple boxes and whatnot. Sitting, she opened the drawer on the left and skimmed through utility receipts, ordinance laws, and inspection results. The center drawer was full of pens and pencils plus new lease agreements. Sitting back, she draped her arms over the armrests. Nothing of a personal nature in the desk and no obvious clues to the supposed killer. She swiveled in the chair with a gaze scanning the office.

On the floor alongside the two filing cabinets sat several stacked cardboard boxes. She opened the first box and was rewarded with an array of thick envelopes. *Tax returns*! She shifted through the large manila envelopes clearly marked with the year, but they were too old. She needed last year's return. She secured the lid to the first and opened another. File folders filled the interior, past tenants at a guess. *Rats*. The last box showed more of the same. She understood the need to save tax returns, but why tenant folders?

Her stomach growled...well, more like gurgled. She drank too much coffee and ate nothing to absorb the liquid. Tomorrow, once she returned from the lawyer's office, she would tackle the filing cabinets. Hopefully, she'd find what she needed since the desk and her aunt's bedroom were eliminated. At the moment, her number one priority was to answer her stomach's call for sustenance. With luck, she wouldn't burn her dinner.

Chapter Ten

Sky burned her dinner. She never claimed to be the best cook in the world, but over the years, she acquired a taste for burnt food. Some was quite good, thank you very much. After adding extra butter to her sad-looking pepper-and-egg omelet, she washed the dishes and then opened some of the flat boxes Fay delivered. With all the knickknacks, the bottoms of the boxes needed reinforcement, and she remembered seeing masking tape in the garage. She stepped onto the rear patio, but from this angle, she could see the garage doors closed for the evening. She'd need the keys, and those were hanging in the office. After grabbing the ring, she headed out the office door and followed the side path to the garage.

A movement toward her left caught her eye.

Philip Santini emerged from the front of the manor on his way to the parking lot.

The man was dressed in suit and tie and looked every bit the professional lawyer. With his good looks, he probably mesmerized female jurors. Right now, though, he had the look of an annoyed man with his brows creased toward the center of his straight nose. *Another mommy dearest problem, no doubt.*

Catching sight of her and doing a quick double-take, he approached with a smile stretching his lips. "I was hoping to see you again. I dropped off my mother's pills."

The man had a relaxing air and put her at ease with his beautiful smile. He'd be a nice friend to confide in, legal and otherwise. But like Logan, she knew so little about Philip. Suppose he had a key to one of the doors and snuck in to bop off a tenant or two? Or even worse, Maria let him in to do her dastardly deeds. Gad, she hated all these random thoughts. Shaking herself, she smiled. "Aren't you staying for pizza?"

He slapped a hand to his chest. "Dear Lord, no. If I ate with you commoners, my mother will think I've descended into the depths of hell." Dropping his hand, he chuckled. "Her words, Sky, not mine. I love pizza. Mother prepared her own dinner, of course."

"Why is she here, Philip? Why not rent her a small apartment at a nice senior center?"

Hissing softly, he stuffed his hands into his trouser pockets. "We're not rolling in dough, Sky. Senior centers want too much of a deposit, and I can't afford the high monthly fee on my public defender's salary." He huffed out a breath and then stared into the distance. "My father was a small-town mayor. After he died, his pension transferred to my mother, but the monthly amount is hardly enough to put food on the table." He met her gaze. "If Mother socialized more, she'd make me feel better, but she'd rather sit at the window and mope."

Since she faced the manor, Skylar glanced at the second-story windows. One of the curtains fluttered in Mrs. Santini's room. Above her, Logan leaned against a balcony post with his arms crossed over his impressive chest, watching. Even at a distance, his gaze had a way of jump-starting her heart.

Shifting her gaze to Philip, she felt nothing from the man. Why? Philip was the obvious choice for a friend. He had a job and lived at his own place and, hopefully, didn't suffer from erectile dysfunction. She nodded toward the house. "Your mother caught us talking."

He waved his hand. "Don't let it bother you. She has this mental block about who I should date, and trust me, she doesn't approve of too many women." With a gleam emanating from his gaze, he stroked her arm. "Once you're settled, I'd like to take you out."

Oh! An actual date? What a lovely idea—as long as he didn't expect her to wear anything dressy. She smiled. "I'd like that." His mother wouldn't. She'd chop off Sky's head and post it on a stick in the yard. *Talk about entering the depths of hell.*

With a finger, Philip lifted her chin.

His gaze was dark and—*wow*—glowed. *My, goodness gracious.* She shot a quick glance downward and was rewarded with the sight of a bulge in his zipper area. No erectile dysfunction for this man.

Philip brushed a finger along her chin. "You're very beautiful, Skylar Dawson. I want to know you better." He lowered his head. "Soon, I hope."

The soft touch of his lips against hers startled her. It felt nice, but she was too surprised to respond.

As Philip headed for his car, he glanced over his shoulder and winked.

Well, hell, a date might change everything.

That night, another dream clouded her sleep. The duel again. She swore it was the same scenario, but farther into the scene, something was different. This time, she wasn't standing nearby. Her silhouette appeared on the horizon, as if watching from afar. Yet, she distinctly pictured Philip in his suit and tie. He appeared so regal and flashed his sword with a yawn. Dirt and sweat covered Logan. Fumes emanated from his odoriferous work clothes, and yes, by golly, she sneezed in her dream. The prince versus the commoner. Two swords clashed. The commoner won and then…she woke up.

All right, that was weird. Why Logan? Philip was no slug in the looks department, and his career as an attorney was a far cry from a guy on welfare. Yet, Logan won the duel. *Go figure.*

With no urge to get out of bed, she rolled onto her back and stared at the ceiling. Before this inheritance, she never thought of anything from one day to the next. Not only had she no ambition to better herself, she also had no desire to marry or be burdened by children. Her urge to travel was non-existent, and it took all she had to pack a bag and head to New Jersey. A few years ago, on a dare from a bar patron, she stepped into a martial arts studio and never looked back, which came as a surprise considering how lazy she was. In a way, being here in this house was another dare, and it forced her to think more about what she wanted in life. Marriage and children were still off the table, but was being alone the way to live? Frustrated with a lack of answers, she threw off the covers and headed for the shower to begin her day.

Her cell phone rang. After slipping a T-shirt over her head, she glanced at the caller ID and then swiped the Accept button. "Morning, Lieutenant."

"I hope I didn't wake you."

"Not at all. What did you uncover?" Last night,

after she retrieved the masking tape from the garage, she phoned Monroe and had him research her dueling suitors. Even though she leaned a little more toward Logan, she'd rather have some concrete information under her belt.

"Logan Greene is his real name. Doreen Hashoff's ex-husband, Kyle Markham, resides in New Mexico."

His information lifted one doubt from her mind. She bit her lip. "Do you think I can trust him?"

"The decision is yours. Greene has no criminal record nor does Philip Santini. You established Greene's alibi at the time of Margaret Caine's death but not Santini's." Papers shuffled. "I'd use caution around Santini. He knows his way around the manor, and his mother gives him a good excuse to visit. Greene wasn't a tenant at the time of the other accidents."

Monroe told her nothing new. "Any information about his injury?"

"Not a thing."

"All right, Lieutenant, thank you. I'll be in touch." She disconnected.

Logan told the truth. He wasn't Doreen's husband. Maybe deep in her subconscious, he won the duel because he could be trusted. How she arrived at that conclusion, she'd never know—except for a gut feeling.

After a relaxing breakfast of toast and coffee and an hour of packing some of the knickknacks, Skylar locked the rancher and headed for the parking lot. She debated whether to wear something more respectable for her appointment with the lawyer—like pants—but when did she ever worry about people's opinions? Cargo shorts would do, and a tank top was a must. People called her crazy for wearing all black, but she had one purpose in mind with a one-color wardrobe. She never had to worry about mix and match—another lazy habit.

On the way toward the parking lot, she slowed, and her throat went dry. Well, wasn't this a pleasant sight to see early in the morning?

Logan leaned against a black sports car with his crutch between his legs. He wore a light-gray T-shirt with black jeans that showed every enticing muscle on his chest and legs. Looking up, he slid his gaze over her body.

Oh, my. The heat emanating shot straight to her core, and she wasn't sure why she shivered. At the bar, men often stared, as if she was the last woman alive, but this muscled man stimulated some foreign sensations. What those sensations were she had no clue. The man was incredibly sexy—despite the handicap.

Approaching, she smiled. "I might take longer than your barber."

He pushed away from the car. "That's okay. I can always shoot the breeze with the guys." He opened the passenger door. "You're the only woman I know who doesn't carry a purse. How come?"

"Because I hate them. Everything I need I carry in my pockets." She patted her hips.

With a chuckle rising from deep within his throat, he waved her into the car.

She ignored the gesture and eyed him through narrowed lids. "I don't know where I stand with you, Logan. You're hot and cold." She folded her arms across her chest. "One minute, you push me away and the next you're offering to drive me around. I'm afraid we'll reach the lawyer's, and you'll switch to your go-away mood."

Lips pursed, he leaned on his crutch. "I'm having second thoughts, Sky."

"Oh?" She raised her brows. "About driving me?"

"No, about pushing you away." He quirked his lips. "I'd like to be friends."

Well, okay. Friends might work. No expectations and all that. Smiling, she slipped on the sunglasses she had clipped to her front pocket. "All right, *friend*, let's go." She slid onto the passenger seat.

Black car with black leather seats—a man after her own heart. She wouldn't even question how a man on welfare afforded such a beauty.

After he closed her door, he hobbled to the driver's side, tossed his crutch onto the rear seat, then took his position behind the steering wheel. With a push of the Start button, the engine roared to life.

She buckled her seatbelt. "Do you want to tell me how you injured yourself?"

"No." Shifting into Drive, he eased the car onto the street.

"Friends talk, you know. Share secrets." She tilted her head toward him, hoping to make eye contact.

He kept his gaze focused on the road.

She sighed. "Okay. Don't expect me to be completely honest, either."

Glancing her way, he said nothing.

Rather than dwell on the issue, Skylar relaxed to enjoy the short ride.

When she first hopped on her motorcycle and headed east, she had no idea what to expect. Since Chicago was her home for so long, she thought nothing of the constant noise of a city. Here in Woodstown, the area had a quiet and relaxed feel. The closer he drove toward the center of town, the older the houses became. Old salt-box homes sat alongside even older colonials. Many were large, stately homes with name plates tacked near the front door. Charles Pancoast House—1883. Josiah Davis House—1850. Nicely kept homes, too, but not what she'd call mansions. Her aunt's estate, with its wide front lawn, was far bigger than the others and might have been a mansion long ago. "I don't suppose the rest of New Jersey looks as quaint as this town."

Logan slowed for a parking vehicle. "I'd say here and there. Certainly south of us in Greenwich and Salem." He clicked on his turn signal and turned left.

"Are you from around here?"

"Princeton." He draped one hand over the top of the steering wheel. "That's in central Jersey. My parents still live there."

Turning her head, she studied him. "Then, why are you here?" She wouldn't say the words to his face, but many disabled people stayed close to family for support.

"Oh, you know, a migration of sorts. A place to put my head together."

Or a place to be alone. He didn't have to say the words for her to understand. Families could be a little overbearing.

At the main intersection, Logan continued straight. A short distance after passing a series of small shops, he aimed for an open spot along a tree-lined street and cut the engine. Her lawyer's office was a large, gray Victorian two houses down.

Logan jerked a thumb over his shoulder. "The

barber shop is around the corner. We'll meet here at the car."

"Right." She stepped onto the sidewalk.

As she approached Nathan Kirby's office, she paused to remove her sunglasses, then glanced in Logan's direction. She caught his gaze as he stood in the middle of the sidewalk, watching her. Again, an odd sensation swept through her. Ever since she arrived, she found him staring. Under different circumstances, she'd call the look creepy, but somehow, the man acted more like a guardian angel. Was he aware of the problems at the manor and kept an eye on her for safety reasons? True or not, a sense of comfort rose with the thought. She might never hit the bedsheets with him, but she recognized a steadfast friend. She had absolutely no doubts she could trust him and high time she listened to her heart. Before entering Kirby's office, she waved to Logan and received a nod in return.

An enduring hour and a half later, full of mind-boggling paperwork, Skylar exited the lawyer's office with a manila envelope loaded with legal documents. Mr. Kirby explained the New Jersey state requirements for filing estate taxes, federal inheritance taxes, and when to use the state waivers. Her main responsibility was to locate her aunt's assets and gather the information for Kirby's tax consultant. The will specified Skylar Dawson receive all of the estate. What *all* meant still required confirmation. So, no more delays. Once she returned to the house, she'd tackle the filing cabinets.

Clutching the fat envelope to her chest, Skylar glanced toward the car to see Logan leaning against the fender. She approached and pointed toward his head.

"Your hair doesn't look any different."

Shrugging, he passed a hand through his hair. "Too crowded. I'll try another day."

With a tilt of her head, she fought a smile. "Something tells me the barber shop wasn't your objective." Standing directly in front of him, she narrowed her gaze. "You're watching over me, Logan, and have been since I arrived. Why?"

He toyed with his crutch. "There's a lot of talk at the dinner table about accidents at the manor. I want to make sure nothing happens to you."

Brow arched, she shifted her hip. "What kind of accidents?"

"Like falling down stairs or drowning in a tub."

So, the tenants suspected foul play? *Interesting.* "What makes you think I'm in danger?"

"Let's say I'm concerned."

Aw, shit. That warm, fuzzy feeling filled her chest. She'd like nothing more than to have someone as a sounding board and, even more importantly, someone to watch her back. Why not choose the guy who already elected himself for the job? She scanned the tree-lined street. "Is there some place we can talk?"

Brows creased, he shifted his crutch. "You mean other than inside the car?" He jerked his head to the left. "Woodstown has a lake with a walkway and benches—unless you'd rather go to the diner."

"No, a private place where I won't be overheard."

He shot her a one-eyed glare.

Oh, good grief. She rolled her eyes. "I won't jump you, Logan. I want to talk about these accidents."

"Okay, let's go to the lake." A short drive later, Logan guided the car into a small parking area where only one other vehicle sat.

Leaving the manila envelope tucked under the seat and her sunglasses on the console, she alighted and joined Logan on a shaded concrete path that circled a small lake. Tall elms and oak trees fluttered their leaves with the breeze, and wooden benches were spaced far enough apart to allow a private conversation. A few people were about. One, a jogger, sprinted across a stone bridge on the far side. A man and a little girl threw bread cubes to quacking ducks floating on the water. Overall, a quiet place to reflect.

"What's bothering you, Sky?"

Funny how her name on his lips sounded so intimate. She pointed to a bench. "Let's sit."

His crutch clicked and rattled as he rested it on the ground. Using the bench's backrest for support, he lowered onto the seat. "Rumors have been flying around the table for months, Sky. Margaret's death brought out even more speculation."

She stared at her sneakers and the white legs showing from her shorts. She wasn't one to bask in the sun, and being a bartender meant working nights while sleeping during the day. She should have a Vitamin D deficiency. She cleared her throat. "The other day, at the supermarket, two detectives approached my car just as I pulled in. Lieutenant Monroe wanted to talk to me in private. So, they drove me to the state police barracks. Monroe told me of my aunt's suspicions that her tenants had been murdered." She glanced his way to check his reaction. He had none and simply eyed her with an expressionless face. "Margaret Caine's official cause of death was natural causes."

Still expressionless, he leaned back and crossed his

arms over his chest. "Go on."

She let her gaze drift across the lake to a road on the other side. "He said my aunt was in the process of gathering proof, but so far, I haven't found anything."

He grunted. "What proof could she have? From the talk at the table, none of the accidents were witnessed."

Shifting on the bench, she faced him. "But what if she had suspicions and confronted someone, and that someone locked her in the basement in retaliation?"

He shook his head. "From what I heard, she was locked in the basement by mistake and had a heart attack because of her fear of the dark."

"But don't you see?" She finally had a chance to verbalize all the questions rolling around in her head. Even if Logan thought she was crazy, he made a great sounding board. He helped ease the tension from her shoulders, and that, by itself, was worth risking this conversation. She tucked one leg under her butt. "Someone probably knew of her weak heart. Why else was the light off and door locked? No one apologized, right?"

With a grimace, he rubbed a hand on the nape of his neck. "You've got a point."

That damn T-shirt outlined the muscles on his chest, and she itched to touch him. For a brief second, she wondered if steroids were to blame for his impotence.

"What are you thinking, Sky?"

Oh, wouldn't he like to know? She snapped her gaze to his face. Heat flooded her cheeks at the smirk on his lips. She coughed and then plastered on as neutral a face as possible. "Do you work out?" Well, *that* wasn't an innocent question. *Stupid, stupid.*

Gaze twinkling, he lowered his arm and flexed a bicep.

The muscle looked like a boulder popping under his skin, and she practically salivated.

"You can touch it."

She shook her head. One touch wouldn't be enough.

Relaxing his arm, he smiled. "I keep in shape with arm weights. Sometimes, I lower one to the floor a little too hard, which prompts an irate call from Santini." He leaned toward her. "She wasn't too happy with Philip's kiss yesterday. Since I was on the balcony, and she had a window cracked open, I heard every word when she called his cell phone. The poor man hadn't even left the parking lot." He straightened. "Why tell me about Monroe, Sky?"

Dropping her foot to the ground, she rotated to face the lake. "I've no one to watch my back, Logan. All the tenants—except you—were present in the time frame for the accidents. I can't even trust Philip." Sighing, she glanced his way. "I don't know what the lieutenant expects from me. I have no idea what to look for, and I'm sure my aunt didn't write her evidence with big red arrows pointing."

With a fist, he nudged her arm. "You have good instincts. You're bound to hear or see something to pique your curiosity. From what I hear and what you find, we can compare notes."

Feeling a huge weight lifting from her shoulders, she smiled. "I'd like that. I won't feel so alone in this sordid mess." As much as she'd love to spend more time with him, she still had a lot to do. Slapping her knees, she stood. "We should go."

He caught her arm. "Count on me to watch your back, okay?"

The warmth and gentleness of his hand solidified her decision to confide in the man. She'd take whatever objection Monroe voiced, but he sat behind a desk all day and had no real argument. If the accidents were indeed intentional, she lived among a killer and didn't like the thought one bit.

Chapter Eleven

While Skylar walked along the path to the car, she stared across the lake. "I wonder if Monroe can give me a copy of the case files?" She looked at Logan. "Between your hearsay and any information we find, we might uncover a connection to the victims. Do you think he would share?"

"Well, it won't hurt to try, but the files could be confidential." Frowning, he readjusted his arm within the crutch holder, then shot her a sideways glance. "By connection, I assume you mean motive?"

She kicked a stone off the path. "If he wants my help, he should give me something to work with." Catching his big grin, she started, brows high. "Did I say something amusing?"

He chuckled. "You sound like a cop."

She grunted in answer.

Stepping in front of her, he flicked a finger under her chin. "You're beautiful."

His maneuver was so sudden, she nearly plowed into his chest. Retreating a step, she stared into a darkened gaze. *Like staring into a barrel of fine ale.* Letting her gaze drift to his lips, she automatically wet her own. Dear Lord, the urge to kiss him was powerful, but one kiss would lead to two and every one a very big mistake. Forcing her feet to move, she took several more steps back. "That's quite a compliment coming from a man who pushes women away. And speaking of pushing…"

He matched her, step for step and slowly inched into her space.

Stumbling from concrete to grass, she thumped her back against a tree. With no place to go, she laid a palm onto his hard chest. "Logan, this isn't a good idea."

"It's a great idea, Sky."

As his head bent, he lifted her chin to meet his lips.

Her heart took off like a rocket, and her breath stopped. His lips felt wonderful. At first, he suckled with tender bites on her lower lip, and she lost all sense of concentration. Then, his tongue urged her to open, and by golly, she obliged.

With a clink, he dropped his crutch to the ground and wrapped his strong arms around her.

Even if she tried, she couldn't pull away. Every nerve in her body fired at once, and she gave in to the sensation of enjoying every second. Slipping her hands into his hair, she melted against his length and felt the bulge press against her belly.

Bulge!

She gasped into his mouth and used both palms to push against his chest. "You lied! That's an erection pressing against my belly."

In answer, he gripped both her butt cheeks and squeezed her tight against his hips, giving her the full effect of his male hardness.

A shudder rippled through her body. "Logan—"

He silenced her with a kiss that weakened her knees. Then, without warning, he dropped his arms and backed away.

Shocked at the sudden disconnect, she blinked.

"What happened?"

Hissing, he bent to retrieve his crutch. "This shouldn't have happened. I'm sorry." He hurried toward the car.

Staring after him, she willed her heart to slow. Was his impotence for real and his erection a fluke, or was something else going on?

****

With a jaw tight enough to crack his molars, Logan entered his room and resisted the urge to throw his crutch against the wall. He'd only make a lot of noise and incite another irritating phone call from Mrs. Santini, the ever-present entity on the second floor. He wasn't in the mood for any of her condescending words, because he sure as hell would rip into her with force. Sucking in a calming breath, he flopped onto the corner of the bed and held his head in his hands.

What have I done? If he hadn't come to his senses, he'd have taken Sky right on the grass. She might have muscles under her clothes, but she was still soft to the touch. And her kiss—*Lord Almighty*. She welcomed his lips with a fierceness that surprised the hell out of him. Her mouth encouraged him to explore, and her body ground against an erection he supposedly couldn't obtain.

Cursing profusely at his weakness, he yanked his cell phone from his rear pocket and hit speed dial. The deep voice answered on the first ring.

"Trouble?"

Logan ran a hand through his hair. "I can't do this anymore."

"Care to explain why?"

"I've lost my edge. She's getting to me."

Tapping sounded on the other end of the line.

The big man wasn't pleased. This lapse in judgment might force his superiors to remove him from his current assignment. He should never have kissed Sky. In fact, he should have kept a safe distance.

"Did she confide in you?"

Closing his eyes, he pinched the bridge of his nose. "Yes. We'll work together, but here's the problem." He dropped his hand. "She has a way of chipping at my resistance. That's never happened before."

"Oh." A long silence. More tapping. "You've worked with beautiful women in the past. Why is she different?"

"Damned if I know." He stared at the rug. "You need to pull me out."

"You're established, Logan, and in a perfect position. I won't remove you."

Logan shot from the bed and paced. "What should I do?"

"I'd say go with the flow."

He bristled. "I won't play games."

"I'm not asking you to."

Every instinct told him not to listen. For years, he followed a set of rules, and those rules kept him alive and detached. But this case was so different from the others. He allowed a weak moment to ruin everything. Stopping by the glass doors to the balcony, he relaxed his shoulders. "What do you want me to do?"

****

Back at the rancher, Skylar headed straight for the bathroom. Naturally, her cell phone rang the second her butt hit the john. Since she slipped her phone on top of the manila envelope and placed both on the kitchen table, she let the call go to voicemail.

On the way home, she'd sent a text message to Lt. Monroe about the case files. She debated telling him about Logan but, instead, kept the news to herself. On the return ride, Logan had clammed up. He gave the impression he was ready to spit nails. At least, he hadn't switched into his go-away mood and left her to find her own way home. No, the safest course of action was to study the files herself and let Mr. Moody be. Finished in the bathroom, she returned to the kitchen to check caller ID—Lt. Monroe. She hit Redial.

"Hello, Ms. Dawson. I got your message." He cleared his throat. "I wanted to give you the information at our last talk but was afraid to push. I'll make copies, but I'd like you to come here. If I came to you, I'd raise a few eyebrows."

Considering the circumstances, she understood perfectly. "Okay. Give me an hour. I need something to eat." She also needed time to clear her head. Something was going on with Logan, and she wasn't in any kind of analytical frame of mind to figure him out. Most men would be pleased to see an end to their impotence problem. Instead, the damn man got angry. Sighing, she assembled a quick cheese sandwich, then tore into it like some mad dog.

Finished with her lunch, she exited onto the patio and headed toward the carport. The garage doors were closed, and Logan's black vehicle was gone, which was good. She'd rather not see him for a while. The man confused her, and she never liked confused.

Bypassing her aunt's car, she threw off the cycle's cover, snapped on her helmet, and slipped on her lightweight windbreaker. With a press of the button, the engine roared to life.

The trip to the barracks took all of ten minutes. Across the road, the Cowtown Rodeo stood empty with the wooden flea market tables bare and buildings closed. Brown bulls roamed in one pasture and horses in another. Alongside the stables, several horse trailers sat parked. Other than the occasional cowboy wandering the grounds, no other activity caught her eye. *Cowboys in New Jersey. Imagine that*. Smiling to herself, she drove into the barracks parking lot, secured her cycle, helmet, and jacket, and entered the building.

Sitting behind a desk, a uniformed officer looked up from his computer. "Can I help you?"

"Skylar Dawson to see Lieutenant Monroe, please."

"Yes, ma'am. He's expecting you." He stood. "Follow me."

Once he reached the door with the lieutenant's placard, the officer knocked three times, swung the door wide, and waved her inside.

Monroe wasn't alone. Another man stood facing the window with hands on his hips. He wore a fitted, gray T-shirt over impressive shoulders, and something about him looked so…*ohmygod, no*! She froze, too stunned to move.

"Come in, Ms. Dawson." Sitting at his desk, Monroe waved her forward. "Allow me to introduce Detective Sergeant Logan Greene from our Princeton division."

Turning, Logan locked onto her gaze with a face devoid of expression.

At this particular moment, she wasn't sure of the emotions tumbling around in her chest. Shock, certainly. Maybe a little anger for being kept in the dark, but her mouth went bone dry for another reason. Pure, simple relief swept through her and weakened her knees. If she collapsed to the floor, she'd be embarrassed as all get out, so she locked her joints and waited, unable to remove her gaze from Logan.

With a smile tugging one side of his mouth, he walked toward her without a hobble or a limp—merely a fine specimen of a man with a powerful gaze to melt her bones. She'd made the right choice to confide in Logan. Who better to watch her back than a cop? She swallowed hard. "There's obviously a story here."

Monroe stood. "Considering how the two of you are getting along, I recommended Logan be upfront." He tossed his pen onto the desk. "I'll let him explain the situation in private. When I return, I'll answer any questions." He left and closed the door with a soft click.

An overwhelming urge to laugh consumed her. Logan played his part well, limp and all, but she was pleased as punch to see him as one of the good guys. She smiled. "I wondered why your limp was so bad without some sort of deformity showing. Where'd you learn to use a forearm crutch?"

His expression grim, he gestured toward the chairs in front of the desk. "A few years ago, I broke my leg in a climbing accident. At first, I used wooden crutches. After a while, I practiced with the metal type since a cripple made for a good cover story. This is my second assignment on crutches. Let's sit." He turned the two wooden chairs to face each other.

Unable to remove her gaze from him, she pretty much flopped onto the chair. Thankfully, she hit the seat, instead of falling straight to the floor.

He sat on the other, leaned forward, and took both her hands. "I wanted to tell you earlier, Sky, but part of my job is secrecy. Monroe believed your aunt's death was too coincidental. On the assumption she was right about her suspicious, he requested an undercover cop from North Jersey."

His thumbs stroked over her knuckles and caused a slew of goose bumps to rise. Dear Lord, the man affected her too easily.

Clearing his throat, he released her hands and leaned back.

Oh, for crying out loud. She should be grateful he wanted to place distance between them, but she had a hard time convincing her ego to chill.

"One of the reasons for a North Jersey cop is because of Philip." He met her gaze. "As the Salem County Public Defender, he knows most of the law enforcement personnel in the area. So, I volunteered for the job as a hard-on-his-luck cripple."

"Does Fay know?"

"Absolutely not." Smiling, he tugged on his ear. "I had a tough time convincing her to rent me a room. She didn't want to do anything without your permission. My saving grace was my offer to care for the lawn." With a frown replacing the smile, he placed his elbows onto his knees and locked his gaze on her face. "I've been here a couple of months and am no farther along than when I started. Mrs. Caine's death told us the killer is still active. Whether her demise was planned to coincide with your arrival, we don't know." Straightening, he broke eye contact and drummed his fingers on his thighs. "I'm going with the assumption the killer saw an opportunity to strike while the rest of us were distracted waiting for you. However, an unforeseen complication developed." He narrowed his gaze. "You."

Brows high, she straightened. "I don't understand."

Again, he leaned forward to take her hands. "When I saw you swing off your cycle, I knew I was in trouble. Your DMV photo gave me an idea who to expect, but nothing beat seeing you in person." He rubbed his thumbs over her knuckles. "After our kiss in the park and your discovery of my impotence lie, I called Monroe and requested to be removed. Instead, he suggested I reveal my identity so we can combine our efforts."

Words eluded her, and her thoughts flew in all directions. But before he released her hands and sent her ego into another dive, she slipped her hands from his and sat back. "If we're working together, then I expect answers to questions when I ask."

Straightening in his chair, he nodded. "I'll do my best. Ask away."

"True relationship status?"

"Honey, I can't have a relationship with undercover work. This assignment is already two months along. Some have taken a lot longer. So, I am not married nor do I have a girlfriend. You can confirm this with Monroe." With brows furrowed, he pursed his lips. "To be clear, I've no intention of leaving undercover work for any woman. Our time together is strictly for this assignment."

Oh-kay. What was it with men and their God's-gift-to-women mentality? Why must every man assume a woman preferred a relationship? She certainly didn't. Shaking her head, she searched his gaze. "You've stated crystal clear intentions, Detective Sergeant."

He humphed. "Hardly. I'm drawn to you, Sky, and I don't understand why. I've met a lot of beautiful women on my assignments, but for some reason, you pop into my thoughts, no matter what I'm doing."

He said the word again—beautiful. Did he mean it, or was he throwing out words to knock her off guard? She cleared her throat. "What you're experiencing is your male protective gene kicking in."

"No, Sky, I'm feeling sexual attraction. I know you feel it, too."

She smirked. "Yes, you're right, but so you know, my home is in Chicago, and I fully intend to return with heart and soul intact."

He gave a quick nod. "Then, we both established our intentions."

Except for the sexual attraction and what to do about it. She couldn't deny her pull toward him, even when she thought he had performance issues. But if he downplayed his feelings, well, dammit, so would she.

Chapter Twelve

A soft tap rapped on Monroe's door. The lieutenant poked his head through the opening. "Everything good here?"

What had he expected, a free-for-all? Sky and Logan were still sitting facing each other, looking like civilized people. Smiling, she waved him in. "I'm surprised but glad. We can compare notes."

"Speaking of notes." Monroe entered and reclaimed his seat behind the desk. After shuffling aside some papers, he handed her a large manila envelope. "Here are the copies of what we have so far. As I mentioned on your last visit, I have no authority to exhume the other bodies for autopsy. In a sense, you'll be flying blind." Sighing, he flopped back in his seat and scrubbed a hand through his crew cut. "I'm praying this hasn't gone on for years, and your aunt just noticed." Face stern, he leaned forearms on the desk. "You'd be wise not to eliminate anyone, and I want you to be careful about what you say to your tenants. If anything, make sure Logan is nearby." With his gaze like slits, he held up a finger. "Please understand why Logan must stay undercover, no matter what. We'll depend on your secrecy."

"You have my word, Lieutenant." She stood.

Logan jumped to his feet. "I'll walk you out." After entering the lobby, Logan nodded to the officer at the desk.

The young man promptly excused himself and disappeared through a side door.

Skylar shot Logan a sly look. "That appeared a trifle staged."

"Sorry, Sky." He wrapped her in his arms. "I'd love to continue where we left off this morning."

Since she clutched the envelope to her chest, she tapped the packet against his. "The moment is lost, Buster. Now that we know each other's intentions, we should cool whatever this is between us."

A commotion sounded in the hall. Voices shouted, and heavy footsteps pounded.

Logan's arms tensed. As the shouts turned angry, he swept her behind him.

A man sporting wild hair and beard flew into the front lobby with a gaze like fire.

She wasn't sure what was happening, but holy moly, the guy weighed a solid three hundred pounds and looked ready to tear someone into pieces. She might have three black belts and have handled men just as large, but she wasn't an idiot. She inched closer to Logan's back.

The crazy dude scanned the small lobby. Then, he locked onto Logan before roaring like a lion and charged.

Taking a standard defensive lineman position by spreading his legs with arms ready to grab, Logan reached.

The man sidestepped but had weight and momentum to his advantage. With one thump, he knocked Logan over the desk.

Uh-oh. Feeling like a trapped animal, Skylar

shifted her gaze between the wild man and the front door. Still clutching the envelope to her chest, she stepped aside to allow him a free run to the outside.

Snarling, the man focused on her and lunged.

Aw, hell. Heart pounding, she slammed the envelope into his face while simultaneously lifting her knee into his gut.

He humphed, growled, then clamped onto her arm and threw her against the wall.

Ouch. Well, now, that wasn't nice. She got the distinct impression he was toying with her. Otherwise, she'd have hit the wall harder. And why the hell didn't he run out the door? Tossing the envelope to the floor, she narrowed her gaze and took a step toward him. The damn man's gaze twinkled. He wanted her to attack? She spread her arms. "Come on, big guy. What are you waiting for?"

Snarling, he charged.

With a quick sidestep, she clamped both hands around his massive forearm and yanked him over her hip.

He dropped to the floor with a grunt.

Using the speed that earned her three black belts, she gripped his right wrist and wrenched to turn him onto his belly. Pulling hard on his arm, she jammed her foot into the middle of his spine.

He let out a piercing scream.

She had him in position to dislocate the shoulder from its socket, but something stopped her. For crying out loud, this crazy man was in a police station. Where were the cops? She looked around to see Logan, Monroe, and four other officers watching the show from the hallway. *What the hell?* She released the man's wrist and glared at Monroe. "You're testing me again." Jaw tight, she jammed her fists on her hips. "I could have hurt him." More like killed him, but hey, she wouldn't brag.

The big man hopped to his feet and rubbed his shoulder. "Damn, you're good." Rotating the joint, he winced.

Monroe approached. "I had to see a black belt in action. I'm impressed."

Clenching her jaw, she hissed. "Lieutenant—"

He stopped her with a raised palm. "Officer Davis volunteered. I'm sure he's happy for your restraint."

Still rubbing his shoulder, Davis grinned. "You bet, and I'd like to learn a few of those moves."

The other officers verbalized their agreement.

Walking toward her, Logan grunted. "Is that all, boss?"

Monroe coughed and urged the others from the lobby.

Bending, she retrieved her envelope. "I'm surprised he didn't have all the officers charge me at once."

While wrapping his arms around her, he raised a brow. "Could you have handled them?"

She rolled her eyes. "You've obviously done your research. What do you think?"

He grinned. "I watched a video of you taking on five men. So, yeah, you can handle them." Wiping the grin from his face, he nodded toward the front door. "I can't be seen going out this way, Sky."

She glanced toward the double-glass doors. "I understand. I guess I should have parked out back, huh?" *Aw, well, too late now*. After giving him a quick peck on the cheek, she stepped out of his arms and waved the envelope. "What do you say we go over these reports after dinner? Meet me on the rancher's patio at seven."

He bent to kiss her cheek. "I'll be there."

Once outside, she paused by her motorcycle and sucked in a deep breath. Monroe took a huge chance just to see her in action. She could have easily killed her attacker with one blow. If he wanted a demonstration, he could have asked. As it was, she used a standard maneuver to control her opponent, not incapacitate. After slipping the envelope into the saddlebag, she jammed on her helmet and, forgoing the jacket, hit the road—grateful for the airy feel of the wind through her tank top.

She had more important things to think about besides Monroe's crazy stunt—like why was someone killing the tenants? Was that someone out to destroy the manor by ruining its reputation and leaving the owner no choice but to sell? Was her aunt eliminated because she refused to be persuaded? But with a new owner coming in, the likelihood of putting the manor on the real estate market was high. So, why kill Margaret Caine? *Too many damn questions*. She slowed for Woodstown's main intersection and waited for traffic to clear before making her left.

The other possibility was a true serial killer living at the manor. The purpose behind those deaths would be harder to prove, and she was super glad to have Logan by her side. Turning onto the side street alongside the manor, she guided the cycle to its spot under the carport and cut the engine. After covering her baby with its fitted tarp and with the envelope in hand, she headed for the rancher's backdoor and let herself inside.

While snacking on some cookies and milk, she skimmed through the police reports. Monroe also included photos. *Ugh.* Nothing like looking at dead bodies while chewing on cookies. Slamming the folder shut, she stuffed everything back into the manila envelope and placed it alongside Kirby's envelope on the kitchen counter.

Remembering Kirby's instructions for the tax consultant, Sky headed to the office and opened the top drawer on the first filing cabinet. Neat folders hung on a wire rack with labels for state, county, and township regulations for operating a boardinghouse, newspaper clippings about the town's long-standing manor, and about a dozen handwritten ledgers listing past tenants and their payments.

The next drawer contained real estate tax receipts, major renovation receipts, and finally, a blueprint for a new garage. Well, that was a surprise. Aunt Ginger decided to park her car in a garage, after all. Skylar definitely liked her motorcycle under a solid roof. Having one attached to her split-level in Chicago was a real godsend.

The last two drawers were empty.

Moving to the top drawer on the second cabinet, Skylar grabbed the handle and met resistance—locked. After pulling all the drawers without luck, she searched the desk for a key. Nothing. The key ring hanging by the door held large door keys with none small enough to fit a cabinet lock.

With her hands on her hips, Skylar stood in the middle of the office and scanned the area. Where would an elderly woman hide a small key? A jewelry box? But she emptied the entire contents of her box and found no key. Fay might have a clue. If not, Logan could break the lock.

Leaving the rancher, she proceeded toward the manor and automatically skimmed her gaze over the parking lot. No black sports car yet. She hopped onto the patio and entered the kitchen. No one about. No dinner started, either. A glance toward Fay's bedroom showed a partially opened door. Hoping Fay wasn't enjoying a nap and forgot to close the door, Sky tapped lightly, then peeked inside to see a large sitting room on one side with the bed on the other side. Nice, but no Fay. Retracing her steps to the kitchen, she stopped when her gaze fell on the slightly ajar cellar door…the place where her aunt died.

Oh, God. Could she do this? Gritting her teeth, she swung open the door and stared into a dark void. *Yes, wow, totally black.* Feeling around the inside door frame, she flipped on the switch and blinked at the bright fluorescent glow. The lights illuminated a wooden staircase with a platform at the top and eight steps down to an L-shaped landing with railings on both sides. Why would her aunt go into the basement at night and not tell Fay? She should have waited for morning when more people were about. For heaven's sake, the black basement would intimidate even the strong-willed. So, logically, for whatever reason, Aunt Ginger was lured to the basement, and she wasn't alone.

Squaring her shoulders, Skylar descended one step when someone threw a shroud over her head and shoved.

****

Logan maneuvered his vehicle into his normal parking slot and killed the engine. The meeting with Sky went well. The woman had a good head on her shoulders, and she took the news of his cop status in stride. He even detected a hint of relief. As far as the demonstration Monroe staged? His boss took a big chance. Skylar Dawson had the agility of a cat and the speed of lightning, and she proved she could stay calm in a tense situation. What did him proud was her lack of fear as her attacker approached. A good trait. But she wasn't a trained cop. At the first opportunity, he'd warn her to always stay on guard.

As his usual habit, he took a quick inventory of the cars in the lot—Rita's sedan, Fay's SUV, Tyrone's hatchback, and Joe's truck. Could their elusive killer be someone who didn't drive, like someone bored of being cooped in the house all day? The possibilities included Gilda—who lost her license after her stroke, Anthony—whose children had his license revoked after an accident, and of course, Maria Santini—who demanded to be chauffeured by her son. Even Tommy couldn't be completely eliminated. Of them all, Anthony seemed the likely candidate. He expressed a strong bitterness toward his adult children and could project his anger onto the other tenants, but from experience, nothing was certain.

Hobbling to the rear of his car, Logan popped the trunk. Since this case wouldn't end anytime soon, he stopped for a few necessities and even swung over to Swedesboro for Sky's six-pack of beer. *To go with her pretzels.* At the thought, he smiled.

Gripping two canvas shopping bags in one hand

and placing the six-pack under his arm, he double-checked for the sedan and cycle under the carport before hobbling toward the rancher's patio. At least now, Sky knew who he was. Initially, he objected to Monroe's suggestion about her involvement. He never once revealed his identity, but Monroe made a good point. They were dealing with a clever murderer, and if she uncovered any shred of information among her aunt's possessions, he'd use what she found and draw this case to a close.

He desperately needed to move on. During his entire undercover career, he never once got involved with a woman. Sex, yes, for the benefit of inside information, but Skylar was different. She wasn't a suspect nor anyone's cohort. She was a beautiful woman with a smile that always put a sparkle into her eyes. She affected him way too much. Slipping his bags onto the patio table, he approached the rancher's backdoor and knocked.

No sound came from within. Repeating the knock and using the doorbell, he again listened. Nothing. The curtains over the windows were opened. After a peek, he glimpsed no movement from within. She might be in the manor. In either case, the beer required refrigeration. Nothing worse than warm beer.

As he rounded the corner of the rancher, he purposely peered inside the office windows in case she hadn't heard the bell. Seeing the room empty, he continued to the manor's kitchen. The strong smell of onions assaulted his nose.

At her usual position by the counter, Fay busily chopped the pungent vegetable on a cutting board. Glancing over her shoulder, she nodded toward the stove. "We're having Sloppy Joe's tonight." She sniffed.

"Sounds good. Have you seen Skylar?"

"Not lately. Did you check the rancher?"

"Yeah, no answer. It's not important." He headed for the staircase when voices from the TV room stopped him. He peeked to see Anthony and Joe in discussion over a ball game. To be sure, he also checked the card room. Empty. He ascended the stairs to the third floor, unloaded his stash, and returned to the lower level.

Because he had been doing undercover work for so long, he developed a sixth sense when something didn't feel right. He could never explain the feeling, but he learned not to ignore it, and right now, his gut told him to search for Sky. Exiting from the front of the house, he turned left toward the gazebo where Tommy and Yapper played. "Hey, Tommy, have you seen Ms. Dawson?"

"Nah. Yapper and me have been busy, but I saw her go into the kitchen a while ago."

"Did she come out?"

He shrugged his small shoulders.

Unease growing, Logan hobbled to the office, entered, and pounded on the main door. "Sky!" Still, no sound from within. He gripped the door latch. Unlocked. Entering, he left his crutch by the inside door and searched the house. She wasn't here. Then, according to Tommy, she was still in the manor. But where?

After reclaiming his crutch, he returned to the manor's kitchen.

Fay glanced over her shoulder. "Find her?"

"No." His gaze fell on the closed cellar door. Hobbling over, he tugged on the knob and met resistance. "Fay, did you lock the cellar door?"

"I never lock it until bedtime. You know the rules." She turned sharply, brows high. "Oh! A little déjà vu?"

"Maybe." He turned the lock and opened the door. The lights were out, so he flipped the switch, and brightness flooded the basement.

His heart stopped.

Skylar was sprawled out on the lower landing, tangled in a white sheet while leaning against the rail and holding her head.

"Sky!"

She gave a weak wave in answer.

Fay joined him on the landing. "What's going on?" Looking over his shoulder, she gasped.

Silently cursing Fay's presence, he hobbled down the steps and pretended to struggle into a squatting position. "What happened?"

She squinted against the bright lights. "Someone threw this sheet over my head, then shoved hard enough so I flew down the steps."

His gut tightened. Glancing toward the upper landing, he willed his heart to calm. "You could have broken your neck." He untangled the sheet and draped it over the railing.

Behind him, Fay leaned over. "Where does it hurt, honey?"

"Everywhere, Fay." Shifting on her butt, she winced. "I blacked out for a while, but I'm okay." She rubbed her left shoulder. "I think I bruised every joint."

Slipping his fingers into her soft hair, he inspected her scalp. "I feel a good lump. Let me call an ambulance." Standing, he reached toward his rear pocket.

She latched onto his forearm. "No, Logan. An ice pack should help."

"I'll get one ready, but you need to get checked out." Fay hurried up the steps.

Taking her outstretched hand, he hoisted Sky to her feet, but she wobbled and fell against him. He caught her by wrapping an arm around her waist. She might have the ability to kick the ass of some big men, but at this moment, she struggled like a woman fighting to hide her vulnerability. Such a simple act gripped his heart.

She shot him a sheepish grin. "Sorry."

"If I wasn't disabled, I'd carry you."

Smirking, she met his gaze. "Yeah, right." Placing a hand on her back, she arched her spine and groaned. "How'd you know I was down here?"

"Because you weren't anywhere else."

Meeting his gaze, she placed a palm on his cheek. "Thank you."

The warmth of her hand combined with her close proximity was enough to drive him to distraction. He cleared his throat. "Someone's trying to frighten you."

She rolled her eyes. "Yeah, well, I'm not eighty-six and not afraid of the dark." Rubbing her butt, she grimaced. "I feel like an idiot. I should never have let someone sneak up behind me." She slowly ascended the steps.

On the upper landing, he took hold of her arm and forced her to face him. "Being caught off-guard is always dangerous, Sky. But we're human. We make mistakes. Keep alert for who and what is around you, okay?"

She studied his face, then nodded and entered the kitchen.

Fay had already tossed several ice cubes into a towel and handed it to Sky.

Lowering onto a kitchen chair, she eased the pack onto her head.

Fay glanced from Skylar to Logan. "Why would someone push her?"

The exact question Logan asked himself. The assault did not bode well. Was it a warning? But for what reason?

Still holding the cold pack to her head, Skylar swiveled on the chair. "Look, Fay. I originally wanted to ask about the locked file cabinet in the office. Do you know where my aunt kept the key?"

Fay cocked a brow. "It's not in the desk?" Frowning, she pursed her lips. "The locked one is Ginny's personal cabinet. Take a look in the kitchen. She has this green bowl on the counter full of tie-wraps and rubber bands. Check there."

Standing, Sky crooked a finger at Logan. "Come with me. If I can't find the key, I want you to break the lock."

"Hold on, woman." He grabbed onto her elbow. "We're not going anywhere except the Urgent Care Center." Even if he had to drag her there.

Chapter Thirteen

Oh, damn him. Sky was perfectly fine, but Logan insisted she get checked out. To appease him, she went. As expected, she suffered no serious damage, just a mild concussion along with multiple bruises. Whoever pushed her—and she had a pretty good idea who—used enough force to throw her off her feet. For a brief second, fear had gripped her throat, but thanks to her martial arts training, she curled into a ball and rolled.

Unfortunately, that maneuver tightened the bedsheet around her body like a cocoon. When she woke and dragged the shroud from her head, she swore she went blind. Not a shred of light showed from anywhere within the basement. She wasn't even sure she *had* her eyes opened until Logan switched on the lights.

Back at the rancher, she found the key exactly where Fay said. She returned to where Logan waited by the desk. "Found it!" She held the key for him to see, slid it into the lock, and opened the first drawer. "Ta-da!" She placed a palm against his bicep and inwardly shuddered from the sheer hardness under her fingers. Then, she squeezed, mainly because she couldn't help but cop a feel. "Thank you for looking out for me." All his fussing should have irritated her, but truth be told, having someone worry over her felt nice.

"That's what friends are for, Sky." He winked and

hobbled toward the door. "If we're still on for tonight, I'll see you on the patio at seven. Call if you want to reschedule. Here, I'll send a text message so you'll have my number." He tapped on his phone.

She smirked. "Obviously, you already have my number."

With a broad grin, he gave a quick salute and left.

Pivoting toward the filing cabinet, she stared at the open top drawer. With a headache nagging and doctor's orders to limit eye use, this wasn't a good time to go through her aunt's files. At least, she had the cabinet key. Sighing, she rubbed her forehead. A quick shower, a nap, and a light dinner should do wonders. She locked the drawer and left the office.

As seven o'clock neared, Skylar stepped outside and placed the tenant folders, along with Monroe's envelope, onto the patio table. A sense of awe filled her chest at the enormous amount of space surrounding her. All her life, she'd lived in a split-level with hardly enough grass for a push mower. Here, she stood on a beautifully constructed patio with a farm field to the rear and a yard big enough for a pool and another garage.

A rabbit hopped by the hedgerow. *So cute.* Somewhere in the neighborhood, a lawnmower sputtered and backfired, causing a dog to howl. With a sigh, she pulled out a chair, tilted her face skyward, and closed her eyes.

Not two minutes later, the clink of his crutch told of his presence. She lifted her head as Logan hobbled onto the patio.

He looked fresh from a shower with still-damp hair and smelled heavenly of soap and his familiar woodsy cologne. A faded pair of blue jeans hugged his thick thighs, and a yellow shirt with two unfastened top buttons allowed her an enticing view of his strong neck.

He plunked a six-pack of beer on the table. "You said you wanted some." He rested his crutch against a chair.

The man remembered. She grinned. "I do." She stood while waving toward the chair on her right. "I'll get the pretzels." Hurrying into the house, she grabbed the pretzel bag from the cabinet and returned as Logan took a seat.

He peered. "Are you allowed to drink?"

"The doctor said no eye strain. I didn't hear a word about alcohol." Grabbing two cans, she flipped the tabs and slid one toward him. "I'll drink only one beer, Logan."

With one eye closed and the other squinting, he nodded. "Okay. One shouldn't hurt." He swallowed a mouthful. "With any luck, no one will interrupt. The gang's favorite reality show is on and should keep them busy for the next hour." He waited for her to take a seat, then leaned toward her to comb his fingers through her hair. "How's the head?"

What was it about this man? Every touch caused a warm, fuzzy feeling to flush through her body, even something as simple as fingers through her hair. Meeting his gaze, she smiled. "Better, thank you. My nap eased the headache." Not to mention a couple of ibuprofen. Breaking the eye lock, she opened the pretzel bag.

He snagged a pretzel that flew halfway across the table. "I called Monroe and told him about the basement incident. Thankfully, you were one failed accident." He popped the morsel into his mouth and chewed.

"Yeah, lucky me." She waggled a finger. "You know, if I wasn't standing on that landing thinking of my aunt, I might have sensed someone behind me."

"That's the danger of undercover work, Sky. You can't let your guard down for a minute." He nodded toward the folders. "Shall we begin?"

While dragging the case folders closer, she shot him a sideways glance. "I don't have to tell you what Monroe included since you probably copied everything."

He grinned. "I knew you'd figure it out. If we're partners, I want you to have as much information as possible. And I already went through the tenant folders." Smirking, he shrugged. "Fay often left the office door unlocked."

So, she figured. He wouldn't be a very good cop otherwise. "And your conclusion?"

"Not a hint whatsoever. How about you?"

"I just found it odd that Michael, Joe, and Tyrone stay here when they have other options."

He pursed his lips. "Good point, but it might be because meals are included."

She hadn't thought of that benefit. Having a meal waiting was nice. She humphed. "I guess we won't need these." After sliding the tenant folders to the side, she opened the first case folder. Grabbing a handful of pretzels, she popped a nugget into her mouth and crunched. Perfectly salted, just the way she liked. She could make a meal of pretzels and beer. Not healthy, but hey, she'd be happy. "Victim One—John Johnson." While holding the typed report, she propped her feet onto the chair and summarized. "Fell down a flight of stairs. Multiple fractures. Cause of death—broken neck, confirmed by assistant medical examiner. Estimated time of death around midnight." She sipped her beer and let the malt coat her throat. "No witnesses. The noise of the fall woke the tenants." Frowning, she paused. "This has all the factors for an accident." She glanced his way. "An elderly man takes a middle-of-the-night trip to the kitchen, miscalculates his footing, and falls head first. Why was my aunt suspicious?"

"From what I uncovered, Mr. Johnson was pretty spry on his feet." Logan popped a few pretzels into his mouth and chewed. "But you're right. Accidents still happen."

She spread the scene photos on the table. "I know Monroe ordered shots of Margaret Caine, but who took these pictures?"

"Whenever anything looks like an accidental death, the responding medical examiner snaps a few for the record. An autopsy is rarely performed unless death is indeterminate."

Studying the photos, she pointed with her pinky finger. "These colored pieces of paper look like candy wrappers."

"They are. According to the tenants, Mr. Johnson always sucked on candy to control his smoker's cough and dropped the wrappers everywhere. The guy drove Rita nuts." He grabbed another handful of pretzels.

Skylar chuckled. "Like Margaret and her cotton balls, eh? Rita probably followed both of them with a broom and dust bin." Crunching a pretzel, she gathered the first folder's contents and set it aside before opening the next. "Darla Winters." *Ah, the Darla mentioned in my aunt's notes*. "Found in bathtub. Bruise on left temple, possibly caused by slipping and hitting head on tub rim. Cause of death—drowning. Estimated TOD between seven and eight in the evening." She scanned the scene photos. "She's soaking in an awful lot of bubbles." Frowning, she tapped the photo. "This also looks like an accident. We might be wasting our time."

"If we believed that, I wouldn't be here." He picked up his beer can and sipped. "What else do you see, Sky?"

Leaning closer, she studied the shots of the tub room. "There's an awful lot of water on the floor." She frowned. "We can eliminate Rita as a suspect. An OCD would never leave such a mess. And here—" Retrieving the first folder, she slipped out the photo of Mr. Johnson. "An OCD can't leave scattered wrappers. They are driven to complete whatever obsesses them. In Rita's case, cleaning." Sitting back, she picked up her beer can and swirled the contents. "Anything to add about Darla?"

He sipped his beer. "According to Fay, Darla's excessive perfume set off Michael Chang's asthma. He often skipped eating at the dinner table."

"Which promptly changed once Darla died. Hmm." She twisted her mouth to the side. "You know, Logan. If I were an asthmatic and had the money to move, I wouldn't hesitate to get out of a house with strong perfumes. I'm sure her bath bubbles were heavily scented, too."

"Again, according to Fay, on Darla's fateful night, the entire second floor had an overpowering flower smell. She and Ginger found Michael on the front porch clutching his inhaler."

"Well, I'd say we have a viable suspect." She pointed to Darla's photo. "I have one big question. Why didn't anyone hear the splashing? With this much water on the floor, Darla had to struggle."

"I questioned that myself until I discovered the gang's interest in the reality show every night." He washed down his pretzels with a mouthful of beer. "With the TV volume so loud, I doubt anyone heard what was going on upstairs."

"Then, someone knew this and took advantage. But isn't there a lock on the door? I'm sure Darla wouldn't want someone walking in on her."

Leaning back, he crossed his arms over his chest. "Fay and Ginger have keys. Ginger's is on the ring inside the office door. With the door always unlocked, anyone can grab the keys off the hook, then return them later."

A low rumble vibrated through the air. She glanced skyward to see the sun gone and whispers of gray clouds floating over the rancher. "That sounds like thunder."

"It is. We're expecting a storm tonight." He checked his watch. "It's probably over the Delaware River in Chester County." Lowering his gaze, he grabbed another handful of pretzels. "Continue, Sky."

Geez, at the rate they're going, the bag of pretzels would be gone in no time. She blamed Logan's large, grabby hands. Imagining what those hands could do for a woman… Clearing her throat, she opened folder number three.

Ginger Dawson. A lump rose in her throat for the woman who left her so much. Sky wasn't even sure she could read the file, but she sucked in a steadying breath and straightened in the chair. "Okay. Aunt Ginger. Found in a locked basement, dead of apparent heart attack. Known history of heart problems. Estimated TOD between seven and nine p.m." Wincing, she met his gaze. "The basement is black even in daytime. There aren't any windows."

"They were sealed closed when the additions were added."

She turned toward Logan to find him watching her…again. For once, she'd like to see burning desire, but the damn man hid his feelings well. The consummate professional. *Just my luck*. "Do you think my aunt was lured?"

Hissing through his teeth, he rubbed the nape of his neck. "I've considered the possibility because of the time of night. Your aunt rarely joined the gang for that reality show."

Skylar extracted the photo. Her aunt's body lay prone on the basement floor, and her heart squeezed at the sight. Had Ginger died instantly or collapsed to the floor gasping for help? Shuddering, she replaced the photo inside the folder and slapped it shut. "This is not a way to remember my aunt."

Logan pushed the folder to the side. "Fay told me she checked on your aunt around nine every night. When she couldn't find her in the rancher, she searched the house and found her around nine thirty." Resting a hand on her shoulder, he squeezed. "You okay?"

She swallowed hard and nodded. "I'm so sorry I never met her."

In the distance, more thunder rumbled. Louder this time. Simultaneously, she and Logan lifted their gazes toward the sky. Black clouds hovered over them. She jerked her head in the direction of the backdoor. "We should finish inside."

"Since we're sitting on metal furniture, I highly recommend it."

Gathering the folders and pretzel bag, she hurried into the rancher, placed her armload onto the coffee table, then held the door for Logan.

He hobbled in with the six-pack and two beer cans. Once inside, he rested his crutch against a chair and headed for the kitchen, pulled a can from the pack, and slipped the remainder into the refrigerator. Popping the tab, he joined Sky on the sofa as thunder rumbled again. He pointed toward the folders. "Where were we?"

A bolt of lightning brightened the living room. She cringed from the inevitable thunder clap and jumped when it hit.

Logan smiled. "We should have a downpour any second."

As if on cue, the clouds released a torrent of rain, taking with it any remaining daylight. She rose to turn on some lamps and close the drapes on the windows. Afterward, she reclaimed her seat and opened Margaret Caine's folder, reading quickly. "Liver temp put her death somewhere between nine and ten in the morning." She extracted the photos and stared at all the cotton balls. "People and their strange habits."

Chuckling, he tugged on his ear. "The one place we didn't find her little balls was on the third floor."

Brows drawn, she chewed on her inner lip. "We have similarities with three victims. Two drop stuff and the third left a puddle—all an OCD's nightmare. So, we effectively ruled out Rita. But my aunt doesn't fit." She tapped her fingers against her beer can. "What we need is motive." She twisted her mouth to the side. "Michael Chang might have a reason to eliminate Darla, but what about the others?"

"I can't answer that."

Neither could she. Talk about frustrating. "Okay. So, we need to make a list of who was home and when, right?"

"Already done." He reached into his back pocket and extracted a folded sheet of paper. "This isn't part of the official file yet." He opened the paper and handed it over. "I can't pinpoint anyone. Each death occurred on a different day of the week and none on the weekend."

She skimmed over the list. Really, all the different times were mind-boggling, and another headache threatened. She handed him the sheet. "If you can't figure it out, I certainly won't." Fighting off a wave of disappointment, she gathered the case files and slipped the stack into the manila envelope. What in the world made her think she'd come up with any ideas? She was just a bartender. Her biggest mental exercise centered on mixing cocktails without a mixing guide. Finished with the last of her beer, she placed the can onto the coffee table and rotated to face him with her back resting against the sofa arm and one leg tucked under her butt. "Anything you want to add?"

Gulping his beer, he crushed the can and smacked his lips. Sitting forward, he placed the can next to hers, then nodded toward the envelope. "Don't let anyone see those files, Sky. I don't want our killer to know you're helping the police."

Their gazes locked.

He was right. She'd have absolutely no excuse for having the files in her possession. "Maybe you should take them with you." Not that the information helped all that much. She was still stumped. Reaching across the sofa, she brushed a finger along the jagged scar on his right forearm. The tissue felt like bumps of gristle, and she shuddered.

Thrusting out his chest, he rotated his arm. "Knife wound. Some jackass in a bar on another assignment."

Ouch. And not stitched by a physician. Her heart ached for this man, and why he'd put himself in so much danger. She shook her head. "You live a dangerous life, Logan." She lifted her left arm onto the sofa back and, with a fist to her temple, rested her head. "Have you ever considered leaving undercover work?"

He shrugged. "Only once in a while. Usually, the thought comes when a gun is pressed to my temple." He fussed with his pant leg before meeting her gaze. "The lifestyle suits me, Sky."

Some lifestyle. He lived in a world with no one to trust and never knowing if today was the last day of his life. How could anyone exist like that? She toyed with her black lounging pants. "I used to think being alone was the best way to live. After coming here, I'm not so sure anymore." She shot him a sideways glance.

He smiled. "I'm used to being alone. My job doesn't leave a lot of room for a relationship, but sex is always on the table." He leaned toward her with a gaze scanning her face. "I'd very much like to have sex with you."

Whoa. Judging from the bulge near his zipper, he meant business. Well, why not? He was single, incredibly attractive, and in great shape. How could she possibly refuse?

Chapter Fourteen

Dear Lord! With a mere sweep of his gaze, Logan heated the air around the sofa, and Sky damn near ripped off her clothes. Would she dare break her rule and sleep with a man who was still a stranger?

She'd be out of her mind. After one too many bad experiences, she learned to temper her impulsiveness. Sure, sex was fun, but once the sated feeling subsided, emptiness followed. Not one of her so-called lovers connected on an emotional level. Logan would be the same. His job alone kept him detached. So, as enticing as this muscled man was, she refused to succumb. At thirty, she was too old to act like some hormonal teenager. Call her a fool, but so what? A coupling between two people should be filled with love and not merely a desire to experience the moment. Stretching across the sofa, she squeezed his hand. "I don't do casual sex anymore, Logan. I'm sorry."

One brow cocked, he shook his head and smiled. "Don't be sorry. I wouldn't be much of a man if I didn't respect a woman's right to refuse." He grabbed hold of her hand and returned the squeeze. "I'm also forgetting your concussion. You shouldn't do anything to raise your blood pressure. And hot, sweaty sex would definitely make a blood pressure cuff explode." He waggled his eyebrows. "At least, I hope so." He chuckled and then met her gaze. "The doctor also said to have someone with you for the first twenty-four hours. We can spend the night cuddling."

Flopping back against the sofa arm, she stared. Cuddling? Had she heard right, or did he toss away his man card? She peered through one eye. "Men don't usually cuddle."

While stretching his arm across the sofa back, he crossed his legs and winked. "We'll keep it as our little secret. Okay?"

Her cell phone mooed. *Kevin, darn it*. She should let it go to voicemail, but he'd keep calling. One of these days, he might actually have an emergency. "Let me get this. It's my boss." She hit the Accept button. "What?"

"Hey, is that any way to answer a call?"

Clenching her teeth, she bit back the snippy retort and willed herself to relax. "Sorry, but I can't accomplish anything if I keep answering my phone."

"Making any progress?"

"Some, but it's only been a few days."

"How long does it take? You rent a dumpster, load the old lady's junk, and put the house on the market. Come on, Midnight. We miss you. The tip jar isn't the same without you."

Should she tell him she might never need to work again? He'd drop onto the floor in a faint. "Look, Kevin—"

"You promised to keep me posted."

She pinched the bridge of her nose. "I'm not calling you every day. Be patient. You and the bar will survive while I'm gone."

He humphed. "All right, but give me something. When can I expect you? Everyone is asking where you are."

By everyone, he meant the regulars who stopped in for their nightly beer. She sighed. "I need the entire month. I told you that." And possibly longer, but she'd keep that tidbit to herself.

"Pah. I'll replace you by then."

With a hand tightening on the phone, she bristled. "Considering the circumstances, I don't give a damn."

"Okay. How about a raise? The customers are anxious to see your face."

One minute, he threatened to fire her and, the next, give her a raise? Sure, she earned the most tips, and his rule for splitting the money between the employees—himself included—made for a nice cash payout at the end of the week. If she wasn't so unsure of her future, she'd tell him to take a dip in Lake Michigan...during winter. But so many questions remained about the value of her aunt's estate. Once she had all the facts, she could make an informed decision as to her future. She rubbed her forehead. "We talked on Monday, Kevin. This is Thursday. You need to give me time."

"All right, you're upset. We'll talk when you've calmed down." He disconnected.

The man was beyond infuriating. He used to be so easygoing, too. What changed? Since she worked six days a week and practically ran the bar, was she discovering his true colors, like how incredibly lazy he was? She tossed her phone onto the table.

"Midnight?"

She shot Logan a glance. "You heard him, eh?"

He shrugged. "He talks loud."

Too loud at times. She tugged on her pant leg. "Midnight Sky is my name at the bar. A lot of sleazy characters wander in, and some can be downright dangerous. So, my real name is kept under wraps. The fact Kevin called me Midnight tells me customers were nearby." She cocked her head. "I thought you knew everything about me."

"I thought I did, too." He chuckled. "Wait 'til I tell Monroe."

Plopping her head onto the sofa cushion, she closed her eyes. "Kevin almost had a stroke when I requested a month off. He has no idea how I almost quit."

"After inheriting all this, you can quit any time you want." He tapped her shoulder. "So, any cuddling rules? I can't promise I won't sneak in a kiss or two."

Tilting her head, she met his gaze and smiled. "No rules." After her conversation with Kevin, another kiss would definitely make her night.

****

Without wasting a second, Logan tugged her across the sofa, then lifted her onto his lap. Her floral scent had been driving him crazy all night. Outside on the patio, he had the advantage of a slight breeze, but in the confines of the living room, her enticing fragrance was sheer torture. Now, with her in his lap, he could bury his nose in her neck.

She screeched and then laughed.

The woman was so damn beautiful. Even though she had three black belts to her name, she was light and soft—muscular, yes, but the muscles of a woman, not a bodybuilder. He captured her mouth, playful at first, and when she responded, he felt like a man awakening from a long slumber. For the first time in his life, he longed to savor a woman and not do his usual in-and-out disappearing act. Skylar was fun, and this revelation startled him. When was the last time he had *fun* with a woman?

As the kisses eased into a gentle exploration, he lowered her back onto the sofa. A breeze hit his chest, and he looked down to see she'd unbuttoned his shirt. Meeting her sparkling gaze, he shot her a one-eyed glare. "You're playing with fire."

"I seldom see a man who takes such good care of his body." She slid the shirt off his shoulders. "Do you mind?"

He released her long enough to yank the shirt off his back and toss it. Her appreciative gaze got his heart pumping, and because women enjoyed a built chest, he jiggled his pectorals.

She gaped. "Oh—my."

Ever so slowly, she palpated the hardness by squeezing here and there, but when she stroked the nipple, she caused a chill to shoot straight down his spine. No sex, huh? Other women had played with his chest, but Skylar's touch was somehow more stimulating. Goose bumps sprang across his skin, and he lifted the hem of her T-shirt. "Tit for tat?"

She shook her head. "If I take my shirt off, you know where we'll go."

So true, especially since she wasn't wearing a bra. *Aw, well*. Couldn't blame a man for trying. He lowered the T-shirt hem and recaptured her mouth.

Her soft moan nearly tumbled him over the edge. *Christ Almighty*. This undercover assignment might prove to be the most difficult of his career.

****

Skylar couldn't keep her hands still, and why should she? She had never squeezed so many beautiful muscles, like she was in a supermarket testing melons. And his kisses…so perfect. Who had she kissed all these years? Boys? Gasping, she broke away from his mouth. "Are you trying to weaken me?" Her voice sounded foreign, as if someone else said the words and used her throat. But, she never had a man so powerfully built handle her like a fragile egg. She loved it.

He lifted his head and grinned. "I like kissing you, but we go no farther unless you say so." He nuzzled her neck. After another minute, he popped up his head to gaze at her face. "Do you know your eyes turn into brilliant crystals when you're aroused?"

They do? No one ever mentioned it, but boy, yeah, the man had her turned on with just the skillful use of his mouth. God help her if she dragged him to bed. Smiling, she traced a finger across his lips. "Possibly because this is the best kissing I've ever shared."

"I'm glad." He nudged aside her shirt collar and suckled her clavicle.

By morning, Skylar woke to the aroma of coffee. She was still on the sofa…alone with one of her aunt's afghans covering her. She hadn't expected him to stay, but after all the titillation, they talked. Then, they both fell asleep—at least, she had. Easing to her feet, she stretched and winced. Every bruise protested. No headache, though, and that was nice. She shook her limbs to get some blood flowing and followed the rich coffee scent.

A handwritten note rested next to a mug near the coffeemaker. Yawning, she read.

Sky,

I left before dawn to avoid the gossips. Please keep our night to yourself. I locked you in via the backdoor with a key I found hidden in the garage. I suspect this was your aunt's extra key in case she locked herself out. I'll gladly return it, but for your safety, I'd like to keep the key handy. If this makes you uncomfortable, just tell me.

I had a wonderful sex-free night and can't imagine topping it, but I'll try—if you let me.

Logan.

P.S. Destroy this note.

Oh, she had every intention of topping last night. In her bedroom next time. She'd break her own rules for this man. Chuckling, she poured coffee into the mug.

While sipping the robust brew, she re-read the note, then turned on the burner to the gas stove, and held the paper over the flame. When the heat nearly singed her fingers, she dropped what remained into the sink and watched until only ashes remained. All this secret agent stuff felt so weird. Shaking her head and with mug in hand, she headed for the shower.

Dressed in shorts and T-shirt, she settled at the kitchen table to eat a light breakfast of toast and cream cheese with another cup of Logan's wonderful coffee. Outside, a beautiful day beckoned. After last night's storm, everything—the trees, grass, and flowers—glowed under the sun with all the dust and pollen washed away.

For the first time in a long while, her heart felt light. Not because of the weather, either. Knowing she wasn't alone in this sordid mess worked wonders on her psyche, especially with the dread of so much to do. Did she mind if Logan had a key to the door? Not in the slightest. She hardly thought he'd abuse the privilege. More than likely, he already searched the house for clues to their elusive killer. That left her to concentrate on her aunt's estate and leave the sleuthing to him. After cleanup, she headed to the office.

With the small key, she unlocked the file cabinet and opened the top drawer. The last three years of tax returns filled the front of the drawer, each clearly marked. Lifting last year's from its slot, she returned to the desk chair and skimmed through the numbers. Compared to her own simple tax return, her aunt's resembled a book. Page after page was loaded with mind-boggling numbers.

Judging from the information, her aunt ran a profitable business. The boardinghouse held no mortgage, and the rent charged on the farm field paid the real estate taxes on the entire property. Even after deducting expenses, including Fay's salary, the adjusted gross income amounted to double Skylar's annual salary plus tips. This phenomenal piece of news was a bit of a shock.

The dividend and interest page listed her aunt's holdings. All Skylar had to do was find statements from the banks and a brokerage firm. Keeping the page open to use as a checklist, she stood and examined the rest of the first drawer. Nothing but annual reports from a bunch of companies. She opened the second drawer and hit the jackpot. The first folder had a bank label, so she extracted the latest statement—which was three months old—and gasped. Her aunt's account showed a savings balance of $440,000!

While staring at the paper, she flopped onto the desk chair, too stunned to fathom such an amount. Tears filled her eyes. Her aunt left so much. Granted, part of the money would pay the estate taxes, but wow!

"If I had only known you, Aunt Ginger." She snapped a tissue from the box on the desk and blew her nose. She might need an entire box of tissues before she was through.

After tossing the tissue into the trash bin alongside the desk, she stood and continued with the rest of the second drawer. A business checking account folder was next—same bank. An old statement showed the account balance at $64,000. Another nice chunk of change.

Brokerage statements were next, and the tears returned. The account held $600,000 in stocks and bonds at a firm in town. While sniffling, she rummaged through the rest of the folders. Nothing but old statements dating back fifteen years.

The third drawer contained warranty and instruction books for every appliance purchased from the beginning of time. The fourth drawer was empty. She returned to the chair.

Fay knocked on the door and entered. Spotting Skylar at the desk, she cocked a brow. "You've been crying!"

Skylar plucked another tissue and dabbed her eyes. "My aunt left me a lot of money." She blew her nose. "You, too. Your name is in the will."

"Kirby told me, and I didn't expect it." She closed the door. "This came from Kirby's office. He forgot to give it to you." She held out a sealed brown envelope.

Before taking the small packet, she tossed her used tissue in the trash. *FOR SKYLAR DAWSON* was handwritten across the face. "Thank you, Fay. While you're here, can you tell me if my aunt has a safe deposit box?"

Resting a shoulder against the closed door, Fay

folded her arms over her chest. "She canceled the box when she gave Kirby the deed to the property to keep with her will."

"And you have the checkbook, right?"

"Yes. Do you want it?"

"Not yet. When I'm ready, I'll let you know." Leaning back, she draped her arms over the armrests and released a long breath. "At least, I'm making some progress."

"You're doing fine. Just so you know, after your aunt died, the bank and your aunt's brokerage firm stopped sending statements until the next of kin presents herself. The bank made an exception for the checking account because my name is also on it." She pushed away from the door. "Let me know if you need anything."

Alone once more, Skylar opened the brown packet. Probably more paperwork. Too much legal shit in her opinion. With a heavy sigh, she extracted a handwritten letter and read.

My Darling Skylar:

You might find it odd why I left everything to you when you likely have no memory of me. The truth is I've loved you from the moment we met. You were two at the time and so cute, but the second I looked into your beautiful blue eyes, I saw myself and couldn't believe the resemblance.

Even though we met a half-dozen times before your father transferred to Chicago, I'm sure you don't remember me. I'm also sure you have no idea why your father spoke so little of his family. After he married your Methodist mother, he was shunned by his Catholic family. He, like me, became outcasts—him for marrying the wrong woman, and me for owning a tavern that contributed to the drunkenness of the sinners. Those were my mother's words, not mine. We might be Irish, but alcohol wasn't allowed in the house. When I sold the tavern to buy this house, I was still viewed as a pariah. So naturally, I had little to do with the family.

A few years after your father's death, I talked to your mother about making you beneficiary of my estate. Don't be mad at her for keeping my secret, but I think this news allowed her to die in peace because, dear child, she worried about you being a bartender for the rest of your life. She also complained you didn't date and you preferred being alone. You sounded so much like me, I had to laugh, but I also recognized her concern. I told your mother I would force you here to experience the family feeling the tenants provide. She thanked me for that.

Everything is yours, Skylar, to do with as you please. I've provided for Fay, so no need to worry about her should you decide to sell. A word of caution, my dear. Watch yourself around men. This inheritance will attract them like flies to sugar water. When I sold the tavern, I fell for a sweet-talker. Thankfully, I realized what he was up to and sent him packing. You'll find the engagement ring in my jewelry box. But I know you have a sensible head on your shoulders—just like me.

With all my love,
Your Great-Aunt Ginger

A postscript was included on another piece of stationery, written in different ink and slightly shaky.

Skylar,
We've experienced some peculiar accidents at the

manor, two of which resulted in deaths. After twenty-five years with hardly an incident, suddenly, window glass is falling or an electrical outlet causes a shock. I've talked to Lieutenant Robert Monroe of the New Jersey State Police, but the fool man wants proof. I have a good idea who's behind these accidents, but I'll do as Monroe suggests and get my proof. If you're reading this, then you know I've met with an untimely end. So please, have Lieutenant Monroe kiss my dead ass. And you, dear girl, must be very careful.

I also want to leave you with one other thing. It's the perfect analgesic for my rheumatoid arthritis. Mix a shot of coffee liquor with honey, amaretto, nectarine juice, and gin. Fay uses it all the time. Just ask her. Pleasant dreams, dear.

Leave it to a former barkeep to create an analgesic laced with booze. But wow, the news of more accidents came as a shock. Did Logan know? She must find him and ask. After folding the smaller note, she tucked it into her shorts pocket. The personal letter she returned to the envelope and carried it to her bedroom. Returning to the office, she locked the filing cabinet and exited through the front door, only to run smack into Philip Santini—again.

Chapter Fifteen

Strong hands gripped her bare arms, surprisingly as rough as Logan's. Like yesterday, Philip wore a business suit and tie and looked every bit the male model—tall, trim, and incredibly handsome. All he needed was a hand slipped into one pocket, a cocked head with a sexy smile, and he'd make the perfect picture. Skylar stared at a brilliant set of white teeth. "Oh."

He slid his fingers down her arms. "Can I talk to you?"

Yeah, sure, after the goose bumps subside. Stepping back, she lowered her gaze to his tie and cleared her throat. "If it's business related, you should talk to Fay."

"It's personal, Sky."

When Logan used her shortened name, she got all tingling from the warmth in his voice. Why not Philip? He had a nice voice.

"Sky?"

Oh, yeah, personal. She coughed. "Walk with me. I need some air." She closed the office door, then turned and smiled. "What can I do for you?" She led him along the brick path toward the manor's patio.

He darted his gaze toward the second-story window. "Let's walk around to the side of the manor. My mother doesn't know I'm here."

"I doubt that. She has radar where you're concerned." She waved a hand. "Lead the way." She followed him across the grass along the north side of the manor. She shot him a glance. "Aren't you a little old for your mom's scrutiny?"

"I can't stop her." He stuffed his hands into his trouser pockets. "She obsesses over everything I do. Why do you think I'm still single?" He stopped and glanced skyward. "I'd love to have a wife and family, but my mother puts my girlfriends through a living hell." He stopped midway where the shade of the elm trees covered the grass.

From this position, his mother had the vantage point of spying through the TV room windows. Skylar scanned for a face pressed against the glass—just in case. "I'm afraid I don't make the grade, either, Philip. Your mother has an extreme aversion toward working women."

He arched a brow. "She said that?" Cringing, he shook his head. "It's time I have my mother evaluated by a professional."

"Good luck with that." No way in hell would the woman cooperate. She'd probably drive the psychologist batty.

The familiar clink of a crutch forced her attention toward the front of the house. Logan hobbled along the brick path with a rake over his shoulder. His moist T-shirt hugged his muscles, and yes, an odoriferous stench blew with the breeze. She rubbed her itchy nose.

Catching sight of her and Philip, Logan pursed his lips and approached with a narrowed gaze focused on Philip. "Well, well, look who's here—again. This is the third time this week, Santini. What does *Mommy* need today?"

Philip shot Logan a glare. "Button it, Greene. I'm having a private conversation with this beautiful woman."

The two men locked gazes.

Wow! She hadn't seen male posturing since a PBS gorilla special. These two guys better not thump their chests or draw swords...hey, she was living her dream! Biting back a grin, Skylar stepped between them. "Logan, I'll talk to you later, but right now, Philip has asked to speak to me privately."

With a smile tugging on his lips, Philip stuck out his chest.

Logan sneered.

Oh, good grief.

"Philip!"

As if caught with her hands tucked into Philip's pants, Skylar jumped to the side and whirled toward the woman standing on the edge of the patio with her fists jammed on her hips. *Oh, boy*. Maria practically had steam puffing from her ears.

Snickering, Logan shot Philip a wide grin. "Duty calls."

Philip growled and turned to Skylar. "Later." He ran to his mother.

And this was why Skylar preferred Logan over Philip. No way would any sane woman tolerate Maria's domineering nature. Crossing her arms over her chest, she glared at Logan. "You were rude."

He thumped his crutch into the grass. "I don't like him."

"I don't care. Tone it down or avoid him. Hear?" Dropping her arms, she pivoted toward the front of the house, all the while hiding the involuntary smile breaking onto her lips. She had two men vying for her affection. *Will wonders never cease?* Unfortunately, her aunt's warning about men and their motives popped into her mind. Her ego deflated.

"That's right, Missy. Put the boy in his place."

Lifting her gaze, she squinted to see Anthony, Joe, and Tyrone leaning on the front porch rail like three old biddies.

" 'They have sown the wind, and they shall reap the whirlwind.' "

Anthony rolled his eyes at Joe, then waved a crooked finger in Logan's direction. "You should pick Philip. He's a lawyer and no slug like Logan. His mother's a pain-in-the-ass, but she can't live forever."

"I agree." Joe waved a hand in Logan's direction. "That man needs to get off welfare and find a decent job."

Poor Logan. If they only knew. Skylar glanced over her shoulder as Logan stomped toward the garage. She originally left the rancher in search of him, but to turn toward him now would raise a few eyebrows. "I'm not here to cause trouble."

Tyrone chuckled. "You did that by being pretty." Straightening from the rail, he held the small of his back. "I can see Logan going after you and your money, but Philip's supporting his mother. That says something about his character."

Joe waggled a finger. "Philip could be after her money, too, but he won't have any luck with a woman unless he puts his mother in her place." He also straightened. "The boy needs to grow some serious backbone."

Skylar silently agreed. All Philip had to do was tell his mother to wait while he finished his conversation. Evidently, pacifying his mother was more important. With a smirk, she looked up at the three men. "I don't have time for either of them, but whatever you do, don't discuss this in front of Mrs. Santini. The woman will be out for my blood."

****

Unable to contain his anger, Logan threw the rake halfway across the garage. The handle hit the wall with a bang and sent several garden tools crashing to the floor. Another mess to clean, but so what? This damn assignment turned into one of the biggest challenges of his career, and not because of some criminal mastermind. Hell, no. His troubles began with that beautiful woman. He actually experienced a surge of heat to see Philip talking to Skylar. Talking! When had he ever felt so jealous? She had a right to converse with whomever she pleased, and he had no right to feel such possessiveness. But they shared a wonderful night kissing and cuddling—the best in his life, in fact. Damned if he'd let Philip have a chance. He jammed both hands through his hair and tugged.

"Logan?"

He whirled toward the open garage doors and saw Skylar standing just inside the opening. He scowled. "Sorry. I acted like a jerk."

Snickering, she entered. "I was flattered, but you have no reason to be jealous."

"I'm not jealous." Great, what a friggin' liar. He sighed and caught her dancing gaze. "All right, I was jealous but shouldn't be. Philip's an okay guy."

Smiling while shaking her head, she slipped her

hand into her shorts pocket and held out a folded piece of paper.

Her gaze no longer danced, and her face lost all expression. Curious, he took the note and read. *Well, I'll be damned.* He raised his brows. "What other accidents?"

"I was hoping you knew."

While re-reading, he sucked in a breath through tight teeth. "Failed attempts. Directed at whom?" He refolded the paper. "Monroe never said a word. I'll see what I can find out at the dinner table." He returned the note and grinned. "Will you try her analgesic?"

She laughed. "I'll keep the recipe handy for when I develop arthritis in my old age." She replaced the paper into her back pocket. "I hate gin, though. I wonder if the analgesic works with Irish whiskey?"

"Gin isn't one of my favorites, either. Here, Sky." Reaching into his jeans pocket, he extracted a key. "This is for your door."

She placed a hand on his arm. "Keep it, at least for a while." Nodding toward the key in his hand, she met his gaze. "Promise me you won't abuse the privilege."

Her touch sent a few goose bumps up his arm. He liked the feeling…way too much. Meeting her gaze, he gestured with a finger to his chest. "Cross my heart. Invitation only." Even if waiting for the invite killed him.

****

Once inside the rancher, Skylar chuckled while locking the main door. Logan was jealous. *Don't that beat all.* For a man who shifted from one undercover job to the next, he sure sounded a little too much like a boyfriend. Where Philip was concerned, Logan had nothing to worry about. Granted, Philip had great looks and might prove equally competent in bed, but he had a mother from the depths of hell. What woman in her right mind fought the devil?

Enough obsessing over two horny men. Time for work.

After packing more of her aunt's never-ending knickknacks, Sky stretched and headed for the kitchen. Dinner consisted of a frozen meal of turkey and stuffing, then she spent an hour vegging in front of the television before calling it a night. Tomorrow was another day. All things considered, her progress improved day by day, slow but steady.

She fell into bed exhausted. Rejuvenated by morning, Skylar stared at the stack of boxes by the front door. They had to go…somewhere. The garage wasn't an option. The manor's basement might be a good idea. Stepping outside into another warm, humid day, she headed toward the manor. A slamming car door caught her attention, and she turned.

"Ms. Dawson!"

Nathan Kirby, her aunt's lawyer, waved from the parking lot and hurried along the brick walkway. "I have great news. A buyer wants to pay seven mil for your entire property!"

Her mouth fell open, then quickly snapped shut. Mind racing, she stared, blinked, and stared again. "Seven? But I haven't decided what to do." Not to mention the ink hadn't dried on the deed transfer papers.

He clapped his hands together and rubbed. "This is a fantastic opportunity and one not to take lightly. You'll sit pretty for the rest of your life."

She already inherited more than she needed, but wow! She shook herself. "What about the boardinghouse? Will it stay?"

"Heavens, no. The buyer plans to level all the buildings and erect a hotel. The area desperately needs one." He plucked out his cell phone from his breast pocket. "I'll call him. Don't worry about a thing. I'll handle the eviction notices and all the paperwork involved, and, of course, allow enough time for the tenants to relocate and the farmer to harvest his crops."

"Whoa, hold on." She placed a hand over his phone. "Not so fast. I'm still in shock. Why didn't the buyer come to me?"

He replaced his phone into his inside pocket. "Probably because we worked on a prior purchase, and I happened to mention the manor's new ownership." He narrowed his gaze. "I strongly encourage this, Skylar. The buyer wants to put the sale through ASAP."

The offer was beyond anything she'd ever dreamed possible, but if she learned anything over the years, she hated to be rushed. In high school, teachers and counselors pushed her to accept scholarships when she had no desire to continue her education. Her martial arts instructors nudged her toward competitions when all she wanted was to be the best without getting all banged up in the process. If anything necessitated careful consideration, it was Kirby's offer. Nearly a dozen lives would be affected, including her own. She shook her head. "I'll sleep on the offer, Mr. Kirby."

He waggled a gnarled finger. "Don't procrastinate, my dear. I'm sure you don't want to be saddled with a rental property."

Why was he in such a hurry? And who said the

place was for sale? She scanned his off-the-rack business suit. Could he be responsible for the accidents? Maybe not personally, but he had the incentive to hire someone—like one of the tenants? She studied him. "You didn't have to drive here. You have my number."

"Nonsense. Exciting news should be told in person. You don't receive an offer like this every day." He turned toward the parking lot. "Call me soon." He hopped into his car and drove away.

The man was too damn eager. What was his hurry? She hardly had a chance to absorb what she inherited.

"Hey, Ms. Dawson!" Tommy ran toward her, his cheeks and bare knees covered with dirt. "Mom's planting flowers by the gazebo, and her small shovel broke. She needs the one from the garage." He bounced on his feet. "The doors are still locked. It's Logan's day off."

Well, this was Saturday, and Logan deserved a day to sleep in. She smiled at Tommy. "Let me grab the keys." She headed for the office.

Running ahead, Tommy pointed. "There's Logan. Hi, Logan. We're unlocking the garage."

Logan sat on his balcony with a newspaper in his hands. He waved to Tommy and gave him a thumbs-up.

Her heart fluttered at the sight of him in the morning sunlight. His skin already sported a beautiful tan, so he probably stayed in the hot sun to observe the activity to and from the parking lot. She suspected, too, he kept an eye on the office door—and her. Clearing her throat, she waved and stepped into the office to retrieve the keys hanging by the door. "Okay, Tommy, let's see what we find."

Approaching the garage, Skylar shifted through one key after the other—thankfully, all labeled—and held out the two for the garage. She slipped the first one into the lock and met with success.

Tommy cut in front of her. "The doors slide. I'll show ya." Turning the handle, he pushed the door along a metal track. For the other, he unbolted a latch on the inside bottom before shoving the door along its groove. "I know where Logan keeps the shovels."

"I think you mean spade, Tommy. Your mom can't dig deep holes for flowers." She pointed toward the peg board. "There's one."

Using a metal toolbox for a step, Tommy stretched over the workbench and retrieved the hand spade. He hopped down. "Now, she needs a bucket to mix dirt and fertilizer."

While waiting, Skylar took a good look around. Logan hardly had room to move with all the junk cluttering the place. A wheelbarrow leaned against the far wall along with a plow blade and hand-push snow blower. Several wooden workhorses were stacked near the lawnmower, and overhead, the old windows she saw the other day sat slightly askew. From this angle, the load looked precarious. She should tell Logan to get rid of the junk before everything fell in a heap.

Yapper trotted in, looking like he owned the place. He announced his presence with a bark, then began a sniffing expedition.

"I found a bucket!" Tommy emerged from the other side of the lawnmower and hopped onto the seat. "Come on, Yapper. I got Mom's stuff."

A *twang* startled her. She shot her gaze toward the rafters and gasped. "Tommy!"

Chapter Sixteen

The loud crash coming from the garage jolted Logan straight out of his chair.

Skylar and Tommy!

Heart thundering, he raced inside and flew down the stairs and out the front door. Leaping off the porch without touching the steps, he bolted for the garage and froze at the bay doors. The interior resembled a post-cyclone hit. The overhead windows had fallen from the rafters and shattered glass all over everything with the lawnmower taking the brunt of the damage. Chills shot up his spine, but he gritted his teeth and stepped inside. *If she's hurt…* "Sky?" No sound or movement. Were they still in here? *God, please, tell me they left*. With muscles tense enough to ache, he kicked a board. "Sky? Tommy?"

"Over here."

A pile of debris moved near the wooden workhorses. Climbing over planks and broken glass, he threw aside one board after the other to make a path, not giving a damn where it landed. Nearing his destination, he removed the remnants of several window panes and uncovered Skylar curled beneath the arches with Tommy tucked under her. The back of her T-shirt had ripped, and a bloody scrape cut into her left shoulder blade.

Breaking free of her hold, Tommy jumped to his

feet. Whirling in place, he stared with wide eyes. "Wow, look at the mess!"

Taking Logan's outstretched hand, Skylar stood with a wince.

His heart twisted to see the pain on her face, and at the same time, a surge of relief hit. She was hurt, but they were both okay. Taking hold of her uninjured shoulder, he turned her to assess the wound on her back. "You've got one bad scrape here."

Rotating her shoulder with a grimace, she faced him. "A plank caught me the wrong way."

"Tommy!"

Doreen ran to the garage opening and darted her gaze in all directions until settling on her son. Entering via Logan's path, she grabbed Tommy and hugged him tightly. Then, she held him at arm's length and brushed the hair off his forehead. "Are you hurt?"

"Nah, Ms. Dawson saved me. I never seen anyone move so fast, like some ninja. Ha!" With an open palm, he chopped the air. Pulling away from his mother, he cupped his hands around his mouth. "Yapper, where are you?"

Logan jerked. *Oh, shit, the dog.* "He's in here?"

"Yeah, somewhere."

"I'll find him, Tommy." Hopefully, he hadn't thrown a plank and killed the poor mutt.

Afraid to move anything without knowing the location of the dog, Logan tread gingerly over the debris while calling for Yapper. He found the white fur ball cowering behind the snow blower. "Come on, boy. Let's check you out." With one hand, he scooped Yapper and gave him a quick inspection. The little guy shook in his hand, but nothing showed injury-wise.

"Other than a grease mark on his hind leg, he seems okay." He handed the dog to Tommy.

The boy took the animal into his arms and cooed into his floppy ear.

Logan returned his attention to Skylar.

She watched him with a cocked brow and then pointed at the garage opening.

All the tenants, including Fay, stared not at the mess but at him.

Uh-oh.

Logan stood in the middle of a pile of debris, minus his crutch, and hadn't one good excuse to give the accusing glares. In the span of thirty seconds, he destroyed his undercover identity. Faced with the damage done, he put on his best humble face and slumped his shoulders.

Gaze narrowed, Tyrone pointed. "He flew off the front porch and hit the ground running. He ain't no more crippled than me."

Maria stepped forward. "I saw him, too. Wait until I tell Philip."

Oh, like Logan really gave a shit about Philip. Catching a glimpse of someone moving toward him, he lifted his gaze to meet Fay's.

With her eyes like slits, Fay jammed her fists onto her hips. "Explain yourself, Mr. Greene."

Joe waggled a finger. " 'Let thy speech be short, comprehending much in few words.' "

Damn. How could he possibly salvage this situation without revealing his true identity? He shot a glance at Skylar, who stood to the side with an impassive look. She probably hadn't a clue what to say or do, either.

Then, like a cloud lifted, she raised her chin. "You're a fraud, Mr. Greene." Sky folded her arms across her chest. "You're pretending to be something you're not, and I'll bet it's all for the welfare money."

Well, damn, what a smart woman. She gave him an out. Focusing fully on Fay, he shrugged. "Yes, I'm sorry. I injured my leg a year ago and stayed on disability for the easy money. I'm not proud of it, but the opportunity was too hard to resist."

Huffing, Fay turned to Skylar. "What should we do? If we—" Brows shooting into her hairline, she dropped her arms and ran to Skylar. "You're hurt!" Spreading the torn T-shirt, she inspected Skylar's back. "Gosh, honey, this is a nasty scrape. How about I clean it?"

The woman barely survived an avalanche of debris, and yet, she stood there like she just took a walk in the park. Most women would be crying their eyes out. Then again, Skylar Dawson wasn't an ordinary woman.

Sky patted Fay's forearm. "We'll head to the kitchen in a minute. Let's settle this first." She shifted her gaze toward Logan. "What do you plan on doing about this fraud, Mr. Greene?"

After glancing from one angry face to another, Logan hung his head. "I'll turn myself in. If I'm allowed to stay, I'll continue with the yard work and see about a job at the supermarket to pay my room and board." He met Fay's steady gaze.

"The disability people will demand repayment," Michael said.

"Yeah, you might need a *real* job," Anthony bellowed. "High time you made something of yourself, young man."

This twist to his undercover assignment could succeed. He shot a quick plea at Skylar. *Thank God, she knows my true identity.*

Pursing her lips, Skylar turned toward Fay. "I'd rather give him a chance than make him homeless."

Fay snorted. "You sound just like your aunt." Facing Logan, she chewed her lower lip. "He saved us a lot of money on lawn care and maintenance." She shifted on her feet. "All right, Logan, you can stay. Same room rent."

A flood of relief relaxed his muscles, and he flashed a smile. "Great. You won't be sorry." He stared at the mower. "In the meantime, I'll clean this mess." He faced Skylar. "I'm truly sorry."

Fay squeezed Skylar's arm. "Meet me in the kitchen, and I'll fix you right up."

"Thank you, Fay. I'll follow in a minute."

Moving around the others gathered at the garage opening, Gilda entered and crunched on the broken glass to reach the mower. She tilted her head up and then down. "Ya-ya." She pointed to the lawnmower seat and then the rafters.

Logan walked over and patted her arm. "Yes, Gilda, a lot of stuff fell. No one was seriously hurt, and yes, I see where the glass cut into the seat. It's ruined."

Lips pinched, she shook her head. "PPE." Again, she pointed up and down.

What the hell? He cast another quick plea toward Skylar.

Shrugging, Skylar waved Gilda away from the mower. "He'll figure it out, Gilda. Let's leave him alone."

After watching them leave, Logan sighed. Skylar

was damn lucky, first, with her staircase fall and now this. Both times and despite injuries, she remained cool as a cucumber. She made him proud.

Looking upward, he studied the rafters. A dangling board sat at an odd angle, but an awful lot of junk fell. Glancing down, something caught his eye by the wheel of the mower. Bending for a closer inspection, he jerked. *Well, son of a bitch.*

****

After some pampering from Fay, Skylar tossed her torn T-shirt into the trash and changed into another. What the hell was it with this place? Was this another unexplained accident? Although, she had a hard time believing it was intentional. All that junk shouldn't have been up on the rafters in the first place.

Opening the fridge, she grabbed a beer as a knock rapped on the rear door. Judging from the shadow through the curtain, she'd recognize his broad chest anywhere. "Door's open."

Looking a little worse for wear with grimy shirt and blue jeans, Logan entered. He stopped on the inside doormat.

Holding her beer can in the air, she waved him toward the kitchen.

"I'll take the beer, but I'll stay here. I'm filthy, Sky."

She opened the fridge and grabbed another can, flipped the tabs, and walked into the living room. She handed him his drink. The poor guy needed more than a beer. He had smudges all over his face, cobwebs in his hair, and dead bugs stuck to his moist forearms. She'd bet any amount of money she'd see some creepy-crawly creature hop from his clothes and walk across the rug.

Ugh.

With a nod, he guzzled half the contents before coming up for air. Meeting her gaze, he glared.

Uh-oh. Judging from the flare to his nostrils, Logan looked mad as hell. Plus, the muscles and veins in his neck protruded to the point of imminent explosion. Something was up.

He cleared his throat. "The rafters were rigged. I don't know how yet, but I found a wire that doesn't belong." He wiped his forehead with a few fingers and left another smudge. "I notified Monroe. He's sending a forensics team. The trap was meant for me."

Shit, shit, shit. She hissed through tight teeth. "Do you think our killer knows you're a cop?"

He scrubbed a hand through his hair, then stared at the cobwebs between his fingers. He wiped his hand on his jeans. "Hard to say. I can't think of any reason why I was targeted."

For Logan or not, the accident could have killed her and Tommy. She shuddered. "Before everything fell, I heard something that sounded like a metal spring. I think Yapper triggered it. I need to sit down." She curled into the corner of the sofa and rested the beer can on a knee. Never had the feeling of returning to Chicago been so strong as it was at this moment. All her life, she stayed in a neutral zone, but these accidents put her front and center, and she didn't like it one damn bit. She rubbed her forehead, then met his gaze. "Won't a forensics team raise questions?"

"They'll come in the guise of insurance investigators. Very discreet."

Guzzling the last of his drink, he crushed the can and placed it on a side table by the door. "I found a wire connected to the rear of the mower, but how it triggered the overhead stuff, I don't know. One way or another, those windows were meant to fall as I shifted the mower into gear." Cursing softly, he stared in the direction of the kitchen window. "I've been allowing Tommy to drive it out of the garage. All that debris would have killed him instantly." He pressed his lips into a thin line.

The trap to kill Logan was bad enough, but to inadvertently kill a little boy tightened her gut into a painful knot. She swallowed a mouthful of beer, then stared at the can. "Somehow, you have a connection with the others." She locked onto his gaze. "What's the common factor?"

"I don't know." Sighing, he again passed a hand through his hair. "The only thing I do know is I blew my charade because of you. The crash nearly stopped my heart."

Yeah, well, her heart wasn't too steady, either. She'd never zipped so fast to grab Tommy and dive under the workhorses. The poor kid probably got whiplash. If those wooden horses weren't sitting there…

Maybe she should consider Mr. Kirby's suggestion and write out a will.

Several hours later, with a cup of coffee in hand, Skylar propped herself on a patio chair to watch the activity by the garage doors.

One CSI woman, who introduced herself as Lizzy, had arrived in a plain white SUV. She talked to Logan for several minutes, then they both entered the garage.

Fay meandered from the side of the rancher, looked into the open hatch of the SUV, and then spotted Skylar on the patio. She approached. "How in the world did you get an insurance investigator here so quickly and on a Saturday?"

"Lucky, I guess." She hadn't a clue about what company insured the premises. Hopefully, Fay wouldn't ask too many questions. Skylar gestured to the chair on her right. "Have a seat. Want some coffee? I made a fresh pot."

"No, thanks, I've had my allotment for the day." She pulled out the chair and collapsed onto the seat. "Whew. I'm exhausted. How's the shoulder?"

"Sore." One of the falling boards had scraped from the top of her scapula to the middle of her spine. Luckily, the impact broke one area of her skin but not enough to warrant a bandage. She still had the bump on her head from the basement fall. What was next—a sprained knee?

Fay placed a tube of antiseptic onto the table. "Use this before you go to bed."

Picking up the tube, Skylar read the directions. "Okay. Thanks." Since the broken skin was at the top of her scapula, she shouldn't have difficulty rubbing on some cream.

While drumming her fingers on the patio table, Fay nodded toward the garage. "I can't imagine an insurance company paying for a bunch of old windows, and if the lawnmower is totaled, the price of a new one wouldn't even meet the deductible." She shifted on the seat. "Did something happen I don't know about?"

Oh, boy. Now, Sky had to act all innocent. With the woman as a possible suspect, how much should she reveal? Her gut told her Logan was trustworthy. It was high time she listened to her gut about Fay. Sky took a sip of coffee, then glanced at Fay. "The overhead windows were rigged to collapse."

Fingers flattening on the table, Fay gaped. "Rigged?" She shot a glance at the garage and shook herself. She met Sky's gaze. "You know, Ginger wondered about some accidents we've had. She said they were rigged. I thought she was suffering from dementia, but after I found her in the basement..." Fay leaned on the table, and with elbows propped, she used two fingers from each hand to rub her temples. "Ginny was right. I'll never forgive myself for doubting her." She looked at Skylar, gaze narrowed. "How do you know so much?"

Skylar told her about Ginger Dawson's personal note. "Aunt Ginger promised to find Lieutenant Monroe proof, but she died too soon. That's why he showed up when Mrs. Caine died." She swallowed the last of her coffee and set the mug on the table. "Aunt Ginger mentioned the other accidents but wasn't clear about what they were."

"Well, for one, the window pane in Darla Winters's room. The glass fell out and missed Darla by inches. She usually lounged near the window to read, and being on blood thinners, she'd have bled to death." She sighed. "Ginny and I studied the window. Someone cut the putty. To this day, I don't know who."

What sadistic mind would try to harm an older woman in such a manner and for what reason? She shuddered. "Aunt Ginger also mentioned something about an electrical shock."

Fay nodded. "Margaret Caine. She always used a curling iron in the bathroom. One day, she plugged in a small nightlight and received a shock. An electrician found the ground wire disconnected. If she had used her curling iron and touched any sort of moisture, she could have been electrocuted."

Both women had attempts on their lives, and now, both were dead by other means. Someone was determined. Sky frowned. "So, whoever is rigging stuff knows everyone's routine."

"That's what Ginny said. She never told me about the police, though." She bit her lower lip.

"Did my aunt ever comment about Mr. Kirby?"

"Oh, heavens, yes." She folded her arms across her chest. "Not a year passed without him encouraging her to sell." Squinting, she pursed her lips. "Wasn't he here earlier?"

Skylar shifted on the seat cushion. The one under her butt felt a little flat. She made a mental note to buy new ones. "He's got a buyer for the property. A man wants to build a hotel." Skylar met the woman's wide gaze and smiled. "No, I haven't changed my mind about selling, but Mr. Kirby is under the assumption I'll return to Chicago. I still don't know what I'm doing, but if tenants die off like they are, I might not have a choice. Someone is on a vendetta, possibly to ruin the manor's reputation." She told too much to a possible suspect, but she and Logan needed more eyes and who better than Fay? If Logan disapproved, well, so what? He could fire her.

The investigator lowered the SUV's rear hatch, then walked toward Skylar while patting dust from her pants. "I'm done here, ma'am. You should receive an estimate in a few days."

"Okay, thanks." She watched the woman hop into the SUV, start up, then drive away.

Fay slapped the table and stood. "I'd best start some dinner. You joining us?"

"No, thanks, Fay. I'll eat here and do a little more packing. And please, don't mention our conversation to anyone. I don't want anything to happen to you." God forbid if anything should happen to Fay. Sky wouldn't know what to do. "By the way, I'm accumulating boxes. Should I put them in the basement until the next yard sale?"

"Definitely. We have our annual sale in September to coincide with Woodstown Day. Ask Logan to carry them over." With a wave, she stepped off the patio and disappeared around the house.

Once alone, Skylar slipped all ten fingers into her hair and tugged. The accidents had no semblance of pattern and no real reason why one person was targeted over the other. Granted, two victims had messy habits—candy wrappers and cotton balls—both irritants to Rita. The bathtub lady wore too much perfume, which pointed to Michael Chang's asthma. What was Logan's fault, not cutting the lawn in a straight line?

Of course, she mustn't forget her aunt and herself. Did Aunt Ginger confront the killer and had to be silenced? As for herself, she had a pretty good idea who shoved her. Proving her suspicion might be impossible, though. "Aggh." If she didn't stop this analytical mumbo jumbo, she'd drive herself crazy.

As the sun set, Skylar re-entered the rancher to make a quick dinner. A shower followed. Afterward, she relaxed on the sofa with the TV on. Somewhere between two uninteresting reality shows, she fell asleep. A tap on the rear door stirred her awake, and she recognized the wide silhouette. *Oh, hell.* Did she really have to move? She felt stiff as a board. "Use your key. I'm not moving."

Entering, Logan smiled. "Hi, beautiful. How you feeling?"

"Achy." Yawning, she stretched and felt her back skin pull. *Ouch.* "What time is it?"

"A little before ten. I saw your lights on."

The man was targeted for death, and he still stopped by to check on her. He might deny an emotional attachment, but she sure had one. Her big problem was how to protect her heart. Any relationship with Logan Greene would end before it began.

He flopped onto the sofa. "Can I do anything for you?"

Oh, he could do so much, but should she take the chance? The little devil on her shoulder said *Hell, yes*! Reaching toward the coffee table, she grabbed the tube of antiseptic. "You can put some of this on my wound."

"No problem. My hands are clean." He reached for the tube.

"Not here, Logan." She stood and took his hand. "Bedroom."

Standing, he cocked a brow. "Are you sure? The temptation might be too much."

He could deny from here to eternity, but she'd bet any amount of money he felt something for her. One way or the other, she was about to find out. "I'm sure."

Chapter Seventeen

While pouring her morning cup of coffee, Skylar smiled to herself. For such a muscular man, Logan was surprisingly gentle. He gave her one fantastic orgasm that defied description. Yes, just one. No second round followed. She didn't ask for more nor did he insist. Instead, he cuddled her—just like their night on the sofa. The man had a way of making her feel cherished and…loved.

The revelation startled her, and she overflowed her coffee. *Oh, shit.*

She was right. He might deny it, but they had an emotional connection that went beyond two people working together to uncover a killer. The feeling wasn't love, of that she was certain, and she'd be a fool to over-think his actions. He had a job to do, and any liaison would end as soon as he left for his next assignment. Still, after being dormant for so long, her girly parts were grateful for the activity. Come to think of it, he never smeared the antiseptic onto her wound. She chuckled.

After cleaning the coffee spill, she took her usual chair at the kitchen table with her mug in both hands while staring out the window. The new flowers Doreen planted around the gazebo were in full bloom—peonies, both pink and white. *Cute.* The view from her Chicago kitchen windows was the neighbor's dilapidated yard—

which was too close. All the houses in her neighborhood were crammed together. As a child, she had friends a backyard away. As an adult, she had no privacy except behind closed windows and doors.

For the first time, thoughts of remaining at the manor entered her mind. Her aunt had willed her a successful business. With Fay and tenants nearby, she always had someone to talk to, and when talking became too much, the rancher would provide the privacy she craved. If boredom hit, she could find a job or maybe do a little traveling or something meaningful, like volunteer for a worthy cause. Never in her life had she so many options to consider.

Standing, she placed her mug in the sink, then turned to the living room to begin her day. But damn, she needed more boxes. *To the manor I go*.

"Sky?"

Halfway along the path to the big house, she turned toward the parking lot to see Philip heading her way. "Hi." The poor man appeared a little frazzled, as if he were about to jump out of his skin. "Are you all right?"

"That's what I'm here to ask *you*. Mother told me what happened."

Knowing Maria, she probably exaggerated every word. Sky smiled. "I'm fine. Just a scraped shoulder."

"Mother's using these accidents as an excuse to move in with me."

Well, now, she understood the strange look on his face. The man was in a panic. She almost laughed, but when she thought about it, Philip's statement cleared him. He'd be out of his mind to rig the accidents. *Another suspect eliminated*.

"Mother also told me of Logan's phony injury."

Peering through one eye, he shook a finger in her face. "I *knew* the guy wasn't trustworthy. You should kick him to the street."

"Fay and I agreed to allow him to make amends."

He hissed. "You women are too soft. Logan's nothing but trouble." After pinching the bridge of his nose, he placed a hand on her shoulder. "Look, Sky. In today's real estate market, the manor and surrounding property is worth a lot of money. Guys like Logan will see dollar signs, and he'll squirm into your life without you realizing."

He already has. Temporarily, anyway. And what a nice squirm it was.

"Philip!"

Simultaneously, she and Philip jumped at the sharp tone. Dear Lord, the woman would give her a heart attack one day. Rolling her eyes, she turned toward the manor's patio.

Maria Santini stood with fists jammed on her hips—her usual stance.

"Mother, you scared the daylights out of us." Philip squared his shoulders and stretched to his full height. "We're discussing yesterday's events. You *did* call to tell me of Skylar's brush with death."

The old woman stomped her foot. "I was emphasizing the danger of living here. If I inadvertently expressed concern for this woman, who has absolutely no taste in clothes, then I apologize for my error." She tromped down the steps and stopped directly in front of Skylar. "I suppose since Logan's a complete fraud, you'll dig your claws into Philip. I won't have it." She jutted her chin.

Claws? Skylar checked the length of her

fingernails. The damn bitch had gall threatening the new owner. Maybe the old biddy hoped to be tossed onto the street. Then, what would Philip do? Was Maria so desperate to move in with her son that she created accidents in order to make the environment dangerous? At the thought, Sky shivered and touched Philip's arm. *Oops, big mistake*. Maria's sharp air intake almost sounded like a freight train. Ignoring the old crow, Sky smiled at Philip. "Thank you for your concern." Desperate for an escape, she hurried along the path toward the manor's front porch when she stopped and stared at the grass. She still needed boxes, but she wasn't about to follow Maria and Philip into the kitchen. Sighing, she continued along the path.

The creak of a rocker drew her gaze.

From the porch, Anthony hailed her with a wave. "Come keep an old man company." He patted the rocker to his right. "Sit. I wouldn't go inside right now. It sounds like Maria is on another tirade."

Yeah, Sky could hear the shrill voice all the way out here. Flopping onto the seat, she draped her arms over the armrests and plunked her head onto the backrest.

"How's the packing going?"

"Slow. I need more boxes."

"Yeah, Ginny collected a lot of crap. Tell you what." He slapped the armrest. "I'll get Tyrone to drive me to the supermarket, and we'll grab a bunch of boxes from the loading dock."

Rotating her head, she smiled. "That's so nice, but you don't have to do that."

"Why not? It's better than hearing Maria yelling at her son." He winked. "She's complaining about you."

He patted her arm. "Don't take it personal. The man can't have a decent conversation with any woman, and the man's got a keen interest in you, little lady. He's no fraud like Logan."

Gilda rushed through the front door, spotted them, then hurried over to stand directly in front of Skylar. "PPE. Ya-ya." She pointed toward the side of the house.

Growing tense from her tone, Skylar straightened in the chair. "What is it, Gilda?" *Please, Lord, not another accident.* But Gilda's face showed no fear. She made strong eye contact and nodded toward the steps. Waving her hand, she urged Skylar to follow.

Anthony grunted. "This woman is crazy as a loon."

"Hey!" Turning toward Anthony, Skylar tapped a knuckle on the armrest. "Just because we can't understand her doesn't mean she can't understand us." She stood and faced the woman. "What? You want to show me something?"

Gilda grabbed Skylar's hand and tugged her off the porch. "Ya-ya." She practically dragged Skylar toward the garage.

This was turning into one heck of a morning. Wasn't this Sunday? Shouldn't everyone be in church and praying for their souls?

At the garage, Logan had just pushed the lawnmower onto the concrete slab. As they approached, he glanced in their direction and cocked a brow.

She could only shrug in answer.

Gilda urged her inside the garage and stopped at the spot where the debris fell. She released Skylar's hand and pointed toward the floor. "Ya-ya." Then, she pointed to the rafters. "PPE."

Oh, God. The woman repeatedly pointed up and down, and Sky followed Gilda's finger like her head was on a string. Yet, she had absolutely no idea what Gilda meant.

Logan stepped alongside. "What's going on?"

"I don't know. She gestured like this yesterday."

Gilda stomped a foot. "Ya-ya." She pointed to the same two spots and clapped her hands. "Boom!"

A new word! Skylar gasped. "She knows something." She grabbed Gilda's arm to draw her gaze. "It wasn't an accident, Gilda. Someone meant to hurt Logan."

"Ya-ya." She bobbed her head, eyes bright, and placed an open palm level with her forehead.

Logan scratched his ear. "What the hell does *that* mean?"

Skylar shushed him. "Do you know who, Gilda? Is that what you're trying to tell us?"

The woman clamped her lips shut and darted her gaze toward the garage opening.

In unison, Skylar and Logan turned.

The yard was full of people. Fay, Doreen, Rita, and Tommy walked from the parking lot with arms loaded with shopping bags. Michael and Joe were bent over the lawnmower, and Anthony and Tyrone had just come from the front of the house.

Without another word, Gilda ran into the manor.

Skylar whirled to Logan and, keeping her voice low, gasped. "She knows!"

Watching the crowd beyond the doors, he frowned. "This isn't good. She could be our next victim."

"But who did she see?" She followed the flurry of activity in the yard. Where had everyone come from all of a sudden? "We should gather the tenants in the living room and have Gilda point out the guilty person."

Logan shook his head. "Because of her medical condition, her testimony will be dismissed. She'd be better off telling me, so I could look for evidence."

"Then, we should ask her to write the name on a piece of paper." Folding her arms across her chest, she scanned the rafters. Without the two-by-fours supporting the old windows, the entire area looked almost barren.

"What are you thinking, Sky?"

She dropped her arms. "Gilda is a retired physics teacher. She probably understands how the trap worked." She faced him. "We're dealing with someone who has a working knowledge of physics."

Lifting his gaze, he stared at the overhead beams. After a minute, he frowned. "Tyrone ran a hospital maintenance department. Anthony, from what I heard, was a damn good engineer." Lowering his gaze, he released a long breath. "Joe's a retired navy machinist. All three are viable suspects, but without proof, we have nothing." Meeting her gaze, he cursed softly. "I have never worked a case with so few clues."

She wouldn't know a clue even if it slapped her upside of the head. She sighed. "I feel so helpless."

"We are, Sky." With a gentle nudge on her elbow, he guided her toward the workbench against the wall, then took a quick look over his shoulder. "I talked with Monroe this morning. The trip wire was connected to a board supporting the windows while a secondary wire went over to the wood planks. Once the mower shifted into gear, everything was rigged to fall. And you're right. Yapper tripped the wire."

Hugging herself tight, she met Logan's gaze. "Isn't the garage usually locked?"

"Only when I'm finished for the day. The doors remain open while I'm in the yard, and anyone can walk inside. But a trap this well-placed had to take time. I'm guessing the perp made a copy of the garage key."

"And he or she worked in the cover of darkness while everyone slept." She chewed on her inner lip. "My bedroom is closest to the garage. I never heard anything." Of course, she had a habit of sleeping like the dead. She slumped against one of the wooden horses. "We're back where we started."

"Not necessarily. The killer's attempt to eliminate me failed. He or she might try again."

Well, gee, couldn't he say it with a little bit of concern? For crying out loud, he was talking about his life. She pushed away from the horse and headed for the garage opening. With all the excitement, she forgot the original reason why she left the rancher. She pivoted to face Logan. "When you get time, can you take my packed boxes to the manor's basement?"

"Sure. How about when I'm done here?"

"Okay. Thank you." Again, she turned to leave.

"Sky?"

Stopping near the garage opening, she glanced over her shoulder with a brow raised.

Grinning, he winked. "I like your shorts."

She narrowed her gaze to feign disapproval but couldn't help wiggling her ass as she left. Since she had no keys to enter through the rear, she retraced her steps to the unlocked front door and stepped into the office. She stopped. Someone had pushed the desk chair away from its position and placed a folded piece of paper onto the seat. Brows high, she opened the sheet and read a handwritten note.

Meet me at the gazebo at 10 o'clock. Don't tell anyone and no lights.

Philip

A secret rendezvous? Like two forbidden lovers hiding from a witch of a mother? Skylar chuckled and placed the note into her pocket. Oh, she'd meet him, all right, and something told her she'd have a very interesting conversation.

Chapter Eighteen

Ugh. Despite the lower nighttime temperatures, humidity hung in the air like a thermal blanket. A lovers' rendezvous could be a sticky situation—no pun intended. *Oh, yeah, I'm a real comedian.* If what Sky suspected was true, she'd solve one problem hanging over her head.

Because every flying creature known to man might enjoy a bite of her skin, Sky wore a pair of cargo pants and slipped on a jacket. She had absolutely no desire to be a bug's late-night snack.

Oddly enough, she hadn't seen her property after dark. Until now, she had no reason to venture outside once the sun set. And what a surprise! Tiny solar lamps lined the perimeter of the parking lot and each of the brick walkways. As expected, the gazebo sat in darkness, even though she remembered seeing a small fan with a light fixture in the center of the ceiling. Of course, the note specified no lights, so she didn't take a chance carrying a flashlight. No moon glowed overhead to help, but the streetlamps illuminated enough of the yard so she wouldn't fall into a hole and break a leg.

Nearing the gazebo, she slowed her steps and, despite herself, she tensed. She knew what to expect, but the rigid silhouette standing in the middle of the floor made her wonder why she agreed to meet. Even in darkness, the heated glare cut through Sky like a saw.

"I knew you'd come. You can't stay away from him."

How could one deal with a jealousy so deep it bordered on madness? Skylar thrust her hands into her jacket pockets and shook her head. "He's a handsome man, Mrs. Santini." She stopped near the steps.

The older woman shifted on her feet. "You were expecting me?"

"Yes, ma'am. I recognized your handwriting from your complaint notes in my aunt's file folder." Sky shot a quick scan of Maria's hands, but in the dark, she couldn't tell whether the woman held a weapon. In all probability, Maria kept the weapon hidden in the folds of her dress. She swatted at some creature on her cheek.

Maria snorted. "Then, why did you come?"

"To convince you I'm not interested in your son."

"But he's infatuated with you, and I can't allow it to continue." She stomped a foot.

"Is that why you hoped I'd break my neck on the cellar steps?"

She humphed. "I didn't push hard enough."

Skylar almost laughed. From the moment she opened her eyes, she suspected Maria. The hands on her back had felt small, and three people in the manor had small hands—Gilda, Tommy, and Maria. She ruled out Tommy. The kid ran everywhere and made enough noise to wake the dead. So, of the two women, only Maria showed hostility toward the new owner.

Okay, so now what? Mrs. Santini hadn't moved from the shadows. She stood in the center of the gazebo floor with her arms straight by her sides, like an automaton waiting to be activated. Skylar placed one foot onto the bottom step. "Why don't we sit and talk?"

She motioned toward the built-in benches along the rail. Not like she'd enjoy a happy little chitchat with the woman, but her mother raised her to be polite.

"I have no intention of sitting with you. I will not accept you as my daughter-in-law, and I must take care of this problem before Philip loses his head completely."

Wow. Daughter-in-law even, and before a first date.

The woman crept closer to the steps with her right arm slowly rising.

Even in shadows, Skylar caught the shape of a knife in her hand. A butcher knife from the length—the kind all the crazy movie stars grab. Despite knowing the lady hadn't a chance in hell against a woman with three black belts, Sky felt her heart rate kick into high gear. A deadly weapon showed Maria meant business. "So, Mrs. Santini, you intend to kill me, and then what? Bury me in the backyard?" She tsked. "Philip will be so disappointed."

"If I'm caught, you mean."

Oh, please. Did the woman honestly believe she'd get away with murder? She didn't look strong enough to dig a grave, let alone drag Skylar's body somewhere.

With the knife poised over her head in a striking position, Maria approached the opening to the gazebo.

Easing away from the structure, Sky waited on the soft grass. She didn't want to hurt the old woman, but she wasn't about to stand still and take a knife in her chest.

With her glassy gaze riveted on Skylar, Maria descended the two steps.

At the possessed look, Sky inwardly shuddered.

The woman definitely needed professional help. "And the others, Mrs. Santini, were they after Philip, too?"

Maria's steps faltered, and she blinked. "There are no others, dear. From the moment you arrived, my Philip lost all common sense."

Nice to know she had that effect on a man. Maybe she should pay more attention to the men crossing her path.

Screaming like a banshee, Maria charged.

With training ingrained from years of practice, Sky relaxed her muscles. Fear and panic had no place in the mind of a martial arts expert, but her heart refused to listen. She wasn't standing on a mat waiting for the next opponent to approach, and her heart pounded within her chest. As the weapon descended, Skylar took one swift step to the side and clamped onto a thin wrist, twisted, and easily yanked the knife from Maria's grip.

"Nooooo!" Maria collapsed into a heap onto the ground.

A few seconds later, Logan vaulted over the gazebo rail but stopped at the steps. Shifting his gaze from Maria to Sky, he grinned. "I can see I'm not needed."

Skylar looked at Logan and smirked. "Always nice to have company." Earlier, she showed Logan the note and relayed her suspicions. He agreed to stay in the background as a witness to Maria's insanity.

Covering her face, Maria bawled like a baby.

Whipping out a handkerchief from his back pocket, Logan took the knife from Skylar and carefully wrapped it.

She pointed toward his little bundle. "Don't cops use plastic bags?"

"If I was a cop, you mean?" He winked. "I'm just the gardener, ma'am." Staring down at Maria, he sighed. "I was hoping for a confession." He slipped out his cell phone, switched on the flashlight app, and swung the beam around the yard.

Skylar arched a brow. "Who are you looking for?"

"Not who, Sky, what. Skunks wander through here at night."

Now, he tells me. She rotated and sniffed. "We smell them first, right?" She wasn't someone who lived with nature. City born and bred, she could mistake a skunk for a cat.

Maria's bawling changed to soft sobs.

Logan squatted in front of Maria. "Why'd you kill the others, Mrs. Santini?"

With a blank stare, the woman met his gaze. "What others? I want this woman away from my son." Her chin dropped to her chest.

Logan stood and, taking Skylar by the arm, guided her to the side. "I'm legally bound to report this."

"Yes, of course." She glanced at Maria and sighed. No matter what Logan might think, he was wrong about Maria Santini, and Skylar was willing to prove it.

****

As was his habit, Logan stayed in character and explained the situation to the arriving cops, then repeated the spiel to the ambulance crew. The butcher knife was properly bagged and labeled, and while the EMTs worked with Maria, he took a position next to Sky. After the conclusion of a case, he never once revealed his identity, and he wasn't about to start now. Whenever possible, he preferred to fade away.

Before long, windows in the manor lit up, and the

patio light clicked on. From his position near the gazebo, he watched as some of the tenants gathered near the covered grill. Anthony and Michael were fully dressed while Doreen, Tyrone, and Fay stood in house robes. Missing were Rita, Joe, Tommy, and Gilda. On Sunday night, all the tenants should be home.

Fay approached while tugging on her robe sash. "What's going on?"

Logan stepped in her path. "Maria attacked Skylar with a knife."

Slapping a hand over her mouth, Fay shot her gaze toward Skylar.

Skylar shrugged. "I'm all right, Fay."

The housekeeper wrapped Sky in a tight, bear hug.

He wanted to do the same. Even as Maria raised the knife, Sky had remained cool as a cucumber. He knew Sky could handle herself, but even so, he had a hard time remaining in the background. He squeezed Fay's shoulder. "Please call Philip and explain what happened. His mother will probably go to the psych ward in Woodbury."

Sniffing, Fay released Skylar and extracted a tissue from her robe pocket. "Yes, I'll call. He won't be happy." While blowing her nose, she hurried toward the house.

As Maria was strapped onto the stretcher, the woman stared with a face devoid of emotion, and not once did she look at the crew fussing over her.

Skylar stood watching with her hands stuffed into her jacket pockets.

Even in the dark, she had a beautiful profile. He wrapped an arm around her shoulders and squeezed. "You did well."

Leaning against him, she smirked. "Maria wasn't much of a threat." Glancing up, she met his gaze. "Shouldn't you call Monroe?"

"Already did. He's walking toward us." He pointed.

The big man gestured toward the rancher.

Placing a hand on the small of her back, Logan urged Sky to follow Monroe. Once inside the rancher's living room, Logan closed the door, turned, and smiled. "We have our killer."

****

Without removing her jacket, Skylar flopped onto the corner of the sofa and shivered. What in the world temperature did she set the air conditioner? The breeze coming through the vents felt like the inside of a freezer. An even colder chill came from Logan's bold statement. Time to set the record straight. She waggled a finger at both men. "Maria is not our killer. She is a woman stuck in the 1950s when a wife doted on her husband and stayed home to care for the children. Plus, I doubt she has the knowledge to rig a garage trap. Her main objective was to keep me away from Philip." She stuffed her hands into her jacket pockets.

Frowning, Monroe slipped onto a side chair and crossed his legs. "Who then?" He shifted his gaze between Skylar and Logan.

Still standing, Logan shrugged. "Sorry, Bob. Sky and I disagreed." He peered at Skylar. "You're wrong."

"Not to appear arrogant, but I doubt it." She stifled a yawn. "Gilda knows but was afraid to tell us. If you remember the crowd outside the garage, Maria was not among them."

Stiffening, Logan stared. "Damn, I hadn't thought

of that. She's right, Bob." He relayed Gilda's actions in the garage.

Monroe gaped. "The stroke woman knows?" Uncrossing his legs, he whipped out a small notebook from his rear pocket and flipped through the pages. "Even if she told us who, we'd still need proof."

A loud pounding on the front door caused Sky to jump halfway off her seat.

With a brow cocked, Logan hurried to the door.

Looking frazzled and still in her robe, Fay rushed inside. She darted her gaze from one person to the next. "It's Gilda! I can't wake her. The ambulance already left with Maria, so I called 9-1-1."

Sky's heart shot straight into her throat. *The killer again*? She jumped to her feet and, motioning for Logan and Monroe to follow, she hurried after Fay.

Gilda occupied Room Number Five, which stood in the far right corner next to the tub room. Everything about the small apartment appeared neat and orderly, including the woman tucked in bed. By all accounts, she looked peacefully asleep.

Fay rushed to her bedside. "I hope she didn't have another stroke."

Sky grabbed the woman's hand and squeezed. "Gilda!"

A garbled moan escaped from Gilda's throat.

Well, at least, she was alive. Placing two fingers on the side of Gilda's neck, Skylar palpated for a pulse. "Weak." She glanced at Logan. "Very weak."

Monroe took out his cell phone. "I'll check on the ambulance's ETA." He stepped into the hall while urging Rita and Michael to move away from the doorway.

Skylar lifted a folded piece of paper from the night table. She opened the sheet and read.

I killed all of them. I'm sorry. Gilda

Her heart flipped. *No way*! Of all the suspects, Gilda was last on Sky's list.

Fay read over Sky's shoulder and gasped. "This isn't possible." She pointed toward the note. "Gilda's handwriting is gibberish. She *thinks* she's writing legibly, but she's not."

Using a two-finger hold on the corner of the paper, Logan took the note from Sky and looked at Fay. "How many people know this?"

Running her fingers through her hair, Fay frowned. "Me, her doctor, and Mr. Kirby. Everything involved with language is gone—except for comprehension."

Dangling the note, Logan faced Sky. "Do you recognize the handwriting?"

Frowning, Sky shook her head. "Not really." She quietly cursed. Whatever happened to Gilda was no coincidence. She would bet money this was the work of their unknown killer.

Gilda gurgled.

Cringing, Sky shifted her gaze from Fay to Logan. "I'm no expert, but does Gilda sound like she's getting worse?" Turning toward the night table, Skylar picked up the water glass by the bedside. For some strange reason, she sniffed. Jerking, she sniffed again. "This smells like cilantro."

Fay shook her head. "That's not possible. She's severely allergic to that herb."

Taking the glass, Logan sniffed. "Smells like soap."

Fay released a cry. "Oh, my God! Cilantro smells

like soap to a lot of people—Gilda included. If she sniffed and smelled soap, she probably thought she didn't rinse the glass well enough after washing." She yanked open the top drawer in the nightstand and rummaged. "She keeps epinephrine in here." She cursed. "The syringe isn't here!"

Logan ran to the door. "Monroe, STAT on the ambulance. Allergic reaction to cilantro."

Knowing they were helpless until the EMTs arrived, Sky grabbed the blanket at the bottom of the bed, doubled the fold, and stuffed it under Gilda's pillow. Somewhere, she remembered reading about elevating a person's head to help them breathe. She hoped it worked.

The sound of Yapper's barks echoed behind a closed door. The poor mutt probably wanted in on all the activity. If Tommy wasn't awake, he would be soon. Sky faced Fay. "Does Gilda always keep a glass of water at her bedside?"

"Yes. She takes her blood pressure medicine at night."

Monroe entered. "Ambulance will be here soon."

"Do you have an evidence bag?" Logan dangled the note by its corner and explained Gilda's inability to write. He pointed to the glass. "The glass needs to be bagged, too. Sky and I just handled it."

Monroe shot a quick glance around the room. "I've nothing on me. Put the paper by the glass. I'll call CSI and have them go over the room. Don't touch anything else." Again, he left the room with his phone held to his ear.

Logan turned to Fay. "Why'd you check on Gilda?"

She waved a hand toward the window. "Her room faces the gazebo, so I was surprised she slept through all the commotion. I almost let her be, but ever since her stroke, I question when something isn't right."

For the second time in as many hours, an ambulance crew arrived. They immediately shot Gilda with epinephrine.

Sky urged Fay to move to the side of the room. All this excitement in one night was getting to be a bit much, and Fay looked a little too pale. Sky squeezed her arm. "You want to sit?"

Fay rubbed her forehead. "I've got a whale of a headache. I need a few aspirin."

"Well, after all this is over, maybe Ginger's special analgesic will help you sleep."

With one raised brow, Fay faced her. "What analgesic?"

The question startled Sky. Was Fay simply flustered by the events of the night and couldn't remember? Sky tilted her head. "You know, the one she took for her rheumatoid arthritis. It's laced with booze."

Fay widened her gaze. "Ginger didn't have rheumatoid arthritis. Oh, they're taking Gilda to the hospital. Let me change out of these nightclothes and follow." She hurried out the door.

Ginger didn't have rheumatoid arthritis? But her aunt specifically said to ask Fay.

A cry of anguish pierced the air.

What in God's name is wrong now?

Doreen rushed through the bedroom door and clamped onto Logan's arm. "Tommy's gone! I can't find him. He was sound asleep when I went outside."

Giving her a faint smile, Logan patted the hand on

his arm. "He's a curious little boy. He's probably outside." He turned to Sky. "Go get some sleep. You've had more of your fair share of excitement for one day. Doreen and I will look for Tommy."

Skylar opened her mouth to protest, but really, cops were everywhere. Logan didn't need her help. She answered with a yawn. When she returned to the rancher and locked the doors behind her, she leaned against the doorframe and released a long breath. Unbeknownst to the killer, Mrs. Santini's murderous outrage saved Gilda. If all the flashing lights hadn't stirred the residents, the little post-stroke lady would have been dead by morning. Lucky for Gilda. Unlucky for the killer. With another yawn, Sky pushed herself from the door.

Fay's reaction to Aunt Ginger's analgesic bothered her. The woman sounded as if she had no idea what Sky meant. Had her aunt left a clue after all, and her niece was too blind to see? Closing her eyes, she recalled the note word for word.

Mix a shot of coffee liquor with honey, amaretto, nectarine juice, and gin. Fay uses it all the time. Just ask her.

Where was the booze to make the concoction? And why wasn't her aunt's Irish whiskey included in the list?

With a loud gasp, Skylar froze. *Holy shit*. She finally figured it out!

Chapter Nineteen

"You should learn to lock your doors, Ms. Dawson."

At the sound of the familiar voice coming from the kitchen, Skylar whirled. Her muscles tensed, her hands curled into fists, and she was pretty sure her hair stood on end. *Yeah, I figured out Aunt Ginger's clue a little too late.* Now, she was about to confront the killer while everyone was preoccupied with the events of the night. Sucking in a calming breath, she lifted her chin and straightened her shoulders. "All right, you can come out. No sense hiding."

A shadow moved within the dark kitchen. Dressed entirely in black, Michael Chang stepped into the light with a gun aimed in her direction. He grinned. "You don't sound too surprised."

Uh-oh. She might have ninja speed, but a bullet was faster. She gulped. "What do you want?"

"We have a few things to discuss, but I'll make it as brief as possible." He waved the weapon toward the center of the living room. "Stand near the sofa, please."

Well, geez, he was still polite. But he was holding a pistol that looked more like something out of a museum. Granted, she knew very little about guns, but did the thing really work? Heart racing, she obeyed and positioned herself behind the sofa back. Not the most advantageous spot, for sure. She stood fifteen feet from the front door and ten feet from the rear door. A quick escape was out of the question, especially with a bullet chasing her. In a flash, she recalled Gilda's frantic gestures in the garage and gaped. "You saw Gilda putting her hand to her forehead. She was indicating someone around her height!"

With his gaze never wavering from her face, he shifted his grip on the gun. "Yes, and lucky for me, she can't speak. I had to get rid of Gilda before you figured it out."

"You want to tell me what's going on, Michael? Why are you killing the tenants?"

Jerking, he raised his brows. "How do you know about the others? Aw, hell, never mind. Your aunt probably left some sort of message." He waved the gun. "It's all for Doreen, you see. She's wonderful, but some people don't see her that way. It started with old man Johnson. That nasty man labeled her an unwed mother, and he wouldn't shut his pie hole. Doreen was divorced because of a deserting husband, but would he accept that? Hell, no. So, one simple push on the stairs, and he fell like a rock." He snickered. "It was quite easy."

A cold chill slithered up her spine. The man made murder sound like a walk in the park. "What about the bathtub lady?"

He cocked his head. "Wow, you do know everything, don't you?" He sighed. "Darla was driving me batty with her perfume and god-awful bubble baths. All her crappy floral scents permeated the entire second floor and set off my asthma. I've been so much better since."

This wasn't real, right? She wasn't into any psycho-babble, but damn, the man was nuts. She glanced at the backdoor. Did she remember to lock it? "Why'd you kill my aunt? You said you liked her."

Nodding, he smirked. "I did, but the night I killed Darla, Ginger found me on the front porch with my inhaler. She's the only one who commented on my wet clothes. She figured it out right quick."

And the knowledge got her killed. Damn the man. Sky furled her hands into tight fists as she inched to the side. "So, you lured her to the basement."

"Of course. Can you believe she demanded I surrender? So, I came up with the bright idea to discuss my terms somewhere private. Fool that she was, she agreed." Smiling, he rubbed the back of his neck. "Easiest thing in the world to leave her in the basement. Knowing her fear of the dark, the outcome was inevitable."

How could her aunt be so gullible, and why didn't she tell Fay about her suspicions? Instead, she walked into a basement with a suspected killer. Sky hissed. "And Mrs. Caine?"

He waggled a finger. "She was pushing to have Doreen and Tommy evicted. She said children shouldn't be at the manor. After Ginger's death, she campaigned hard to get Fay to cancel their lease."

What a heartless man. Michael had an excuse for every murder. In his mind, they were rational reasons. She rubbed her forehead.

"Keep your hands by your side, please."

"Sorry. Headache brewing." Not really a headache. The throb was more a buildup of anger to the point where her head wanted to explode. She dropped her hand and met his gaze. "I suppose you targeted Logan because Doreen was interested in him?"

"Bingo!" Grinning, he tapped the tip of his nose.

"But Mrs. Santini spoiled your plans for Gilda."

He rolled his eyes. "That lady is a royal pain in the ass. I went through all the trouble to coat Gilda's glass with cilantro oil, and the old battle-ax woke up the dead."

This man was certifiably crazy. He believed in justifiable murder. Were there others besides the tenants? Maybe where he worked? She stole a glance at the wall clock. What was taking Logan so long? Hadn't they found...*aw, crap*. Her chest tightened, and she shot Michael a glare. "You took Tommy, didn't you? That's when we heard Yapper barking."

He grinned. "See? You're smart. Yes, I took him and hid him where no one will think to look. As for Yapper, I had to stomp on his little throat."

She gasped. *Dear Lord Almighty*. She might enjoy strangling the man. "How could you do that? Tommy will be heartbroken." The man was so cruel. But ten to one, if he liked Doreen, he wouldn't hurt Tommy. She strolled to one end of the sofa.

Squinting, he extended his gun hand. "I said don't move!"

She froze. Damn, he caught her. Somehow, she had to get around to the front of the sofa. "Sorry. I forgot. I can't wait to hear your reason for killing me."

He snorted. "I happened to step out onto the patio when Nathan Kirby paid you a visit. I overheard about the prospective client who wants to buy the manor. I can't let you sell."

Mouth agape, Skylar blinked. "I haven't decided what to do, but thanks to Mr. Kirby, I know something about estate law. If I die without a will, all my property goes to the state for disbursement. The state has no choice but to sell the property."

His jaw turned to stone, and he glared. "That's unfortunate. Now, I'll have to kill you for what you know."

Well, golly gee, a real catch-22. Like she hadn't seen the obvious. Flexing her fingers to keep herself focused, she took another step to the side. "I don't understand why you involved Tommy."

"You, of course. The boy is my insurance policy." He moved closer. "You see, I know all about your martial arts skills." Turning the gun sideways, he patted the barrel with his other hand. "This is my grandfather's gun. It's a 1943 Japanese *Nambu* pistol. When Japan invaded China during World War Two, my grandfather killed the officer carrying this gun. Can you believe they still make bullets for these relics?"

"Actually, I don't know a lot about guns." Except they kill. Dodging a bullet would be tricky, but she had to try. "If I die with a bullet in me, I'll become a definite murder case. Cops will be all over this place."

"Not if the shot is precise, and you die with the weapon in your hand."

Oh, sure, good luck with that scenario. No way in hell would she allow him to get close enough for a suicide shot. She again glanced at the backdoor.

Sneering, he followed her gaze. "Don't expect Logan to waltz in. He's busy searching for a lost, little boy who—I might add—is heavily sedated with some liquid antihistamine. I wrapped him nice and tight to hide him. When I'm done here, I'll take Tommy from his hiding spot and become the hero."

Well, damn, she'd better make sure she didn't

deliver a fatal blow. If Tommy had too much antihistamine, he might be in danger, and the sooner they got him to a hospital, the better he'd be. But she sure couldn't stand here all night avoiding the inevitable nor could she wait for Logan to stroll in. Daring Michael, she walked to his side of the sofa and spread her arms wide. "Take your best shot."

Waving the gun, he snarled. "I want you to face the door and stand still."

Yeah, like that will happen. "What's the matter? Don't want to see my face wither in pain?"

With both hands, he gripped the gun handle. "Just turn around."

The coffee table stood between them. He had to close the distance by rounding the table, and in order for her murder to appear like a suicide, he must position the gun to the side of her head and fire a close-range shot. Anyone who watched a cop show knew such a critical detail. But how close would he dare?

She had only one way to find out. Reaching for her inner calm, she relaxed her muscles and turned toward the backdoor. With a glance to her right, she caught his reflection in the picture frames mounted on the dining room table. *My goodness, how convenient.*

Moving closer, Michael raised the gun.

Sweat dripped down both sides of his temples, and the gun shook even while holding it with both hands. *Well, well.* The man was nervous. He was still too far for a suicide shot, but two steps around the table should place him within striking distance. *And there he goes.*

Skylar whirled to the side in the split second the gun fired. The bullet shattered the backdoor window. Before another bullet fired, she flew, feet first, kicked the gun from his hand with one foot, and smacked the side of his head with the other.

He stumbled, then fell, rolled, and jumped to his feet, staging quickly into a standard karate stance.

Oh, how nice. The man had a little ninja skills. This should be fun. She waited for him to make the first move.

"If you kill me, Tommy dies!"

Skylar smiled. "You do realize I have the power to torture you, right?"

"Yaaahh!" Arms whirling, he charged.

Oh, for the love of… Moving like a flash of light, she kneed his side to knock him off balance, clamped onto his wrist, then flipped him onto his back.

Again, rolling and jumping to his feet, he swung a leg toward her head.

Ducking, Sky caught his ankle and twisted.

His right shoulder hit the floor with a thud.

Not wasting a second, she stepped on his right hand and grabbed the left. With one spin, she yanked him onto his stomach while wrenching his arm behind his back. For good measure, she jammed her heel into his spine.

He screamed.

"That was a bit of a girly scream, Michael."

"I should have shot you as soon as you stepped through the door. Oww! That hurts!" He struggled against her grip.

Stronger men couldn't break her hold, and Michael had nowhere near the strength of the guys she threw around. For good measure, she bent his hand at the wrist. "Tell me where Tommy is before I rip your arm out of the socket."

A crash drew her gaze toward the backdoor.

Logan stood poised in the doorway with eyes flaring. "What the hell is going on?"

Jerking her head toward Chang, Skylar grinned. "We have our killer."

Michael struggled under her foot. "I'm not saying where Tommy is unless you let me go."

Skylar looked at Logan. "Did you find Tommy?"

"Not yet. I heard the shot and hightailed it over here." He turned to two officers who hurried in behind him. "Cuff him, will you? I'll call Monroe." He took out his phone.

Michael strained to see Logan. "You're a *cop*?"

Logan winked. "Surprise, surprise." He talked into his phone.

The entire Woodstown police department might as well park on the property for the night. She'd bet any amount of money the manor never caused so much excitement. Before she released Michael to the officers, Skylar gave his arm a good twist.

"Oww, dammit! Stop!"

"That was for Ginger Dawson." Sighing, she released her hold and let the officers do their job.

Monroe rushed in along with several more officers.

Cursing worse than a sailor, Michael was cuffed and hauled to his feet. On the way out the door, he glared over his shoulder. "I'll never tell you where Tommy is!"

Skylar fell onto the sofa and threw her head onto the back cushion. This had been one hell of a night. First, Maria, then Gilda, and now Michael. Her whole body felt like lead.

Logan kicked out the gun from under the dining

room table, and his brows shot into his hairline. "Holy cow! This is a *Nambu*! Doesn't Michael know how valuable this is?" He lowered his brows and looked at Sky. "How was he going to explain a bullet?"

"He planned on putting the gun in my hand."

Monroe approached and stood before Skylar. "You all right?"

"Oh, sure. He surprised me, but yeah, I'm fine." She sighed. "He told me everything, and you won't believe his motive." Waggling her fingers toward Logan, she extended her hand for an assist. Afterward, she squeezed his hand. "Thank you." She straightened her shirt. "Michael is in love with Doreen."

Both Logan and Monroe stared.

"Hey, I said you wouldn't believe me." Glancing beyond the two men, Skylar gasped. The backdoor had been busted from one hinge and dangled. The jamb with the lock was totally splintered, and four of the six panes of glass were shattered. She stared at Logan. Obviously, he hadn't wasted time fumbling for a key.

He shrugged. "I saw red."

Fighting a laugh, she stroked his cheek. "Thank you. No man has ever come to my rescue. It feels nice."

He snorted and jammed fists onto his hips. "Any ideas where he hid Tommy?"

"One guess. With all the people around, Michael would have difficulty walking out with a child in his arms. He said he wrapped Tommy tight and gave him antihistamine to keep him asleep. All that takes time. So, Tommy is still in Doreen's room." She touched Logan's forearm. "He killed Yapper."

"Aw, damn." Logan clenched his jaw. "I'm sorry I didn't have a go at the bastard." He nodded toward the front door. "Let's see if you're right."

Leaving via the front door, Skylar led the way. Once inside the manor, she gestured for a pale-faced Doreen to follow. The poor girl was pacing the hall like a caged animal.

Doreen caught up on the stairs. "Where are you going?"

"How thoroughly did you search your room?"

"I—" She gaped. "He wasn't in his bed, so I checked the bathroom." She tripped on a step. "You think he's still in the room?"

"Yes."

Once on the second floor, Doreen rushed through her open door, then stood still.

Skylar pointed. "Check the closet." She grabbed Doreen's arm. "Michael killed Yapper."

Gritting her teeth, she ran over and threw the door wide. After tossing out several canvas bags and a suitcase, she cried out and fell to her knees.

Tommy was tucked into the corner, wrapped in a blanket—and sound asleep.

Poor Yapper was dumped on some shoeboxes, lifeless. *That heartless bastard.* She should have broken a few of his bones.

Reaching in, Doreen swept the boy into her arms and cried.

Monroe patted Doreen's shoulder. "I'll have one of my officers drive you to an urgent care center."

After the formalities of statements, Skylar and Logan returned to the rancher. She was beyond exhausted and could barely keep her eyes open. "By the way, we had my aunt's clue all along."

He raised a brow. "Where?"

"Her analgesic recipe. *Coffee liquor, honey, amaretto, nectarine juice, and gin.* If we take the first letter of each of the ingredients, it spells *Chang*." She entered the rancher.

"Son of a bitch." Jaw tight, he shook his head.

Hammering stopped her. She looked up to see Tyrone and Anthony working on the damaged door. Good grief, it was four o'clock in the morning!

Tyrone grinned. "Just finished. We couldn't let you miss a good night's rest by worrying about an open door."

With a heart ready to explode, she blinked back the moisture in her eyes. "You guys are wonderful. Thank you."

Anthony closed the toolbox. "Fixed it the best we could, but the wood should hold 'til you buy a new one." Hands on hips, he eyed Skylar. "You hurt?" Unable to form words, she shook her head.

Both men said "good night" and left.

After inspecting the door, Logan swung it on its hinges, then closed and bolted the lock. Turning, he swept her into his arms and carried her to the bedroom. He lowered her to the bed. "I'll hold you until you fall asleep, Sky."

Which wouldn't take long. Once she slipped under the sheets, she felt Logan tug her close. The strength of his arms did more for her than any balm or pill could ever do, and she soon drifted off to sleep.

In the morning, he was gone.

Chapter Twenty

As the days passed, Skylar wasn't stupid enough to ignore the inevitable. The capture of the manor's killer meant Logan's much-anticipated reassignment. He was no longer the handyman, and the garage stayed closed until Anthony or Tyrone wandered in to find something. Because no one heard a word from him, and she wasn't one to call and ask what the hell was going on, she gave Fay permission to hire a lawn service.

She'd never forget him, though. He awakened a part of her that believed being alone was her preference. Not anymore. She had the gang, and several times during the week, she found herself at the dinner table with her extended family.

After rinsing the last of her breakfast dishes, Sky grabbed the hose and gave the sink a good squirt to wash the remaining residue down the drain. She hardly ever used the rancher's dishwasher, and why would she when one person used one plate, one cup, and maybe a side dish? She just shut the tap when a knock sounded on the backdoor. While snatching a dishtowel from the counter, Skylar turned from the sink to see Logan's silhouette through the new door drapes. Her stomach flipped, but reality was a bitch. He wasn't here for her. He had a lease to terminate and a room to clear. She swallowed the lump in her throat. "It's open."

Logan entered wearing his usual blue jeans and

snug, black T-shirt.

He looked as handsome as ever with his tousled hair and day-old beard. She'd miss him, and damn, her heart squeezed. Realizing she might tear the dishtowel into shreds, she tossed it onto the table and dropped her hands to her sides. "Want something to drink?" Well, geez, what else could she say? The least she could do was offer him fluids. Hydration and all that.

"No, thanks." He placed a key on the kitchen table. "I won't need your door key anymore." After clearing his throat, he stuffed his hands into his front pockets. "I packed up my stuff and gave Fay the key to the room. I—huh—stopped to say goodbye."

Her heart wrenched. So, this was the end of a relationship doomed from the start. She wasn't in love—at least, she didn't think so—but he had turned into a partner of sorts. Swallowing what stuck in her throat, she forced a smile. "Onward to the next assignment?"

A brief smile touched his lips. "I've already aired out my Princeton condo." He met her gaze. "I want to thank you for your help."

Thank me? She expected a goodbye speech but nothing so impersonal. Hiding a grimace, she grabbed the dishtowel and folded it. "I owed my aunt, Logan." She'd met men like Logan. Work took precedence over everything—including relationships. But didn't she do the same? Back in Chicago, she lived alone on purpose, worked every night except Sunday, and came home to an empty house. The manor's gang had changed her mindset, and like it or not, she had some serious decisions to make. Facing him, she leaned against the counter while folding her arms across her chest.

Logan cleared his throat. "About us, Sky."

Here it comes. She almost cut him short since he so aptly insulted her. Instead, she scratched her nose and waited.

He shifted on his feet. "It's time for me to return to Princeton." He strained a smile. "I'll never forget you."

"I'll never forget you, either, Logan." Her damn lump grew and threatened to close off her airway. She coughed.

"Are you staying?"

"I'm still thinking about it." Like he cared. She wished he would just leave. This was why she avoided relationships. Men got bored and moved on. "I'll continue with my aunt's stuff until I decide what to do with myself." For the first time since the death of her mother, she felt like this was the place where she should be. What did she have in Chicago? Nothing but a job with too many hours, no family, and no real close friends.

She met Logan's steady gaze. If he struggled with any internal conflict, he hid all emotions behind a guarded expression. *Ah, well.* Breaking the eye lock, she pushed away from the counter and approached to give him a hug. "I wish you well, Logan."

Wrapping his arms around her, he returned the hug. "You, too, Sky." Dropping his arms, he stepped away, turned, and left without a glance over his shoulder.

The roar of his sports car filled the air and faded as he drove away. She just watched a friend walk out of her life. No way in hell would she cry, but her eyes were so full of fluid, a tear escaped anyway.

The next day, Lieutenant Monroe called. He needed her to approve and sign the case file on Michael

Chang. Anxious for a chance to hop on her bike and let the wind blow away her troubles, she readily agreed to drive over. So, after a light lunch, she started her cycle and headed for the barracks.

Once again, an officer escorted her to the lieutenant's office.

When she entered, for some reason, she expected to see Logan. *Silly me*.

Monroe sat alone at his desk. He glanced up and smiled. "Hi. Thanks for coming. Everything is typed and waiting for your signature. Read it first to double-check the facts." He slipped the paper and a pen across the desk.

Still standing, she took the report and read. Since she was the one who heard Chang's reasons for murder, she made sure the details were there. Finding no errors, she signed and slid the paper back.

Monroe placed the paper inside a folder. "Michael Chang plead guilty. Your testimony will not be necessary." Propping his forearms onto the desk, he intertwined his fingers. "Do you have any future plans?"

What an odd question! She cocked a brow. "Why?"

"I have a proposition that might interest you." He motioned toward the chairs in front of his desk. "Have a seat."

"Hmm." She narrowed her gaze. "The last time you used that tone of voice, you asked me to find my aunt's killer. Maybe I should walk out now." She was joking, but truthfully, she was curious as hell. She lowered onto one of the wooden chairs.

With a probing gaze, he pursed his lips. "I'm retiring at the end of this year."

Was she supposed to make a comment? Oh, well, maybe. "That's nice, but you look a little young to retire."

"Thank you. I am, but I have my pension time in with the state police, and my retirement means I can concentrate on my business." A faint smile touched one side of his mouth. "Ever hear of Monroe Security Solutions?"

"Can't say I have." Where was he going with this?

He leaned back. "We handle all types of security— from camera surveillance to bodyguard duties. I want all my agents trained in martial arts, but I need an instructor. What do you think?"

Eh—what? She opened her mouth, then slapped it shut. "Me?" He must be out of his mind.

Smiling, he rocked his chair. "You can't say you're not qualified. If in the future you want to become a full agent, you already have a code name, *Midnight*." He grinned. "Logan told me. Midnight Sky. It suits you." His expression serious, he sat forward. "I realize I'm asking you to make Jersey your permanent home, but you'd be a great addition to the firm. Any thoughts?"

Too many to verbalize. She ran a hand through her hair. *I need a haircut.* "This is quite a surprise, Lieutenant." Really though, what better chance to put her extensive skills to use? While her inheritance afforded her an easy lifestyle, she wasn't one to sit around and eat chocolates all day. She met his gaze. "Where are you based?"

"On Route 40 in a small town called Newfield. That's about twenty minutes east of Woodstown. We help with a lot of security for the casinos in Atlantic City when some big-name celebrity comes to town. Our location also places us near the Atlantic City airport for ease of catching a flight somewhere." He picked up his pen and tapped it on the desk pad. "We're still a small operation, but we're gaining a good reputation. We haven't gone national yet, but we will someday. I already have eight full-time employees of which six are agents, and a half-dozen police officers on an on-call basis. Sound interesting?"

"Yes, it does." Brows drawn, she tapped a finger on her knee and met his gaze. "Do you have a large room to use?"

"I purchased a sizable building that contains my living quarters, and I have room to expand, but I was thinking about gutting the entire second floor to make it a workout area. Before I proceed, I'd want your input."

"Okay, then." She stood. "I'll let you know by tomorrow. Is that okay?" If she took the job, she'd have no recourse but to permanently close her life in Chicago and establish roots in South Jersey. Was she willing to take such a giant step? Really, what did she have to lose?

****

A month passed. July turned into August, and the heat wave came with a blast—ninety-plus degrees everyday with humidity thick enough to curl the stiffest board. Logan entered Monroe's office and sighed with relief at the cool breeze blowing from the air conditioning vents. He'd been waiting for this meeting. About time, too. He closed the door. "You wanted to see me?"

Without removing his gaze from his paperwork, Monroe waved Logan forward. "I have an update. Take a seat."

An update didn't sound definitive, and his heart sank. Logan had done nothing for the entire month of July except needless paperwork along with once-a-week sessions with the department psychologist—a requirement after every undercover assignment. Then, he hung around in his Princeton condo watching reality TV. He had nothing else to do but grumble about wasting time. Never had a transfer taken so long, and he cursed the holdup.

What the hell was the problem? He actually considered returning to the manor to continue Tommy's lessons on the mower. Sure, he missed the quirky tenants, but in the end, he dismissed the whole idea…because of Skylar.

Every night, his thoughts drifted to her beautiful face and floral scent. She was special, and he would probably never come across another woman like her. They shared one glorious night of sex, but the intimacy whenever they were in the same room was something he never experienced. He liked holding her or sitting at the table talking. He missed the vividness of her blue eyes whenever they turned into sparkling crystals. To be honest, he missed everything about her. But an undercover cop was best as a loner. He fully intended to remain status quo, no matter how painful the memories of Sky. The ache would ease in time. Hopefully, the meeting with Monroe would finalize his transfer. He took a seat in front of the desk.

Monroe threw his pen onto a pile of papers and leaned back, his chair giving a loud screech in the process. "Seen or heard from Skylar?"

Logan crossed one leg over the other and toyed with the denim material. "I haven't spoken to her since

I left."

"You had a lot of free time on your hands. What happened?"

Throat thick, he stared out the window. "It's over, Bob."

"Oh—sorry to hear that. I guess the sparks flying between you two were nothing more than retinal flashes." He cleared his throat. "The department psychologist tells me you have anger issues."

Tensing, Logan snapped his gaze to meet Monroe's. "He's full of shit."

"You know I can't authorize your transfer north until he gives the okay. Nobody wants an angry undercover cop."

"I'm not angry!" He jumped to his feet and paced. "I'm frustrated, dammit, and bored out of my skull. I've nothing to do." He stopped and sighed. "Look, I've cleaned my condo from top to bottom. If this goes on any longer, I'll repaint the whole damn place."

The older man nodded. "I get it. No life outside of your job. A common problem for a lot of us." He rocked his chair while intertwining his fingers. "I was like you. Still am, in fact. Never knew what to do with myself if I wasn't at the precinct."

Logan clamped his hands onto the back of his chair. "We take pride in our work, Bob."

"No, we don't prioritize what's important until it's too late." Dropping his hands to the armrests, he shook his head. "For years, I worked undercover until a knife took out my spleen. When I recovered, I transferred to Vice and then settled in Homicide until a promotion put me behind this desk. I loved every one of my jobs." He shrugged. "Maybe a little too much." He tapped a finger on the desk pad. "You know what the worst part is? I'm retiring at the end of the year, and I'm as alone now as when I started with the force. The only thing I have to occupy my time is my business—Monroe Security Solutions. I started it several years ago with the idea of doing something useful in retirement. We're doing very well, but regardless, I still go home to an empty house." He stared at his desk pad.

Logan couldn't ignore the deeper meaning behind Monroe's words. Far too many cops retired single or divorced because nothing was more important than their job. This past month proved he had nothing outside of work. But Monroe obviously had his shit together. Starting a business while still working took a lot of guts.

"How long have you done undercover?"

Monroe's question broke into his thoughts. What was this, another psychology session? Fighting a wave of irritation, he flopped onto his seat. "Four years."

"Then, you know the odds of survival decrease over time."

He crossed his legs. "Yes, sir, I'm aware."

Monroe picked up his pen and tapped the tip on the desk. "I know why you're angry, Logan, even if the psychologist doesn't. You miss Skylar."

Avoiding eye contact, Logan shifted on the seat. "That's ridiculous."

"Tell me you don't think of her."

"I don't." Shit, what a liar. He tried everything in his power to forget her. Workouts at the gym. A binge at the bar. Nothing but sore muscles and a headache. Even the image of another woman in his arms repulsed him. She wouldn't be Skylar.

Logan watched Monroe tap his pen. *Tap-tap-tap.* He was about to seize the pen and snap it in half. "Look, Bob, I'm fine."

"Uh-huh. If you want to be cleared by the shrink, you need to face what's bothering you." Monroe cocked his head. "But is giving up the love of a lifetime wise just to stay undercover? I never took the time to fall in love, Logan. That's why I'll bury myself in my business. If I'm lucky, I'll die at my desk because no one will give a damn."

"Who the hell said I'm in love?" With his nerves firing all at once, Logan again jumped to his feet and paced. "Whether I stay undercover or not isn't the issue, Bob. I don't know if I can give a woman what she wants—you know, children and a house with a white picket fence. I'm not that kind of guy."

Although, he had to admit the manor case was his best ever. Instead of his normal cloak-and-dagger world, he spent time as part of a family. He enjoyed tending the lawn and teaching Tommy about cars and motors. Sure, Tyrone and Anthony busted his chops about the lawn, but he liked and respected those two guys. He jabbed his fingers through his hair. "What am I supposed to do? I won't return to patrol."

"Come work for me."

The statement stopped him cold. A lot of cops did security as a side job, but Logan considered the occupation akin to a desk assignment. He stared. "Are you joking?"

"Not at all. You won't have your pension time in, but you'll probably live longer. I offer all my agents a pension. If you have a death wish, you might as well stay undercover." Monroe shuffled through the papers on his desk. Extracting a sheet, he slid it toward Logan and pointed. "The home office wants you to use some accumulated vacation time."

Oh, holy hell, no. Logan snatched the paper and read. *One hundred and twenty-seven hours! Are they shitting me?* Wincing, he tossed the sheet onto the desk. "I'm still on leave because of the shrink."

"I know. Once you're cleared, you start vacation. From the amount of time on record, I'd say you don't take a day off very often." Returning the sheet to the pile, he straightened the rest of the papers. "Once a reasonable amount of vacation time is used, I'll authorize your transfer to Princeton. In the meantime, why don't you talk to some of my people and get a feel for life in a security firm?" He extracted a business card from his breast pocket and handed it to Logan.

Logan took the card and read it. "How many employees do you have?"

"I signed my ninth this week. You know her, too. Midnight Sky. Martial arts instructor."

He gaped. "She's staying in Jersey?" He wasn't sure how he felt about it, either.

"She's already given several of my guys a demonstration of her skill." Monroe cocked his head and smirked. "She's damn good, Logan. I can see her becoming a full-fledged agent." Swiveling toward his computer, he tapped the keyboard to activate the view screen. "Think about my offer. Now, get out of here and make plans for some fun."

Fun? Who the hell had fun alone? And doing what? His main reason for so much time was because he had nowhere to go. He wasn't one for trips to an exotic beach or to take hikes on faraway mountains. Years ago, he had an itch to learn carpentry, but he couldn't mess with wood in a condo. Was the big man right? Did he want to be like Monroe and retire with no one by his side? Logan still had family in New Jersey, but by the time he turned in his badge, his parents would be dead, and his nieces and nephews would have lives of their own.

He jerked. *Well, hell*. His loner life finally bit him in the ass.

Chapter Twenty-One

With Monroe's job offer nagging him, Logan eased his car into the manor's parking lot. His heart clenched at the familiar sight. Nothing had changed. The lawn was still properly trimmed. Skylar's white car sat in its usual spot under the carport, but—*ah*—the motorcycle was gone. She wasn't home, and a heaviness filled his chest. More likely, she was out for a joy ride. He'd wait—all day if necessary. After killing the engine, he alighted and stood there, unsure which way to head first.

Voices drew him to the rancher's rear patio. He strolled over to see Tyrone and Anthony each holding one end of a large blueprint across the tabletop. "Hey, guys!"

Both turned simultaneously and smiled.

Tyrone moved first, hand outstretched. "How ya doing, boy?"

Smiling, Logan took the hand. "Okay. What's with the blueprint?"

Anthony also extended his hand. "Seems Ginger planned for a new garage, after all. Skylar found the prints and assigned the two of us to supervise. Looky here." He pointed. "The building's designed with enough room for her cycle and two cars."

He studied the blueprint. "What about the old garage?"

"That will stay as is with all the lawn equipment and such. Be nice to get it cleaned out a little more." Anthony peered. "You here for a reason?"

Yeah, but she wasn't home. He cleared his throat. "I stopped by to say hello."

Tyrone jerked his head toward the manor. "Fay's in the kitchen. Go say hello. Anthony and I have an appointment with the builder. You sticking around for dinner?"

"Don't know yet. I'll catch you later."

A new garage meant Skylar wasn't selling. Good news, as far as he was concerned. She already had a house to live in and people to watch out for her. A perfect setup.

Gut jumping like a nervous schoolboy, Logan ascended the manor's patio steps.

While wiping her hands on a dishtowel, Fay pushed open the screen door. "Well, look what the wind blew in. Logan, come over here!" She waved him to approach.

Dear Fay. She had a way of making everyone feel welcomed. He reached the housekeeper.

She wrapped him in a bear hug. "I never had a chance to thank you for proving Ginger right." She dropped her arms.

"Sky deserves all the credit." He straightened his T-shirt.

"I already thanked her. Come in for a while. The sun is hot as blazes today."

He followed into the familiar kitchen to see Gilda stirring a pot on the stove. The sight forced him to recognize how he missed all of them.

Gilda turned from the stove, gaze bright. "Ya-ya."

She hurried over to give him a hug.

The little woman always looked so frail, and with her in his arms, he confirmed what he always suspected. Her protruding bones were hard to miss. Breaking the hug and holding her at arm's length, he smiled. "I heard you recovered very well from when I saw you last."

"Ya-ya." She patted him on the arm and returned to the stove.

Logan turned to Fay. "Where's Skylar? I see her bike is missing." He looked around, as if she'd pop out of the woodwork.

Clucking her tongue, Fay shot him a one-eyed glare. "She left for Chicago last week but not before she and I arranged a partnership."

Well, that was a nice kick in the butt, and his heart sank. He wanted to talk to her before considering Monroe's offer. He stuffed his hands into his front pockets. "How long will she be gone?"

"Until she gets things settled. I'm officially in charge, and I'm pleased to say all rooms are leased." She removed her eyeglasses and held them toward the window. "I have to clean these things." She used the dishtowel still in her hand to wipe the lenses. "Sky's putting her parents' house on the market and will drive back in a rental truck. She said we're her family now, and even though she doesn't need to work, she took a job with Monroe Security."

Sky made a complete one-eighty turn in her lifestyle. She gave up her Chicago home to move to New Jersey, left tending bar to teaching others her martial arts skills, and said goodbye to her loner life to become a landlord to a bunch of nice people. She was brave enough to take the necessary steps. Was he?

After replacing the glasses onto her nose, Fay threw the dishtowel onto the table. "I know Philip is thrilled. After you left, he spent a lot of time with her." She narrowed her gaze. "You let her go, Logan." Smirking, she folded her arms over her chest. "You didn't think I was blind, did you? Every one of us saw how you felt."

"Ya-ya." Gilda pointed to her eyes and nodded.

How could he argue with the truth? Hell, he prided himself on how well he contained his emotions, but Skylar Dawson made him lower his defenses. He never told her how he felt, and right now, he wasn't sure he should. He forced a smile. "I had to, Fay. My job requires anonymity. She knew we weren't meant to be."

"Yeah, you keep telling yourself that. Someday, you'll believe it." She cocked her head. "So, why are you here?"

From her tone, the question wasn't a friendly one. She was protecting Skylar, and his admiration for Fay soared. He rubbed his neck. "I had to see Monroe and thought I'd stop by."

Dropping her arms, she snorted. "Why? To torment her?"

Aw, shit. When she put it like that, he felt like a heel. He slipped his hands into his jeans front pockets. "Do you think Philip has a chance?"

Fay shrugged. "Time will tell. I'm hoping when she starts her new job, she'll meet someone. She deserves to be happy. You, however, are another story."

Yeah, he was a man who chose to be alone for the sake of his job. Where was the happiness in that?

****

Skylar had never been so thrilled to cross over the Delaware River and into New Jersey. On her first trip across Pennsylvania, she rode her cycle and maneuvered around the slower cars, but her rental truck had the maneuverability of a sloth, not to mention the engine had a strange ping that concerned her. Since the back was packed full of her worldly possessions, including her precious motorcycle, she stayed in the right lane and bit her tongue whenever the urge came to hit the gas.

By mid-afternoon, she turned onto the side street adjacent to the manor. A flurry of activity greeted her, and she smiled at the nearly complete new garage. Because so many pickup trucks crowded the parking lot and street, she had no choice but to park along the curb. Alighting, she walked toward the garage.

Two men were on the outside installing gray siding. Two more men were inside doing…

She froze. For a second, she swore the man in a sweat-soaked T-shirt was Logan. But maybe her bleary eyes triggered an hallucination—either that or wishful thinking.

Then, the man turned and smiled.

Her knees weakened while her heart skipped around inside her chest. *Well, I'll be damned.* Why had he returned? She'd think he'd be embroiled in another undercover operation, not here looking like a sexy carpenter with a tool belt on his hips.

Logan approached and stood before her. "Hi."

He was covered in dirt, and Lord Almighty, she never saw anything so wonderful. She managed to swallow what stuck in her throat. "Hi. Didn't expect to see you."

"I've always had an interest in carpentry, and the boss man let me work—for free." He grinned.

"Where…eh—" *Damn*. Words eluded her. He had her discombobulated. She swallowed. "Where are you staying? Fay said we're full."

He wiped sweat from his brow. "I'm renting a room in Swedesboro. Look, Sky, can we talk later? I'll grab a pizza and beer and come by around six o'clock. I've a lot to tell you."

She couldn't imagine what he had to say. But she'd listen. "Yeah, sure. Six o'clock."

"Great."

His steps faltered. She swore he was about to kiss her, but instead, he hurried into the garage. Stunned, she headed for the rancher patio to see Tyrone and Anthony sitting at the table. "Hi, guys."

Anthony pulled out the chair to his left. "Good to see you back."

"It's good to be here—permanent."

Both men flashed big smiles.

Tyrone nodded toward the new structure. "What do you think?"

Since her butt still hurt from the truck's lumpy seat, Sky placed her hands on the chair's backrest and turned to watch the activity. "Everything looks great. Although, I'm surprised to see Logan."

Anthony nodded. "Surprised us, too. The boy's having fun for a change."

She arched a brow. "He's calling this fun?"

"Yeah, but it's a shame his old room is rented. Would be nice to have our gardener again."

She agreed, but no sense getting her hopes up.

****

She's back.

Skylar looked as beautiful as ever, and Logan desperately wanted to wrap her in his arms. He held off, though. With all the sweat dripping, his body was a walking sawdust magnet. Besides, after too many months away, she might tell him to take a hike off a short pier. He hoped not, but with the garage nearly complete, he'd have no reason to stay in the area. The automatic garage doors were scheduled for installation tomorrow, followed by the asphalt truck to lay out the driveway. Skylar would have one fine-looking garage…and his work would be done.

When six o'clock rolled around, he stood by the backdoor with a pizza box and six-pack of cold beer in one hand. He knocked. With no answer, he tapped again.

A moment later, the door swung open. A sleepy and slightly disheveled woman answered with a yawn. God, she looked gorgeous, and his heart squeezed. Fay was right. He let Skylar go, and right now, he mentally kicked his ass. His best option was to apologize and hope she'd forgive him.

Running a hand through her hair, she released a sleepy smile. "Hi. Come in."

Bypassing the sofa, he aimed straight for the kitchen. No way in hell could he sit on the sofa where he held her all night. The memory of how good it felt hit his heart with a pang. After missing her for these past few months, he debated long and hard whether he was in love with her. His answer was a definitive not sure. He'd never loved anyone before and hadn't a clue what it felt like.

After slipping the pizza box onto the table, he

extracted two beer cans from the carton and popped the tabs. The rest he placed in the fridge. His palms were sweating like crazy. Too much time had passed, and being here felt awkward. His own fault, really.

Skylar slipped plates and napkins onto the table, then pulled out a chair and sat. She opened the pizza box and smacked her lips. "Yum. Pepperoni and sweet peppers. I'm starving." She loaded pizza slices onto both plates. "Fay filled my freezer with casseroles, but I'll save those for later, like when I unload the truck."

"I can help." To spend more time together? *Hell, yeah.* It was a great excuse. He sat at the table.

She smiled. "I'll accept, too. I don't have any big pieces. Most of Mom's furniture I sold at auction." After picking up her slice, she took a bite.

He should have been with her. The whole process couldn't have been easy. Shit, he had the free time. "Was it hard to sell your parents' house?"

She chewed for several minutes, then swallowed the food with a sip of beer. "At first, yeah, but the house felt so empty since my mom died. Then, as I stood in the middle of the living room wondering if I was making the biggest mistake of my life, my cell phone rang. It was Fay, asking if I was all right." She toyed with her beer can. "Right there, I realized no one would ask me that question in Chicago. I knew New Jersey was where I belonged with Fay and Monroe and the tenants."

"And me, I hope."

She didn't respond nor look at him. Really, what had he expected? He'd been incommunicado for going on three months now. She hadn't the slightest idea what he'd been up to. He rubbed his sweaty palms on his thighs. Hot pizza or nerves, he wasn't certain. He cleared his throat. "I suppose you're wondering why I'm here."

"The thought crossed my mind." Watching him, she bit into her slice and chewed.

"I'm quitting the state police. After I use all my accumulated vacation time, I'll be finished."

Brows arched, she stopped mid-chew. "You're leaving undercover work?"

"This last assignment taught me a few things, Sky. I don't want to be alone anymore. I accepted a job with Monroe Security Solutions." He glanced her way.

She stared, eyes wide. "You're serious?"

"Very. I want you to know it's not because you signed on—although I like the idea…a lot. I thought it was high time I established some roots—you know, stay in one place."

Frowning, she narrowed her gaze. "What does that mean exactly?"

He heard a slight catch in her voice. He couldn't blame her for being unsure. At this point, he wasn't sure of anything, either. He held his pizza near his mouth. "It means I want to couple up with a nice woman. I might do carpentry as a side job and hobby. In other words, live a normal life and have someone to come home to." He shot her another glance. "Interested?"

Mouth gaping, she visibly jerked and dropped her pizza onto the plate. She met his gaze. "You want a relationship with me?"

To hide the slight tremor in his hands, he slid another slice of pizza from the box. "I know it's a foreign word for both of us. So, let's start with friendship. Am I too late?" Here it comes. The answer to the Skylar-Philip question.

She blinked. "Logan, I'm floored. You left without a word. I put you out of my mind."

"Well—" He nearly crushed his slice of pizza. Before he made a mess on his hand, he slipped the piece onto his plate. "We'll be working for the same company. Even if you say *no* to everything else, I want to count you as a friend."

Staring, she sat back in her chair. "Wow, okay, sure, we'll always be friends."

"Good." One huge obstacle out of the way. Friends he could do, but he had a tough road ahead. He better make damn sure he followed the twists and turns.

****

What was wrong with her? *Really, friends*? The man returned. He didn't have to reconcile anything. Yes, all right, so Sky lied. Not a night passed without him popping into her mind. She even accepted a date with Philip, thinking a night out would help. All she accomplished was to miss Logan more. She grabbed another slice of pizza. "What about your condo in Princeton?"

"It's still there." He swallowed some beer. "The room I rented in Swedesboro is on a weekly basis. When the garage is done, I'll head home, clear out my stuff, and put the condo on the market. I'll look for a place closer to Monroe Security. I don't know the area well, so I'll start with an apartment." Leaning back, he wiped his mouth with the napkin. "Monroe thinks you'll make a good agent."

She humphed. "Yeah, well, he's entitled to his opinion. I'm not so sure." She sipped her cold beer. "I told Monroe I had no need to work, but he said I can make my own schedule. That appealed to me." She plucked a piece of pepperoni from her slice, placed it in her mouth, and chewed. The little morsel of meat had a nice crunch.

"You do whatever you feel comfortable with, Sky." He faced her. "Look. I don't expect us to start where we left off. I know I acted like a jerk, but the truth is, I was scared. Still am, in fact. Scared of how I feel around you. That's never happened before. But I returned to delve deeper into these feelings."

His face was serious. *Wow*. So totally unexpected. She swallowed hard. "What feelings?"

"I don't know yet, but I'm willing to explore them."

Holy moly. She hadn't expected this, and her stomach did a happy, little flip. Should she try a relationship—well, friendship? What would be the harm? Her heart said go for it. Her brain called her crazy. In truth, she had only one way to arrive at an answer. She leaned close. "Kiss me." Judging from the rise of his brows, she surprised him. But hey, he was a great kisser. She doubted he changed.

Grinning, he scooted her chair closer, latched onto her shoulders, and drew her toward him before brushing his lips over hers.

A thrill shot through her at the taste of his mouth. Warmth gathered in her core, and she was damn sure it wasn't from the pizza. Lordy, the man caused an internal heat wave. Should she let him back into her life? Seriously, she'd be a fool to turn him away. And what if everything worked out? Would she be willing to advance beyond friendship to a full-blown relationship?

Lifting his head, he stared into her eyes. "You are the first woman who has ever made me feel, Skylar."

She could say the same but kept quiet. She'd been down this road with men and their fancy words. Besides, her heart and brain were in total disagreement, and Logan would have to prove he had staying power. She licked her lips. "What do you feel?"

He smiled. "Happy. Anxious. Aroused. Mostly, I feel like I'm home." With a palm on her cheek, he kissed her lightly. "What do you feel?"

Like a bed is necessary. The hand on her cheek felt like a soothing balm. She searched his face. "I would say ditto and add scared. I guess I'm willing to try."

He cupped her face with both hands. "When do we start?"

Clamping onto the front of his T-shirt, she tugged him close. "How about right now?"